LIKE WATER

Also by Rebecca Podos

The Mystery of Hollow Places

like water

REBECCA PODOS

Balzer + Bray

An Imprint of HarperCollins*Publishers*

Balzer + Bray is an imprint of HarperCollins Publishers.

John Haines, "Little Cosmic Dust Poem"
from *The Owl in the Mask of the Dreamer: Collected Poems.*
Copyright © 1983, 1996 by John Haines.
Reprinted with the permission of The Permissions Company, Inc.,
on behalf of Graywolf Press, Minneapolis, Minnesota, www.graywolfpress.org.

Like Water

www.epicreads.com

Library of Congress Cataloging-in-Publication Data
Names: Podos, Rebecca, author.
Title: Like water / Rebecca Podos.
Description: First Edition. | New York, NY : Balzer + Bray, an imprint
  of HarperCollins Publishers, [2017] | Summary: When her father is
  diagnosed with Huntington's disease, eighteen-year-old Vanni abandons
  her plan to flee her small New Mexico hometown after high school
  graduation and instead spends the summer keeping herself busy with
  part-time jobs and boys, but that changes after she meets Leigh, whose
  friendship dares Vanni to ask herself big questions and make new plans.
Identifiers: LCCN 2016053584 | ISBN 9780062373373 (hardcover)
Subjects: | CYAC: Bisexuality—Fiction. | Huntington's disease—Fiction. |
  Hispanic Americans—Fiction. | New Mexico—Fiction.
Classification: LCC PZ7.1.P63 Li 2017 | DDC [Fic]—dc23 LC record
  available at https://lccn.loc.gov/2016053584

17 18 19 20 21   PC/LSCH   10 9 8 7 6 5 4 3 2 1

❖

First Edition

For Tom, and for the cantaloupes

Before fireworks from our pack of Roman Candles, Sky Flyers, and Screaming Meemies bloom above the roofs.

Before the booms echo inside of us on the front lawn.

Before she lays her hand on my chest and asks, "Did you feel that one? Did you feel *that*?"

Before I

Before she

Before we

ONE

Before everything else was New Year's morning three years ago, in the subarctic dining room at Silvia's. Crumbs clung to my gloves as I poured tortilla chips into baskets, shivering in my pink peacoat and beanie. The thermocouple on our furnace was broken, so Dad was in the back office, scrambling to get ahold of our repair guy before we opened at noon. In the meantime, my fingers were Popsicle sticks, my breath a cloud. There'd been snow in the air since Christmas, and everything was pale and hard with frost. Even the sun was white in a milky sky.

Out-of-towners were always surprised by the cold in New Mexico. "Isn't this the desert?" they whined. "Isn't it supposed to be sand and sun and margaritas?"

Yeah, right. Winters could be bitter up north—especially on the scrubby plains where our three-traffic-light town squatted—and the wind would blow you away.

While I shivered and poured the chips, Jake Mosqueda leaned across the counter. No coat for him; in his scuffed cowboy boots and with his work apron dangling casually from the waist strings, he looked maximally cool. Which was the whole point, of course.

He tugged on a strand of hair that spiraled out below my beanie. "Princesita! Let me get those." Jake stacked chip baskets three-deep along his brown forearms, the scar on his knuckles shining under the restaurant lights. Tourists who stumbled through on their way to somewhere better probably thought he'd earned it wrangling cattle, or in an old-timey bare-knuckle boxing match.

I happened to know it was from reckless flirting and gesticulating near a pot of Dad's pozole rojo as it simmered on the stove.

"How's school?" Jake asked, drifting alongside me.

"School?"

"Yeah, how's art or fractions or whatever?"

As if I was a four-year-old instead of his bosses'

fourteen-and-a-half-year-old daughter. I was plenty old enough to work regular shifts in the restaurant, child labor laws be damned (not a single business in La Trampa cared about those). And I was old enough to kiss—and occasionally dry-hump—Max Binali behind the high school cafeteria.

"Great. They're teaching us shapes now," I said slowly. "Maybe colors next."

"Cool, cool." He handed me baskets one by one to set on the tables between salt and pepper shakers shaped like little glass cacti.

The tourists loved them.

"So I've got this problem," Jake continued, in a way that told me it was soon to be my problem.

Technically, I owed Jake. After my shift the Friday before, he'd given Diana Reyes, Marilee Smith, and me a ride to a party in the arroyo, the three of us piled on top of one another in the passenger seat of his old truck. This was nothing new. Since preschool, we'd spent most of our spare time piled on top of one another in our backyards, bedrooms, and closets. We ate at the same table in the cafeteria and sat together in every class. On weekends, we played popcorn on Diana's trampoline, even after we were too big and too heavy and Mrs. Reyes was constantly shouting out the back window for us to behave like ladies. We learned to do our makeup in Marilee's bathroom, perched on the rim of her tub, passing around disks of blush she got from her mother; my mom's makeup drawer held nothing but sunblock and the tube of Riveting Rose lipstick she wore when she was especially nervous, but wanted to pretend she wasn't. And Diana's super-religious mom didn't believe in "girls painting themselves like rameras." A ramera was the worst thing you could be in that household (a marihuano was the second).

Anyway, there was a zero percent chance Mrs. Reyes would have given us a ride to the party. My parents were working, and Marilee's big sister was in Albuquerque. Which is why Jake dropped us off on Jimeno Road, already freezing and pinching down the shortest skirts we owned. (Diana's still reached the tips of her fingers with straightened arms.) We crunched along the slope of the dry streambed, rocks and dead weeds rolling away under our boots. At the bottom, Max Binali and a bunch of his fellow juniors sat on overturned shopping carts, gulping out of red plastic cups. "Ladies," Max said, and nodded. Then he pointed us toward the keg.

Typical boy. He'd written my name on his thumb in Sharpie the day before, and all of a sudden he couldn't remember it.

In hindsight, the favor hadn't been worth it, but I

doubted Jake would take that into consideration. He clasped my gloved hand in his. "Talk to your daddy, princesita. He does whatever you ask. Tell him to give me more Friday and Saturday nights."

"Why?"

"The tips! Tell him customers have been asking for me. Please?" He pressed his lips to my curled fingers. "I'm saving for this guitar I saw at that place in La Cienega, Fender Bender. Maybe I'll play for you when you're a grown-up."

I snorted in the most un-grown-up way.

Jake thought he was hot shit, and okay, most girls agreed. With dimples like canyons and blue-black hair waving loosely around his ears, I could see it. I wasn't blind. But I knew him, and he was exactly like every other kid in La Trampa who'd stayed stuck.

Anyone here could tell you that townies did one of three things after they graduated:

1. Skip college and work for the family business, be it a restaurant, a trailer-size plant nursery, or the Turquoise Depot, all contained within the four square miles of La Trampa proper.

2. Go to community college or trade school while living over their parents' garage, then work for somebody else's family business.

3. Move away to a big city, make one scary mistake—
    a lost job, a maxed-out credit card, a DUI—then
    come home tuck-tailed. Maybe get lucky and snag
    a spot at that new mini-golf course in Española,
    or the hotel hiring in Pojoaque.

For Jake Mosqueda, it'd been door number three. Right after high school, where he'd been the only reasonably good football player his senior year, and thus, a star, he'd gone to Austin for six whole months. Then he got busted for drinking underage, when the bar where he worked was raided. In December, he came swaggering back to all this fanfare, like he was some hometown hero returning to La Trampa after the War. But, really, he was just another number three.

Funny(ish) story: Technically, our hometown isn't La Trampa. Its real name is El Trampero, "The Trapper" in English, named after some fur trappers who founded the town. But none of the kids call it that. We call it La Trampa, *the trap*. And for good reason. Jake might've made it out into the world, but he hadn't made it very far, or lasted very long. A common problem.

Me, I had the Plan in place to stop it from becoming mine.

Jake didn't impress me, but I did owe him, so I sighed and followed him to the back to talk to Dad. As if he needed my help. Mysteriously, Dad liked Jake. Maybe because, while I loved my father, he was also townie to the bone.

Stuffed inside the cubby of an office, he sat with his feet propped on the desk and the phone in hand, pleading with our hungover HVAC guy to work on a holiday.

"Ayúdame, Julian. I've got no heat here." He sighed, dropped the phone to his shoulder, and told us, "On hold. Think he went to throw up."

"Gross, Dad."

"Need something?"

"Yeah, just, Jake and I were talking about Friday and Saturday shifts and how me and Estrella always work them, and I thought—"

"Un momento," he interrupted, holding up a palm, then grumbled into the speaker, "¡Por supuesto que estoy todavía aqui!"

I winced at the growl in his voice. My dad wasn't what you'd call "chatty." He'd told me stories about my grandfather, who I never met, and my grandmother, who I barely got the chance to meet. How they moved up to La Trampa from Tijuana before Dad was born. How they knew English when they came, but never mastered figures of speech. If Dad told his parents their football team was "on fire," they'd look at him in horror. "Who was on fire? What fire? ¿Estás bien?" they'd ask. Dad grew up rationing his words and picking them practically, whereas Mom would happily babble to the repair guy, to tourists, to the woman in line behind her at the grocery store.

So sure, Dad is quiet, but he's never been cranky.

"I'll try again later," I said to Jake, and turned to hustle him out of the office, but his stupidly broad body was bottlenecking the door.

"Why, what—"

We both jumped as Dad swept his legs from the desk, his boots thundering against the tiled floor. "Escúchame, pendejo," he yelled. "I've got a freezing-cold restaurant. Get your ass out of bed and do your job. ¿Me entiendes?" He slammed the phone onto the cradle, propped his elbow on the desk, and knuckled his forehead, fingers pulsing into a jittery fist, clenching and unclenching and clenching.

"You okay, Mr. Espinoza?" Jake piped up, as confused as I was.

"Sorry, kids. Just a head-splitter. Too much partying last night."

Sure, that would do it. Except that when Marilee's mother drove me back from their house just after midnight, my parents were already sound asleep, and there was *maybe* a pair of Coors cans shining in the recycling bin.

"No te preocupes," Dad reassured us, slipping into

his usual voice, low but soft. "Vanni, take the trash out for me, would you? You already got your coat on."

By the Dumpster behind Silvia's, the spiny shrubs were swollen with frost. I snapped a tube of ice off one of the branches and let it break at my feet, picturing places where the world really was sand and sun all year round. Not that I knew them from experience. I'd never been east of Texas or west of the Arizona border or north of Taos. Never been on a plane, and the only train I'd ridden was the Rail Runner from Santa Fe to Albuquerque.

But I had the Plan. To not be a one, a two, or a three.

In three and a half years I'd graduate, and then I'd go away to school. Not in the desert. I'd go to the East Coast, or to California. *A coast,* at least. I already knew my parents couldn't give much, but my grades were good, and I had what Mrs. Short, our principal, called "important extracurriculars." Teachers would write nice recommendations when I applied to colleges.

And I had swimming.

I wasn't, like, an Olympic hopeful. No way would I get scouted. To my eternal disappointment, El Trampero High was too small for a team. Decent bodies of water were rare in my little corner of the state, man-made or otherwise. But for years when I was a kid, my parents took turns driving the hour round trip to Bicentennial in Santa Fe to bring me to swim lessons. And I'd done some competitions with the Santa Fe Aquatic Club. I could have Dad film me and show the coach the reel, do well in tryouts, get at least a partial scholarship to squeeze me through. My laptop's search history was stuffed with Division II schools with ocean views.

And after that . . . ?

It's not like I hated life in the restaurant, or in La Trampa. My parents were cooler than expected, and I had my best friends, and a lot of bonus friends besides. I had Max, kind of. At least I was pretty sure he'd ask me to his junior prom in the spring. I was on the baton squad, had been on the freshman Homecoming Court in the fall. So I wasn't miserable or anything on New Year's Day 2014. Far from it.

But I knew with my whole heart I wasn't supposed to be una pueblerina, topping off horchatas and arguing with the HVAC guy at Silvia's when I was Dad's age.

Graduation would be like swim, I was certain. I'd step up onto the block and take my mark, the whistle would sound, and with shoulders relaxed and palms flat out, I'd dive headfirst into the world, warm and waiting, lapping up around my ears, whispering, "Welcome, Savannah Espinoza."

TWO

We stand in the grass-flecked dust beyond the abandoned football field of El Trampero High on the last day of senior year, a fact I'm on the way to forgetting until a husky voice whispers in my ear, breath hotter than the air around us, "What if somebody sees?"

A fair question. We're partially sheltered by a copse of mesquite, but not exactly invisible. I can see the dull gleam of the bleachers through the branches, the *CONGRATULATIONS, SENIORS!* banner still strung up across the scoreboard, the small patch of folding chairs still in neat rows on the field, now cleared of people. If anybody wandered too close to the trees—maybe a janitor cleaning up after the ceremony—and if they bothered to look, I know exactly what they'd see: me, mud-brown graduation cap pressed low on my forehead, mud-brown robes flung open around my jean miniskirt and sleeveless black shirt, unbuttoned up to my bra.

And a tan, muscled hand snaking around my hips, burrowing beneath my skirt, strong fingers sliding against my zipper.

I lean into him, trying to feel Jake Mosqueda's belt buckle through the layers of polyester and denim between us. The ground below burns the soles of my feet, my heels abandoned on the field. "So what?"

"Your mother will murder you." His fingers dip a little lower.

"I'm eighteen."

"Yeah, for three whole weeks," he laughs. Lower, his fingers strum the elastic waist of my underwear. "Well, then she'll murder me."

"Good. Maybe then we can hire a waiter who doesn't bang *all* the waitresses."

The hand starts to withdraw. "Come on, princesita. You know I'm only about you. You're the one who doesn't want a boyfriend."

"Don't call me that." I wrap my fingers around his

wrist, keeping it in place. I know for a fact that he and Estrella rocked Silvia's two-stall girls' room during their shift break last week, because I had to cover my tables *and* the front door, and then I had to help Estrella tuck her tag into her pearl-buttoned shirt when she emerged. But who cares, because he's right.

Jake Mosqueda is not my boyfriend.

Max Binali is not my boyfriend.

Oriel Trejo is not my boyfriend.

Will Fischer is not my boyfriend.

Jaime Aguilar is not my boyfriend.

The hand plunges and I forget them all and the whole world with them.

Plodding down Calle Tamara toward the restaurant, I slightly regret sending Jake and his rust-bucket truck on ahead. I'm hotter and damper now than I was sitting on the football field while Mrs. Short droned on about our bright futures.

As I'm patting my cheeks to check my eyeliner for sweat slippage, a too-familiar car pulls up alongside me. Diana leans over the passenger side of Marilee's red Sebring convertible; her dad's until last year, when he sobered up from his midlife crisis.

"Umm, hey Vanni, do you need a ride or something?" she asks, while Marilee inspects her signature baby-pink lipstick in the rearview mirror. They've ditched their caps and robes for the senior party in the arroyo.

In another world, like a next-door dimension where one tiny butterfly of a thing is different and so everything is different, I would've been in the backseat. In fact, who am I kidding? I never rode bitch. I would've been in the front, Diana happily and obediently scrunched up behind us.

"That's okay. I'm just going to work." I point up the road.

"Right now?" Diana frowns. "But it's graduation! Aren't you coming to the party?"

Marilee cranes her neck around Diana to eyeball me with the barest flash of recognition. I heard she's starting in the teaching program at UNM in September. Diana's sticking around to work at her parents' two-man accounting firm; the only accountants in the county, they do everybody's taxes and know everybody's dirty business, which pleases Mrs. Reyes endlessly. Diana will sit with them every Sunday morning and Wednesday evening in the pews of the Shrine of Our Lady Parish, the church on our side of town—La Trampa has three Catholic churches, almost one per square mile—and probably marry one of the acolytes within a year or two.

In a next-door dimension, I would've dragged her out of town with me by her frizzy brown hair. Instead, I wave them off. "Maybe I'll show up later."

"Okay, well, say hi to your mom." Diana smiles sweetly. Marilee speeds away, hair billowing behind her, the cloud of dust from her tires settling over my sweaty robes.

Probably I deserved that. When I stopped talking to them last year, stopped answering their texts, switched cafeteria tables and class partners, Marilee took it hard. It wasn't a cakewalk for me, either.

But I had my reasons. When the Plan became a non-starter, the last people I wanted around were the ones who'd helped form the Plan in the first place. And who could blame me for that?

I step carefully around a patch of sidewalk glittering with broken glass, keeping my eyes on the ground.

As I push through the door at Silvia's, Jake immediately busies himself brushing imaginary dust off the little podium—today he's playing host. Chalking the specials on the blackboard beside him, Mom turns and blinks at me in the bright doorway. "Vanni? What are you doing here?" Her dark hair beats against her shoulder in a careless braid as she walks toward me. Over the other shoulder, an ancient dish towel with faded flowers. She looks the way she always looks: beautiful and tired and determined. "I told you to go celebrate with your girlfriends!"

"It's Saturday." I shrug. "I close on Saturdays."

"Don't be ridiculous! I had you off the schedule weeks ago. Go enjoy yourself. Have some fun. And maybe you can stop at home and say hello to your father?" She pats her palm against my flushed cheek and smiles into my face. "We're so proud of you. This is your big day."

"Not *that* big," I say, discreetly brushing chalk off my face.

Mom tilts her head. "It's the start of the rest of your life, mija."

"What life?"

It's supposed to be a joke to slow the Vanni Pride Parade a little, but her forehead puckers, and I know right away I've stepped perilously close to the land mine always buried in the ground between us.

I back away from it slowly, so as not to set it off. "Just, because I'm staying here. I'm happy I'm staying, but nothing's really . . . changing."

Mom's forehead smooths over; her smile returns. "Maybe not tomorrow. So? We're glad to keep you for a little while longer. I took a couple of months after high school to figure things out too."

Look how that worked out, I would never, ever say to her.

"Can I take your car?" I ask quickly. "To get to the party?"

"Of course." She fishes for the keys in her skirt pocket and drops them in my palm. "Jake will drive me home later, won't you, cariño?"

He dials the wattage on his smile up to Full Charm. "Happy to, Mrs. Espinoza!"

"Thanks," I say. And when Mom turns away, I lean across the podium boobs-first and murmur below the hum of the swamp cooler, "Hope you washed that hand, cariño."

He goes red to the tips of his ears, lets his blue-black hair flop across his forehead as he stoops to inspect a scratch on the podium. Jake talks big shit in stockrooms and hidden behind trees, but put him around my painfully cheerful, five-feet-nothing mother, and he's a little boy. I laugh and head back into the killer heat, stopping on the way to the parking lot to bundle my graduation robe into the Dumpster.

In the sunbaked front seat of my mom's old Malibu, I weigh my options. I could go to the house, change, kiss my dad on the cheek, and then head to the arroyo. Party with all twenty-six kids in my class, most of whom I've said maybe a handful of words to since junior year. Wish a couple of them well on their way out of town and commiserate with the kids staying behind.

I choose option two. Let it be known, I don't *enjoy* lying to Mom. I always feel shitty about it, even when she does half the work for me by lying to herself.

La Trampa sits just off the Turquoise Trail, a fifty-something-mile-long road that runs down from Santa Fe, through Los Cerrillos and Madrid and so on, south toward the Cibola National Forest. You can drive it all the way to Albuquerque. It isn't as fast as the highway, but all the tourist brochures say it's one of the most beautiful drives in the Southwest.

I don't care about that so much as that it takes me where I need to go. Half an hour later, I pull into the parking lot of the Bicentennial Pool, the nearest and only outdoor public pool in Santa Fe. It's after five thirty, but jam-packed from the tot pond to the mushroom water-falls to the big red slide, even when everyone should be toweling off their kids and taking them home for family dinner. Good thing they set up lanes for a lap swim at six. I take my time in the locker room showering off dust and sweat from my . . . extracurriculars with Jake. By the time I'm done, half the bright blue water is buoyed off, a few grown-ups in swim caps and goggles stroking back and forth. I slip into the cold pool with hardly a splash, maybe showing off a bit.

And why not? I earned this. Dad's parents insisted he learn how to swim, even though they'd come from the ocean to the desert, so Dad insisted I learn. And though Mom could barely frog-paddle, and probably wasn't thrilled to spend a couple afternoons a week driving me all the way out to Bicentennial, there's nothing she wouldn't do for Dad. There never was.

I freestyle to the deep end, fluttering my feet and reaching, reaching with long-but-not-too-long strokes, rolling my hips and shoulders at once, eyes on the bottom of the pool between breaths. I reach the far wall and flip-turn, swim lap after lap before I pause by the ladder in the deep end to catch my breath. Scrubbing my hair back, I blink up at the lifeguard chair a few feet from me, where a guard that Diana would've labeled an Unidentified Flying Hottie watches me.

He tugs down his little white visor and keeps half his attention on the water, half on me. "Nice technique."

I've been told so. Casually, I paddle to the ledge in front of him. "You're new here, right?"

He nods. "Lucas."

"Savannah."

"That's pretty."

I like the way his voice rumbles. Even from below, I can tell he's not tall, but solid, with excellently proportioned biceps. Sandy-brown tufts of hair splay out above his visor; below, his eyes are green, surprisingly dark lashed. My own hair is a bedraggled mass of seaweed dripping down my back, I'm wearing my frumpiest two-piece—navy blue and high-cut—and though most of my makeup washed off in the shower, I suspect my resilient Colossal Chaotic mascara has smudged below my lids, like a football player's eye black.

But fresh blood only comes around so often. I can try to work under these conditions.

"I'm here a lot. You'll be around?" I flutter and twist one soggy curl around my finger.

He smiles, scanning the pool. "Just three days a week. They were only hiring part-time. Other days I'm at the Lost Lagoon. I lifeguard there, too."

"That water park?" I heard one was opening in the desert just north of Albuquerque. There are a few small places in the city, like Cliff's Water Mania, but the big park my parents sometimes took me to called the Beach closed when I was ten. I guess they shit the bucket (maybe literally) on a health inspection. Some other town in New Mexico bought the slides but never put them up, so now they sit in piles off the highway, all cracked plastic and bent ladders and tumbleweeds. "Is that place any good?"

Lucas looks down at me again, eyeing what might be my necklace, a tiny low-hanging pearl Mom let me borrow for the ceremony, but *might* be something else my mother gave me. "It's pretty decent. You should check it out, you know?"

"I guess I should."

In the parking lot a car honks once, twice, lingers on the third blast.

"My little sister." He sighs. "My shift was up at six, but the cavalry's late. . . ." Then he looks past me and waves, and I turn to see a blond lifeguard in her own fire-engine-red suit padding around the pool's edge. "There she is. See you around, Savannah . . . ?"

"Espinoza."

"Clemente." Lucas pats his chest. Then he rises out of the chair and points a finger at me, like a promise, before striding to the locker room. He's shorter than Jake after all, and slightly bowlegged.

It works for him.

I watch a few minutes later as he pops up beyond the pool gate, wearing a loose black-and-white baseball tee and carrying his duffel bag to an ugly green minivan parked right by the entrance. In the driver's seat, his sister's face is half shadowed by the sun visor, the other half streaked with light through the windshield, so all I can really see is her silhouette. Lucas slips into the passenger seat, and together, they crawl forward through the shrieking crowd.

I sink until my nose is submerged, eyes above the surface like a crocodile for as long as possible. Once I run out of breath, I kick off from the ledge and float backward, even though I'm in a lap lane. I'm weightless. I let my arms go, hands curling gently as they drift away from me.

My right thumb twitches.

I drop my legs so quickly I nearly sink, then paddle to the rough-bottomed shallows. Once I'm home free, I slog toward the stairs and out onto the hot concrete and then I plant my legs, flexing every muscle in them, and stand dripping and sizzling under the sun, simply because I can.

THREE

When I park in our driveway on Jemez Road, I wedge the Malibu in beside a boxy blue Dodge Ram whose paint chips and fender dings I know by heart, smiling despite myself. I let myself into the house and call out, "Chris?" kicking my heels off beside our old Navajo print sofa.

Chris Zepeda slowly shuffles in from the kitchen; he toppled a dirt bike and shattered the bones in his left leg when he and Dad were my age, and he's favored it ever since. Squinting small brown eyes bracketed by crow's-feet as splintered as a dried streambed, he holds out his arm. "Vanni, ¿qué onda?"

"Fine. Good," I say, and duck into the hug. "Mom's still at the restaurant?"

"Till closing."

"I didn't know you were staying. You could've called me to come home."

He smiles widely through a black briar patch of a beard. "Happy to stay, cariño."

Maybe it's because they grew up two streets apart, or maybe it's through long exposure, but in his more emotional moments, Chris speaks a little like my dad. It's their clipped sentences, the way the words at the beginning and the end slide away like loose rocks crumbling from a cliff face. They're best friends, so it's not surprising. I can't remember a time I didn't know Chris Zepeda, who I danced with at my quinceañera, who showed me how to drive the ATVs in his shed when I was thirteen and taught me card tricks I've long since forgotten.

"Is Dad in bed?" I ask.

"Resting. But it was a good day. Probably still up, you want to poke your head in."

"Okay." I drop Mom's car keys in a heart-shaped basket on our scuffed coffee table. "Thanks for hanging out with him today."

Usually that would fall to Dad's part-time home aide, Ximena, a tiny little woman with surprising biceps beneath her button-down shirts. Since Dad stopped driving last year, we used Xime whenever I was in school and Mom needed to be at Silvia's, and Dad had to get to PT, or OT, or to the once-a-month psychiatrist who specializes in HD (what a fun alphabet soup life has become). We haven't needed Xime as much since Mom rolled back the restaurant hours—we only serve lunch and dinner Monday through Friday, a full day Saturday, and closed on Sunday—because Mom wants to be there for Dad whenever he needs her.

Anyway, the four locals who made up our a.m. crowd weren't exactly paying the staff's salary with their pancakes and horchatas.

Chris lifts his Windbreaker off the coatrack. "It was great to see you on that stage today, graduating and everything. Only sorry I gotta get back and get packing. I got that flight tomorrow."

"Yeah, how's Sophia?"

"Tired," he laughs. One of the rarest La Trampans, Chris's sister, Sophia Zepeda, split for California after high school, got married, and stayed gone. She's just had her fourth kid, and is apparently adrift in a sleepless haze of formula and diapers and the senseless wailing of their new bundle of joy. Chris is closing up his auto-repair business for the whole summer to sleep on their couch in Monterey and help his sister out.

"Enjoy that." I smile sweetly.

Chris gives me a quick kiss on the cheek. "Left a little something for you in the fridge. Felicidades, Vanni! See you in September, hey?"

As soon as he's gone, I pop my head into the fridge and find a foil-wrapped plate of chocolate-banana empanadas on the top rack. They must've come from the bakery in town, because Chris, who lives the stereotypical bachelor's life out of meals in boxes, definitely didn't bake them. He used to have dinner with us a couple times a month, but now that Dad doesn't really cook, they spend most of their time together slowly sipping beer in the backyard, neither of them speaking. They've never really needed words anyway.

I think it's helped just having Chis around while Dad readjusts to a world that's growing harder and shrinking smaller. We'll all miss him this summer, for sure.

Shoveling four empanadas onto a plate, I carry my sugary riches down the cramped hall, pausing outside Mom and Dad's room. No light seeps out below the door. I ease it open with my free hand and whisper, "Daddy?" into the dark. Squinting toward the bed, I can just make out the shape of him, flat and still. No answer. I know the medication he takes knocks him out, sometimes even in the middle of the day.

We can talk tomorrow.

"Vanni?" a gruff voice calls just as I'm closing the door.

Frozen for a moment in the slice of hallway light, I tell myself to set the plate on the floor and go perch on the very edge of the mattress. "How was physical therapy?"

It usually takes a few extra seconds for him to grasp questions—the medicine that helps with other symptoms actually makes this worse—but he answers eventually. While I wait, I watch him. Though curled in on himself a little, Dad looks mostly the way he did when he was healthy. His wiry hair is still full and dark, he's got the same proud brown wedge of a nose, his knuckles are still strong. Though even before the first signs and symptoms, he wasn't *truly* healthy. This rotten, implosive combination of genes was always inside of him, invisible and waiting.

For Dad, Huntington's started with trembling fingers. A dropped pitcher of water, a fumbled knife while chopping carrots, a dangerous twitch when he went to pull a pan out of the oven at Silvia's. Hand cramps, he claimed. Nothing to worry about, and no need to see a doctor (even before the bills and the shortened restaurant hours and occasional help from Xime, we were never rolling in it).

But soon, he would stagger on flat ground. Smack his hip on a restaurant table a time too often. Just after that New Year's Day in 2014, he missed a step coming off our front stoop and scraped his knee raw. Every now and then, he'd slur his words as if he *wasn't* a two-beers-maybe-on-a-Friday-night guy. And then there were the quick-bright flares of temper, so unlike Dad, who'd always been about as excitable as sand.

Finally, Mom made him an appointment with his doctor, who sent him on for tests and . . . well, here we are.

His answer comes a moment later. "PT was hard." He grimaces. "Did a lot of stretching."

"That's good though, Daddy."

Propped up against two pillows, he shrugs. Or I think he does; sometimes it's hard to tell what's on purpose and what's not. Dad pats my hand above the sheet, then after a pause, "You like your graduation, mi corazón?"

Let's see; it was hot. Dusty. Endless. Pointless. "It was great."

Another long pause. "You see us on the bleachers?"

"Of course I saw you, Daddy." More silence, so I keep going. "Sorry I couldn't stick around. I went to this senior party after the ceremony. It was so much fun."

"All your friends there?"

"Yeah, Daddy. Everybody went. It was great."

We trade white lies and wavering pauses for a few minutes, and then I kiss the hard, tan apple of his cheek and tell him I'm off to bed.

"Proud of you, Vanni."

I wince, glad he can't see me clearly in the dim bedroom. Everybody's just so, so proud of me today.

When I'm safe in my bedroom, I flop onto the sheets with my empanadas and stare up at the ceiling, where Dad stood on his own mattress when he was a teenager and reached way up to scratch *GABRIEL ESPINOZA WAS HERE* into the plaster with a pocketknife. This was Dad's childhood home. I sleep in the bed he slept in. He combed his hair, deep chocolaty brown like mine, in the speckled mirror above the desk. He spread his books out on the same worn red rug and did his homework left-handed, like me.

I swim like my dad. I look like my dad. I write like my dad. I might not walk like him, but I run and laugh just like he used to. There are plenty of differences—for one, it turns out a lack of talent can be passed down through blood just as easily as talent, as I've inherited my mom's unfortunate gift for runny eggs, burnt Campbell's soup, and still-chewy noodles—but the similarities do add up.

Feeling way too tight in my skin, I scoop my phone, silenced for the past few hours, out of my purse. There's one new email (a Nigerian prince needs my help and will share his fortune with me in exchange for a small one-time loan) and a text.

Jake: Not cool, crazy girl! Not in front of the boss!

Me: Like you don't love it

A moment later he answers.

Jake: Pick you up tomorrow?

I drop my phone on my stomach. Tomorrow: the first day of the rest of my life, post–high school. I'm already bored.

To make things worse, for the first summer in three years I won't be working full days at Silvia's. Some days I won't work at all, because even though I'm cheap-to-free labor and despite the cost of keeping on our regular waitstaff, my parents couldn't bring themselves to fire Jake and Estrella and the rest. Instead, they scaled back our hours. Now Jake works a second job at the Trading Post, where you can get a package of T-shirts, juice, and a baby doll in a mariachi costume all within one aisle. You know, the essentials.

When I'm not working, I'll help out at home, of course. I'll do chores and help Mom cobble together breakfast and wash the dishes, drive Dad to his appointments, run errands at the grocery store or the pharmacy. Then before noon a few days a week, I'll head to the restaurant. Except for a new sign outside the Shrine of Our Lady Parish, the route will look just like it always has.

Generally: it's brown.

Specifically: it's old, tiny, dusty, and brown. Grown-ups always complain about how things changed in the cities—how Santa Fe is all white tourists on bicycles and fancy restaurants downtown and B and Bs where families use to live for generations—but it's not like that here. Mr. Binali has always smoked two packs a day on the porch outside his one-room real estate agency. Mrs. Reyes has always handed out *Turn to Jesus* pamphlets by the bronze statue of a coonskin-capped, musket-toting fur trapper in the miniature town square on her lunch hour. Kids have always gathered in the arroyo off Silver Avenue if they're cool, and around the picnic table outside Burrito Bandito if they're not.

Mrs. Short handed me a slip of paper today on a dusty football field, but that doesn't mean anything's changed, not even a bit, no matter what Mom believes. Maybe it's different for Diana and Marilee and the others. I could ask them. They'll be around for the summer at least. But when was the last time I really talked to them? Not this year. Probably not last. There's just too many ghosts of too many promises between us. Like, we swore to each other that we'd go away to school, we'd study abroad in Greece or Spain or Egypt, we'd switch countries as regularly as we changed our tampons.

Unlikely.

Mom might think I'm only staying long enough to help them through a rough patch at the restaurant, to squeeze in more time with Dad, to make Important Decisions about my future. But for all he'll never say it, I'm pretty sure Dad at least knows the truth.

I roll over on the bed and swallow my empanadas, one after the other, wondering how Lucas the lifeguard can help pass the time.

FOUR

The Lost Lagoon's been open only a few weeks, yet somehow it manages to look like a park on the edge of collapse.

Part of it's the whole Atlantis vibe. I follow the directions on the billboard on I-25, park in the half-full lot, and walk the path to the front entrance. It's shaped like a tumbledown coliseum, fake crumbled columns and all. Inside, the ticket stand and turnstiles are bathed in dim blue light like an underwater cave. I flash my El Trampero High ID to get the student price—might as well make some use of my education post-graduation—and resurface in the park. It's big. Not, like, Florida-theme-park big, but it's New Mexico big. I count five waterslides soaring over the tourists, with plastic aquatic plants and vines twined around the tubes. Larger-than-life severed heads of faux-marble statues border an unnaturally blue wave pool. There's an extra-depressing chipped figure of Venus in her sea-shell outside the portable bathrooms, a kid's cherry ICEE upchucked on her toes.

Half the attractions are still fenced off with *Under Construction* and *Coming Soon!* signs on the chain-link fence, so I start my search for Lucas at Neptune's Pool, shaped like a moat around a miniature ruined temple. The lifeguard stationed on the island points me to a sandwich shop near the front of the park, the Sunken Sub, where Lucas is apparently on his lunch break. It's one of two eateries in the park; the other's a seafood restaurant—the sort of place that spells all the crab on the menu with a *K*.

Sure enough, I duck inside the Sub—there's no actual door, but a curtain of streamers like multicolored seaweed—and spot him and his bright red suit in a cor-ner booth.

Turning my back, I stand in plain sight at the front of the café. I study the sandwich case as if I have a great interest in lunch meats, leaning across the glass on tiptoe for maximum length of leg and maximum firmness of ass beneath my cuffed denim shorts. My calves are starting to tremble a little by the time he finally shouts, "Savannah!" I spin around, and he waves me over.

Would it be too much to say that I sway toward him? I don't *not* sway. I take my time strolling to the booth, anyway.

Lucas tips his familiar white visor. "How's the Sub of the Day?"

How should I know? I was concentrating so hard on being looked at, I spared not a glance for anything. I lean against the wall beside the booth, painted with fishes and eels and anemones, and pop my hip to the side. "Looks fantastic. So glad I came all this way just for a sandwich."

He grins, all white teeth. It's going well so far—a little cliché, maybe—but then I'm distracted. Because across the booth from Lucas is a girl hunched over an overly toasted panini that Dad would've tossed in a bonfire before serving, crushing her french fries into mashed potatoes with her fork tines.

"Oh hey, someone I want you to meet," Lucas says. "This is my little sister, Leigh."

She slouches back against her seat and looks up at me, and it's like staring at a smaller, skinnier Lucas. Leigh's hair, ambiguously trapped between brown and blond like Lucas's, is chopped even shorter than her brother's—tufts of it brush her ears and ruffle across her forehead. Same strangely dark eyebrows and eyelashes and big eyes, though hers are a muddier kind of hazel. Even her clothes could be his. She crosses her arms over a baggy boy's tank top, crisp white and high around her neck, huge around her tanned shoulders.

"Do you work here too?" I ask.

He laughs. "God forbid! We're still hiring, but they have this policy. You gotta be eighteen, and Leigh-Bee's only seventeen."

"Don't *call* me that." She scowls, swatting her brother's hand away as he digs for a surviving fry.

"We live out in Los Cerrillos, but she'll be a senior at Santa Fe Prep," he continues.

"*She* has *ears*."

"You like Santa Fe Prep?" I ask Leigh.

"I don't know yet," she says grudgingly. "We're new."

"My condolences."

Lucas looks up. "Why, is it that bad here?"

"No," I lie, biting my cheek. I was aiming for salty, but landed on sad. "There's lots of stuff to do if you know where to look." I grasp for an example. "Have you been to the Mine Shaft Tavern in Madrid?"

He shakes his head.

"It's a lot of locals—bikers and tourists, but it's pretty cool. I could show you sometime." I tug on my necklace where it falls just above the V in my V-neck.

The noise Leigh makes is like the moan of a dying animal in pain.

Lucas winces. He slides his empty glass across the table toward her and points to the soda dispenser across the cafeteria. "Go get me a refill, Leigh-Bee."

"Why?"

"You're eating your lunch free, is why."

"No, it's costing me," she says, and takes his glass and smiles through gritted teeth. It's not Lucas's smile. And her eyes, they're *sharper*. I don't know where the thought comes from, but if Lucas is soft-serve, she's more like a snow cone.

And just a guess, but she doesn't seem impressed by me, either.

When she's gone, he laughs, looks at me pleadingly. "Don't mind my sister. She's shy."

Shy isn't the word I'd use. She's Karen Goodstein, is what she is. Karen was a transplant from Connecticut in eighth grade. Strange enough on its own, since nobody really moves *to* La Trampa, the same way none of us leave. She sat in the back of every classroom, sighing mournfully. She sighed her way through school assemblies. She sighed while meandering back and forth across the basketball court in gym. Hers was an all-purpose sigh that said: *I once had a rich, full, East Coast life, and now, I have* this *place.*

Then again, I heard that even Karen Goodstein went to the party in the arroyo after graduation.

"No problem," I tell Lucas, sliding into the booth across from him. Meanwhile, Leigh's already abandoned her brother's cup by the dispenser and wandered away. Probably for the best.

"But I'm glad you came by," Lucas says, regaining my attention. "I'm driving out to Santa Cruz Lake this weekend. There's supposed to be a meteor shower Saturday night, and maybe you want to come up? It should be something."

My smile slips a little. The stockroom at Silvia's is one thing, or the back seat of a rusted gold El Camino in a school parking lot, or the semi-sheltered patch of desert behind the football field. But a trip up into the mountains with a guy I just met? It's not like I'm Susie Safe Choices, but even for me, that's out there.

Maybe he sees this in my face, because he hurries to add, "Leigh and I are both going. We always watched showers up there, best place in town. Or outside of it."

"I thought you guys were new?"

"New-ish. We moved from here to Boston with our mom when I was thirteen. Leigh was eleven. Dad stayed in the area, and we just moved back to live with him when our school years ended. But I came out a few weeks beforehand, applying for jobs and visiting the college and stuff. That's how I walked into the Lost Lagoon."

"You were in college in Boston?"

He nods. "I started at UMass last fall, but we . . . I wanted a change, and Leigh came too. So I'll be at UNM in September, and Leigh will be at Santa Fe. You'll like her when she settles in. We just, uh . . ." He rubs the deeply suntanned back of his neck and glances over at Leigh, now inspecting an armless plaster statue of a mermaid by the dessert stand. We watch as she scuffs her chewed-up brown Vans, shoves her hands into the pockets of her striped red board shorts, and brings her face close to its ample shell bra.

"Neither of us know many people around here anymore," he finishes. "We could use some friends."

I'm not sure whether to feel relieved or disappointed by our third wheel. I am definitely not relieved by his use of the word *friend* instead of *maximally sexy soon-to-be lover.*

"Maybe," I say. Then I shrug demurely, remembering my mission now that Leigh's not here to salt my game. "I might be busy. I'm hunting for a part-time job and I hear that can take a while, though I *also* heard there's a water park hiring."

He catches on with a lazy grin. "I guess I heard that too."

"I have extra time, since I'm on summer vacation." Though is it really a vacation, if it's just your life? "I work shifts at my parents' restaurant, but other than that, I'm not doing much. Plus I could use the paycheck."

That part, at least, is 100 percent honest. A new cash flow would help. For a while now money has been tighter than tight, with Dad's hospital bills and therapy bills and occasional home aide bills. I know the restaurant isn't making as much, especially with half days, and we've had to hire an assistant manager to help Mom, and a new head cook to take over for Dad. Martin was his assistant, and though Dad would never say so, he must hate that the chef's hat is outside the family for the first time. But it's not as if I and my half-blackened grilled cheese and Campbell's could put it on.

Martin's good, he's just not Dad. Martin doesn't have Dad's sixth sense for picking exactly the perfect jicama and avocados at the market. Martin can't make an amazing menudo out of frozen onions and sheep's feet. Martin can't spin straw into gold. It sounds stupid, but to watch Dad cook was like watching a wizard in potions class at Hogwarts. The way he'd toss an unmeasured-yet-precise amount of spices onto strips of meat, the way he'd pulp soaked chilies in mere seconds, the way he'd juice lime wedges and lemon slices with one hand while stirring a simmering pot with the other. He'd tried to pass it all down to me, but honestly, he wasn't a good teacher. He couldn't explain how to spoon just enough filling into cornhusks, wrap them loosely and seal them just-tight-enough-but-not-too-tight with kitchen yarn to steam perfect tamales. Not when it came so intuitively to him. How would you teach somebody to sneeze? Instead, I'd watch him as he stood at the kitchen counter browning and chopping and stuffing. He probably hoped I'd absorb *some* skills just by being near him. But I never did.

Sometimes that makes me feel strangely hopeful.

Anyway, a little extra income definitely wouldn't hurt my parents. If the rest of the staff at Silvia's has second jobs, why can't I? Besides, I like to keep busy. I like to keep moving. And anything that puts me and my swimsuit in Lucas's path is a real bonus.

"You're looking for something in the water?" he asks.

"Always."

Across the booth, he pretends to size me up; at least, I think he's pretending. "They're full on lifeguards, but one of the attractions is hiring. They're casting for the pool personnel next Tuesday."

"What do you mean, casting?"

"You'll have to show up to solve that mystery."

Right, because wrangling foam noodles in a wave pool or packing children one at a time down a waterslide for four hours sounds delightfully mysterious.

He pops another fry. "But I think you'd be perfect. I'll tell them about you, if you want, so you won't have to apply for the first round."

I don't hear Leigh's catlike approach until she stands beside the table, eyeing me in her seat. "A-*hem*." She clears her throat. So original.

I take my cue to go. "Okay, I guess I'll see you Tuesday."

"Tuesday, or Saturday night?"

"Hmm." I drum my fingertips against my mouth, pretending to deliberate whilst calling attention to my lips, like Marilee once taught me. "Let's say Saturday night."

"Yeah?" There's real happiness in his gravelly voice, which pleases me, so I type my number into Lucas's cell—deliberately not looking over at Leigh—and walk away with an extra sway in my step, just for him.

And maybe just a little bit to spite his sister.

FIVE

I sit on my front steps on Saturday evening and watch our gravel driveway glitter under the still-bright eye of the sun. The concrete is warm beneath me, and I'm sweating a little. I wasn't sure what to wear on a first sorta-date. I went with my standard casual outfit: dark jean capris and a backless orange tank top, though I had to switch the espadrille wedges out for clean-ish sneakers. Tied around my purse strap is a big El Trampero High sweatshirt, through which you can't even tell I have a body, but it'll be cool in the mountains at night.

Not like I spent the afternoon tearing through my

closet for just the right shapeless, sexless sweatshirt to impress Lucas. I don't get that kind of nervous around boys. Maybe I used to, but I had a slow start. Marilee, on the other hand, kissed Taylor Naswood on a field trip to the Cochiti Pueblo in sixth grade. They went at it behind the pottery shop, with tongue, bragged Taylor. When they boarded the school bus at the end of the afternoon, she sat beside me, scrubbing a finger back and forth across her lips as if they felt different. I slumped down in my seat, jealous. Not because of the boy—Marilee found a new boyfriend for the Wheelwright Museum of the American Indian, and for every school trip after—but of the feeling.

Diana was always my date to middle school dances. She wasn't allowed to have boyfriends, though she loved them from afar. She even had nicknames for them, all the boys whose last names she tried on in the margins of her notebooks. Hot Boy, Pretty Boy, Band Boy, Math Boy, Skater Boy. She was uncreative, but devoted. Every time we passed a crush of hers in the hallway, she'd drill an elbow into my kidneys.

I wonder whether she'd go wild if she ever got loose.

I guess I went a little wild the summer between eighth grade and freshman year, when I looked down and found breasts instead of eraser stubs lurking below my T-shirts. I grew two inches before the start of school, and borrowed Marilee's copies of *Seventeen*, and the lady in the curling-wand kiosk at the Coronado Mall showed me a few tricks. I considered cutting back on Dad's chorizo and bean dip or his mole poblano, but who was I kidding? I never could've squeezed my size-twelve hips into Marilee's size-two bandage dresses, nor my muscled shoulders, which I had earned through years of swimming and was proud of. Max Binali liked my curves. He noticed me, and I had liked that somebody was noticing me, especially a junior.

But did I really feel different after my first kiss? My tenth?

Not much. Or maybe I did, just never for very long.

All of this is to say that the instant I hear the crunch of tires grinding over gravel, I vault off the stoop, ready to feel something new. My mood sinks slightly when I see Leigh slumped down in the passenger seat with shades on. Guess I'm riding bitch after all. Ignoring her, I poke my head through the driver's-side window, my elbows on the hot metal. "I like your van. It's really . . . green." A sticky, overpowering shade of green at that.

"Sorry about the seating." Lucas grimaces. "Leigh-Bee gets carsick. Or so she claims."

I slide into the backseat. "Thanks for picking me up."

"You got off at the restaurant?"

"No, Lucas, she's just a heat mirage," Leigh mumbles.

"I told my mom about the meteor shower," I plough on. "I think she was . . . surprised."

He cranes around his seat. "Not your usual Saturday night thing?"

That's an understatement, if ever there was one. I shake my head.

"Well, you're gonna be impressed," Lucas promises. "You'll see."

We take off in silence, sort of. There's no air-conditioning, so the windows are all down, and once we reach the highway, wind roars dully inside the minivan. Plus every time Lucas taps the breaks, they squeal brutally, as if the van runs on piglets instead of gasoline.

Perhaps it's the noisiness of the silence that makes it awkward, but I'm suddenly realizing how long it's been since I've ridden in a car with people my own age (multiple people, that is, not just Jake on the drive to or from our latest round of couch-wrestling). It's like I've forgotten everything I knew about having and making friends. How to talk without flirting. How to ask small questions of people I don't yet know, and how to care about the answers. How to be myself, the me I am when nobody's looking, while Lucas glances anxiously in the rearview mirror and Leigh sits stonily up front.

I scrape my billowing hair out of my face, then sit on my hands because I can't figure out what else to do with them. Staring out the open window, I turn over the life choices that led me here, wondering: Is the glimmer of a potential hookup (with a guy I met two weeks ago but have yet to achieve any kind of play) worth being trapped in a car with strangers, half of whom want nothing to do with me? Is a crappy job in a crappy water park worth it? Is anything?

After a few miles of this, Lucas reaches down and puts on what I think is the CD player, but turns out to be a tape deck. Guitar and a Latin beat drizzle from the speakers. "You like Carlos Santana?" he calls over his shoulder. "Our dad loves him."

"I don't really know him," I shout gratefully above the wind. "My parents listen to, like, Morrissey."

He drums his thumbs on the steering wheel. "I think you'll like him. This is *Caravanserai*. Totally his best. Dad used to play it every time we drove to Santa Cruz to go camping." He laughs. "Hey Leigh-Bee, remember that time with the pop-up tent?"

"Ugh, must we?" she shouts back. "Roll the windows up, already. I'd rather be hot than deaf."

He cranks his closed—the van's clearly too old for power windows—and I do the same in back.

"So this is the story," he starts. "Leigh and Dad and I went camping just after we rented *The Blair Witch Project*. Which I wasn't supposed to show Leigh, who was ten or something, but I did, and I fast-forwarded through the part where it said they were in the Maryland woods. I told her it was the woods around Santa Cruz Lake."

"You idiot," Leigh says, whipping her shades off. "They weren't even the right trees."

"Who's the idiot? Your spongy little child-brain believed me. So the next week we drove up, and Dad had a surprise for Leigh. Her own tent. Usually we all slept in the same room in our old Coleman, but Dad said Leigh-Bee was *becoming a woman*." He reaches over to pinch Leigh's cheeks.

She grunts and swats him off. "He was probably afraid I'd wake up and see you playing with yourself."

"Shut up. Vanni, you should've seen her face when she realized she had to sleep alone with the Blair Witch waiting out there in the dark. And her sad little 'Help!' when I snuck out and pounded on the walls of her tent in the middle of the night. After that, she slept in the backseat of the station wagon with the doors locked."

"That's so mean!" I say.

But Leigh laughs with him. She has a nice laugh, light and high-pitched, like ice tinkling or something. "Dad wanted to drown you in the lake. He didn't even tell you when I peed on your soap."

"Wait. You did that? Did he know?"

"About the soap, yeah. He didn't know about your toothbrush."

"You little sicko!" he cries.

We drive north while the sun dips low in the sky and the air cools, then pull off the highway into the foot-hills of the Sangre de Cristo Mountains. All of a sudden, we come into a town up in the darkening hills. Houses loom above us on the left. On the right where the cliff side slopes down, you could walk off the road and onto the roofs below.

"What is this place?" I ask.

"Not sure." Lucas shrugs and steers carefully. "I guess we should look it up on a map, but we never have. Wait and see what's ahead."

When we round the next bend he pulls off to the side and puts the car in park in front of a house. He whistles, even though he must've seen the place loads of times. Leigh cranes her neck out the window for a better look too. I unclick my seat belt, lean forward, and slip between them to stare through the windshield at a house absolutely smothered in cow skulls—nailed up to the walls and gutter and fence posts, like cracked white stones.

Leigh settles back into her seat and turns to me. "Lucas thinks a psycho ex-cowboy hermit lives here. Like, he's been sneaking out of the hills and murdering the stupid beasts that plagued him all his life to collect their bones."

"It is pretty creepy."

She shakes her head, and her voice is softer. "I bet he really cares about them. He thinks they're beautiful and doesn't give a shit what anyone else thinks. Maybe he's just a sad old guy who loves what he loves."

Up this close, she doesn't look as much like her brother. Her sandy-brown hair is short, her hazel eyes just as big, but Leigh's eyelashes are even longer—they leave fan-shaped shadows on her cheeks in the dim light—and her face is smaller. Slimmer. Baggy clothes or no, she's pretty.

Too bad she's a total Karen Goodstein.

We're not back on the road for long before we pull down a slope and into a parking lot. The last of the sunset fades over the water in front of us, behind a lake cupped by rising hills of pine trees. There are no bonfires down on the beach, no other cars in the lot. It's a quiet place. Kind of a murdery place for a first date, you might say, and I'm almost glad there's three of us here.

Lucas pops the trunk, steps out, and stretches. He grabs a few grocery bags while Leigh hauls out a pile of blankets, and leads the way down to the lake. Beyond the lot is the narrow beach, and stretching out into the water, a long metal gangway leads to the dock. We dump our stuff in the sand around us and I shrug into my sweatshirt.

Farewell, sex appeal.

Lucas spreads out the blankets and says, "Okay, girls. It's just after nine now. The Weather Channel says we should see the shower around nine thirty. So eyes on the sky."

Leigh fishes out a can of Pringles, rolls over onto her stomach on her blanket, and fixes her eyes down the tube. I share a quilt with Lucas, sitting close enough so when we lie back, our elbows are inches apart.

"When were you guys up here last?" I ask, staring up toward the Milky Way, every star visible in the unpolluted darkness.

"Together? Probably when Leigh turned ten—she had her party up here. Was it Barbie themed, Leigh-Bee?"

"It was World Cup themed, butt-munch."

"Oh, yeah." He grins up at the sky. "You had your little Abby Wambach jersey, and that soccer ball cake, and you didn't get to eat it because you had to go sit in the van for trying to drown your friend."

"She shouldn't have worn a Marta jersey," Leigh mumbles around a mouthful of chips.

"We lived in Española then," Lucas explains, "but Dad moved to Naveen's house in Los Cerillos after the divorce, and Leigh and Mom and me moved to Boston, where our grandparents live."

"So you live in Los Cerrillos now?" I ask. "That's ten miles from me!"

"Hallelujah," Leigh deadpans. She throws a chip toward the lake, and because Pringles aren't aerodynamic, it falls short, but not by much. Good arm.

"This might come as a surprise since Leigh's being really subtle about it, but she doesn't like it here." Lucas reaches over to punch lightly at her bicep, and she swats him off dramatically.

"You didn't want to come home?" I ask, tracking the red pinprick of a plane across the sky.

"*Boston's* home," she answers, frost in her voice.

"Oh." Though no part of us is touching, I feel Lucas stiffen beside me, and for his sake I scramble to break the tension. Okay, it's also for the sake of my long game, wherein he and I go for a private starlit hike, leaving Leigh behind to sulk. "A girl in my class was from New England. Karen. She was . . . awesome. She loved it there."

"You ever been?" he asks.

"No closer than Round Rock, Texas, to visit my grandparents." I shrug. "Maybe I'll get there sometime."

Leigh snorts loudly, still staring into her Pringles tube. Lucas bunches the blanket in his fist, and everything's awkward again, more so than the first few quiet miles in the car.

Although *Mistake! Mistake!* blinks through my brain in rhythm with the winking lights of that far-off plane, I can't help myself. *"What?"* I ask her, knowing I'll regret it.

She looks up at last. "Just you."

I roll to my side and stare at her across Lucas's stone-still chest. "What *about* me, exactly?"

Leigh stares back. *"Maybe* you'll get there? Like, *maybe* you'll *someday* get farther than Tex-ass? Have you never partaken in the miracle of flight? Have you never experienced motorized vehicles or blended fabrics or this thing they call electricity? Aren't you eighteen? What are you even—"

"Oh my god," Lucas sighs. "Vanni, I'm so—"

"Don't." Leigh sits up and snaps. "Don't act like I'm your sad little dog who pooped on her front lawn. Don't apologize for me. This tragedy is on you, since I never asked my *brother* to make me friends."

"As if I could work such fucking miracles!" He stands and snatches the Pringles out of her hand. Ignoring her cries of protest, he stalks off and vengefully empties the tube into a trash can up near the parking lot. Though he pauses as if he might come back our way, Lucas shakes his head and walks off down the beach toward the trees beyond the sand, his hands folded behind his head; the living, breathing, dictionary definition of surrender.

In the ringing silence that follows, Leigh turns to me. It seems like she wants to say something more, but I'm already up and shuffling away across the beach. Because I did *not* switch shifts with Jake for this, I did *not* cram myself into a car with strangers just to have a staring match with Leigh Clemente. I had another goal in mind, and for a moment I have every intention of trailing after Lucas. Maybe this night can be salvaged. Boys are pretty good at compartmentalizing when persuaded. I'll catch up to him, grab for his shoulder with gentle fingers, and it'll go something like:

Me: Hey.

Him: Hey. Look . . . I'm really sorry about my sister. She's such a mega-bitch. That stuff she said . . .

Me: It's fine.

Him: She doesn't know what she's talking about. You're awesome, Vanni.

Me: Really, it's totally fine. I didn't come here for your sister, anyways.

Him: No?

And then I'll take his arm, pull him inside the tree line, and we can forget about all this and all about the meteor shower, the sky blocked out by the branches overhead.

But I don't go after Lucas.

Instead I veer right, clank over the narrow gangway to the dock, and drop down onto the cooled metal at the end, my hands shaking against the railing.

For sure, Leigh is a mega-bitch.

She's also right. Not about the blended fabrics or whatever. But even though she's said five words to me, ever, she's right about me. How I'm just *here*, I might always be *here*, scared and bored and waiting for the sky to fall—or not.

Footsteps clomp down the dock, but alas, it isn't Lucas who plops down next to me.

"So this was fun," Leigh says flatly. "When's the second date?"

The lake laps at the dock below the platform. The insects whine.

"You want my brother, right?" she asks.

"If I say yes, will you switch places?" I sneer my coldest sneer, colder even than hers.

Unfortunately, she doesn't take it personally, and doesn't leave. "Just, he sort of has a girlfriend. At least, they're sniffing and circling each other like dogs in a park. She's going to UNM in September too. I guess they met at some orientation thing last month. And she told him about the Lagoon. She's a scoop girl at the Glacier—that's the ice cream parlor at the park. Gives him free ice cream. It's hard to compete with a mating call like that."

I stare carefully into the moon-sprinkled water. A scoop girl and a college girl in one; that is tough to compete with.

"I'm not trying to be mean," she says, which I actually believe, because she must've had to leave her dignity in the sand to come out here and talk. "Are you devastated?"

"Why would I be devastated?"

"I figured you were into him. Everybody's into Lucas."

I wonder: Am I devastated?

It doesn't feel like devastation. Disappointment, sure. Like I said, we don't get a lot of fresh blood around here, and Lucas does have gorgeous eyes. Maybe I feel like an asshole for swaying and hip-popping, if he was never into me in the first place.

"He does like you, though," Leigh adds. "He couldn't stop talking about you this afternoon. '*Vanni's* pretty cool, right?'" she grunts in a low voice. "'You should see if *Vanni* likes soccer, since *Vanni's* such a good swimmer. You should be like *Vanni. Vanni* probably doesn't fart in her brother's sock drawer.'"

I laugh, though I don't mean to.

"Right? Everyone thinks he's cool, but the nerd has no chill." The breeze kicks up and Leigh shivers, her tan skin noticeably goose bumped in the starlight. She only wears another long white tank top—the kind you buy in six-packs at Walgreens, which I suspect she has—and baggy black sweatpants cuffed to the knees. "I just wish he'd give me a fucking week to miss home before he starts matchmaking. But, um, I am sorry."

"Whatever. Don't worry about it." I put her out of her misery, because what good is it to me?

"And all that stuff about you basically being like a modern tragedy—"

"Yeah, we really don't have to talk about it."

"That's cool." She taps her fingers against the railing in no particular rhythm, then glances at me and smiles slyly. "We could go in the water instead."

I look back toward the shore, where signs posted all over the beach demand: *NO SWIMMING.* "We're not supposed to."

"So we can wade. I dare you."

"It'll be freezing."

She glances at me, moonlight ponding in her narrowed eyes. "But I *dared* you."

"But I'm not *twelve*," I shoot back. What's her deal?

Miserable one second and a human amphetamine the next?

Still, when she stands, I follow her. Down the gangway, onto the sand, where she turns deliberately away from me before pulling off her sweatpants and tank top to reveal navy Y-fronts, loose on her muscled legs, and a plain black sports bra.

"I thought we were just wading," I object.

She glances over her shoulder at me, arms wrapped around her waist, then strides into the water. "Oh shit oh shit, that's cold!" she hisses.

I strip off my sweatshirt and jeans, glad I picked the hot-pink panties with black polka dots; according to Will Fischer, they make my butt look like "a sexy watermelon." Part of me wonders whether Lucas is watching; I search for him in the dark and find him up the beach, tossing rocks into the lake. I can't tell if he's looking this way, but I bend over to lay my capris out on the sand, slowly and deliberately. Serves him right. He could've mentioned the scoop girl. He could've told me this was a playdate with his little sister.

When I straighten, Leigh is watching me from the shallows, still hugging herself. Under all those shapeless clothes are narrow hips and small breasts. Nothing like my curves. She's slimmer and straighter, with different muscles than mine; her body's strong, but in different ways.

It's a good body.

"What?" she asks defensively, hugging herself tighter, hollowing her rib cage and bowing her shoulders as if to shrink herself. Now she's shy?

"Nothing," I call back. Already shivering, I tiptoe into the water after her. I was right, of course; it's freezing. I push forward up to my shaking knees and consider myself brave, until Leigh drops her knees and lets herself plunge under.

She surfaces a little farther out, gasping. *"Fu-u-u-uck!"* she splutters, slicking her short hair back. "Come on!"

"Are you crazy?" I laugh around chattering teeth.

But I'm considering it.

Luckily and unfortunately, Lucas barks, "LEIGH!" and jogs toward us, sand kicking up under his sneakers. "What the fuck? The undercurrent's too strong, you idiot! What are you thinking?"

I blush guiltily, because I definitely know better.

"Okay, okay!" She shovels her arms and legs smoothly through the water until she's standing beside me again, dripping, blue lipped. We retreat to the beach, where she pulls her tank top and sweatpants on at once without drying off. I know from plenty of post-pool experience that it's terrible, like you're a snake trying to slip back into too-tight skin. Pushing the hair off her forehead, she grins at me. "Your turn," she says, sweeping an arm toward the water.

"No thanks." I laugh again. Maybe it's because I'm cold, but I feel . . . awake. Like I can feel every part of my body at once, every little blood vessel and bone.

I tilt my face up, toward a million stars you can't see from the city, not even from La Trampa. As I stare, a bright streak crosses it, then another a moment later. "Look," I say, and she does. After a while, there are so many, they look like one great white light behind a shredded sky.

SIX

On Monday I'm taking inventory in the stockroom of Silvia's when a pair of brown arms corded with muscles encircles my waist from behind. "Guess who?"

I clutch my chest. "Culero!"

"Good guess." Jake laughs as I slap him with the ledger. "Oh, don't be like that, princesita. It's dull as shit out there. Just the old guys at table four, guzzling coffee all goddamn day." He steps into me, and his breath smells of Lucky Strikes thinly veiled by wintergreen gum. I imagine the still-glowing stubs scattering the hot pavement behind the Dumpster; he could've at least offered me one. I've been trapped among the pinto beans and flour sacks all morning, with only the knocking of the old swamp cooler for company.

With my thumb and forefinger, I play the world's saddest song on the world's smallest violin. "You can do the inventory if you're so bored."

An animal grin twists his full lips. He hooks his fingers around the neck strap of my apron, dragging me closer. "Sure, boss. I'll get right on that." One strong hand slips below the apron, works its way between the hem of my peasant top and corduroy skirt.

However much he claims he wants to be my boyfriend, fooling around with Jake is the same overall experience as a two-for-two-dollars chili dog from the countertop case at Allsup's. Attractive to the starving, surprisingly delicious, but followed by half an hour of gut cramps and regret. And yet, like the perpetually hungry, this hard-won wisdom rarely stops me. I come back for it again and again.

I cut my eyes toward the stockroom door. If nothing else, it'd be better than tallying sacks of beans. I push him backward, drop the ledger, and shed my apron onto the concrete floor.

We're not even all the way out of our shirts before a voice crackles across the two-way on the shelf beside us. "Savannah, you there?" asks Juno, the assistant manager. "There's a girl up front looking for you. Says she's your friend."

I pull away from Jake as panic spikes my pulse. What girl? What friend? Is it Diana? Marilee? Why would either of them come by? I haven't seen them since graduation.

"Pretend you didn't hear." Jake's breath warms my throat.

I nod, but Juno's an asthmatic smoker, and her wheezing vocals aren't the most sensual sound track. When she calls for me a second time, I shrug Jake off. "I'll be quick," I promise.

Sorrowfully, he watches me go.

Blinking in the bright daylight outside the stockroom, I'm shocked to see Leigh leaning against the vacant host podium.

"Hi?" I say, approaching cautiously.

She straightens and shoves her hands into the pockets of saggy black basketball shorts, cinched tight over her waist. "I'm not creeping or anything. Lucas sent me over."

"He . . . huh?"

"He got the date wrong for that job they're hiring for. At the water park? It's today at three—he's been texting you all morning."

Fuck, my phone's been in the back office. "Well that sucks, 'cause I can't get there this afternoon. My mom's got the car, and I'm working."

She raises one dark, arrow-straight eyebrow and glances toward the old men shuffling conquian cards at table four, sipping the same coffees they ordered an hour ago. Regulars in the midafternoon, they're our only customers at the moment. Every so often they'll lift their mugs for a refill, but that's as much action as we'll see till the dinner rush—really more of a crawl on Mondays— unless Mr. Paiz drops his spoon again.

"Look, I don't know why you want to work at the Pitiful Kingdom, but I'm driving down to see Lucas anyway. We can pick your stuff up on the way. And you don't look that busy."

I almost wish we were busy, or that Juno would forbid me to take off if I asked. The idea of riding all the way out to Albuquerque with Leigh, of finding things to say the whole time, is nerve-racking. "That's pretty unnecessary," I say. "Like, thanks for the offer, but you don't have to be nice to me just because your brother wants us to be friends."

"Maybe I am nice."

It's my turn to raise an eyebrow.

"Maybe I'm trying." She plucks a wrapped peppermint from the dish on Jake's podium and twists the plastic tight between her tan fingers. She's nervous too, I realize.

I could so easily brush her off. Tell her I won't have a break for hours yet. That we're expecting that imaginary rush any time now. That sacks of rice won't inventory themselves. That I mostly asked for this job to get inside her brother's swim trunks. That I couldn't really take on another job, even though the money would be great, and I wouldn't mind a distraction of a different kind.

And then there's Jake.

I try to picture him in back, to remind myself what's waiting for me: He checks the time on his phone, reapplies the ChapStick he doesn't know I know he keeps in the pocket of his apron, texts some girl he met at Sonic. Now, he's arranging his most attractive pout for my inevitable return.

"Okay," I say.

One thing's certain as I shove my apron behind the counter: Jake will be pissed, and I'm not sure if this is a pro or a con. Ditching him feels the way you'd feel walking away from that Allsup's chili dog. You know it's right, but that's cold comfort as your empty stomach slowly consumes itself.

Leigh isn't as good a driver as her brother. She seems to think the pedals won't work unless crushed to the floor mat with every traffic light or stop sign, so the ride starts uncomfortably, in more ways than one. Because despite Lucas's scheming, one semipainful night under the stars does not the best of friends make.

But it *was* legitimately nice of her to fetch me for tryouts.

Besides, Leigh doesn't know my life, doesn't know which awful and sincere questions to ask. None of this *How are you, Vanni? How's your dad, Vanni? What are your plans, Vanni? Why won't you talk about the future, Vanni? Are you gonna take the test, Vanni?* I don't even think she'd care about the answers. Leigh doesn't look at me like Diana does, as though I'm sinking and she's the only one who can save me. Or like Marilee, as though I'm sinking and might at any moment drag her underwater with me.

So I take a breath, and search the car for a conversation starter, anything at all, landing on "I like your sunglasses."

"These?" she asks, patting the top of her head where big blue-green aviators perch in the tufts of her hair. "They're Lucas's. I think I stole them."

"Cool."

"I guess."

Since that's a dead end, I continue the search. In the mirror of my flipped-down visor, I spot a stack of books in the backseat. I recognize the one that tops the pile: *The Poem and You.* "Are you reading that?" I ask.

Leigh cuts her eyes to the rearview mirror, just in time to launch us over a school-zone speed bump. "What, the poetry one?"

"We read it in junior and senior English. Mr. Garza, he was our teacher both years, though he might've been drunk the whole time?"

"Go on," Leigh says.

"It wasn't for sure, but he'd have us read our textbooks while he was 'grading papers.' Except he'd never turn the page on a single report, and he was popping aspirin hard-core. He was also our football coach, but there were, like, thirteen guys on our team, basically every guy in school who could throw a ball in a straight line and take a hit without dying. And they weren't all big or strong, so someone was always hurt, and the rest had to play the entire game, every game. They were about as good as you might think, which could've been one of the many reasons why he was always sipping the juice."

"Scandalous!" Leigh gasps.

"It was. But that's probably why I never learned any poetry, which would've come in super handy bussing tables for a living."

"Same for me. I mean, it's all assigned reading from the Santa Fe Prep summer list, but I haven't looked at it." She waves her hand toward the books. "I'm pretty sure they'll change my life."

"You'll be a senior?"

"Yeah, but I'll be eighteen in September."

"It sucks you couldn't finish school in—" I cut myself off, afraid to poke the bear, as Mom sometimes says.

"It really does," she agrees, her voice quiet, her body stiff. Then she shakes her head, like a dog shakes off droplets of water. "But whatever. Who cares about varsity soccer and actual trees and buildings over two stories, when I can have all of this?" She sweeps one hand across the windshield, palm face out toward the rolling dust and squat brown buildings in front of us, stretching on. "Good thing I'm not the type to sulk."

"What type are you, then?" I ask, because I thought she was exactly the sulking type.

Leigh looks over, draws her eyes up and down my skin in a way that feels familiar, and also not.

My June-hot face flushes brighter.

"I . . . am the type to chauffeur Savannah Espinoza to her casting, obviously."

"Aha! If you know they call it a casting, you know what the job is," I accuse.

"I do."

"Can you tell me?"

"I cannot."

"Great, now I'm scared."

"Good scared, or bad scared?"

"There's a good scared?" I ask dryly.

"Yeah. It's like . . ." Stopping for barely a blink of the turn signal, she pulls us out onto the trail. "When you're waiting for a train, and you see the lights coming down the track, and just for a millisecond your brain wants you to jump out in front of it. And you're scared your body might actually do it, and your heart's going, like, faster than the train."

"How is that good?"

Leigh doesn't have Jake's dimples, or Lucas's easy grin, but with a rare, real smile, her eyes warm up, become mottled slivers of light. "Feels good to me."

It turns out the tryouts aren't actually at the Lost Lagoon, but at the indoor pool at the West Mesa Aquatic Center. A familiar place. I did a few competitions here with my swim club; once, I came in second in my age group in the 100 meter. The pool's Olympic-size, with stadium seating for hundreds, three diving boards, and red, white, and blue pennants strung up across the lanes, all of which are full except for the one blocked off for us. Three dozen girls gather, about two dozen more than I expected to apply as waterslide attendees or inner-tube minders.

But then a middle-aged man with a stereotypical clipboard summons us to the bleachers by bellowing,

"Mermaids, round up!"

What. The. Fuck?

I drift over at the back of the pack and drop my gym bag on the bench beside me.

"I'm Eric, in charge of auditions for our performing park personnel," the man with the clipboard says, "and I'll be casting five mermaids per shift, ten in total."

Now that I look around, I notice . . . similarities between me and the girls waiting to be "cast." We're all eighteen at least and late twenties at the oldest. We're all average in height, and though I'm one of the curviest, we've all got decently muscled shoulders and legs. We're pretty—the girl down the row absentmindedly chewing her long brown hair looks like that YouTube star, the one who matches her makeup to fancy cupcakes she bakes and ices, but never eats. The girl next to her looks like the fifteenth Kardashian sister.

I threw my hair into a hasty ponytail on the car ride, but the rest of the girls have hair that ripples down their backs. I tear my elastic out to match, even as I listen dubiously.

"The job's important but simple," Eric continues. "We don't do underwater stunts like your big fancy parks, so you won't have to mess with scuba lessons or breathing tubes. You don't have to dance or drink underwater. You'll swim around Mermaid Cove, pose on the rocks, wave to the tourists, do a little routine a few times per shift. If selected, you'll begin official training on the twenty-third, and we'll worry about your tails then. Today, we just need to see that you're comfortable in the water and can swim pretty."

I itch to pick up my bag, call Leigh, and on the ride back to Silvia's, text-scream at Lucas for setting me up for this shit. Because *I'm trained, damn it.* I don't *swim pretty.* I'm *strong.* I could get into tryouts at a Division II college, especially if I spent a few months working on my times, and then at the end of summer . . .

Except that I'm doing nothing and going nowhere at the end of summer. So what am I, too good for a mermaid tail? Too good for a C-list water park outside Albuquerque? Too good for a paycheck?

No, I am not. So I shut up and I suck it up. I change into my suit and when it's my turn to try out, I slip into the water. After a few warm-up laps, I pretend that Eric-in-charge-of-auditions-for-performing-park-personnel is a coach at CSU East Bay, or Florida Tech, or Pace. I propel myself off the bottom of the pool and dolphin-kick my damn heart out, knees together, toes pointed, body rolling, my hips more than my legs powering me along. Not my strongest style, but when Eric asks me to use soft hands and a big smile, I do it, even though I much prefer to swim in the zone where I feel like I'll never stop, like I'll never need to.

In the end I emerge dripping and dissatisfied, but at least I swam pretty.

There are only four cars in the lot when we return to Silvia's, and half of them belong to Juno and Jake. I'm guessing I wasn't missed too badly, even if my lunch break has run three hours long.

Leigh throws the car into park, and I jerk roughly against my seat belt. "I release you back into the wild," she says.

I pause before climbing out. Trapped in the heat of the minivan, with all the windows rolled up so we could hear each other on the drive home, Leigh smells generically clean, like Irish Spring soap. I've never much considered the scent of it, but I like it. It almost makes the heat bearable. "Thanks for the ride, I guess."

"You're welcome, I guess," she says, and then "Hold up," as I reach for the door handle. She takes my hand, flips it over palm-up. Fishing a pen out of the glove compartment, she presses down and scribbles across my hand. Her warm fingers trap mine.

I breathe. "What is it?"

"It's my number. You punch it into a phone and then you can text me. In case you need another ride or whatever."

"Six-one-seven?" I squint at the scribbled area code.

"It's a Boston number," she says mournfully.

I climb out into the baking sun and start to wave, but for some reason feel like a goober, so instead I reach for the hem of my skirt, swivel around and moon her with my bathing suit bottom. It's no less stupid, but Leigh fake-swoons against the door, and drives off grinning.

The skip in my step lasts until I duck inside the diner, where Jake glowers at me from behind the counter. "What the hell, we were looking for you!"

I stop in my tracks, deflated. "Is Juno mad?" I didn't really think she'd care. It's not like I'm a flaky employee.

"No," he whispers. "Try the guy you blue-balled in the stockroom! You didn't even tell me you were leaving."

"Oh. Sorry." I start for the back office, but Jake catches my wrist.

"You know there's a way you can make it up to me. . . ."

"Not now," I snap, slipping free.

Maybe it's my imagination, but he looks genuinely hurt, instead of sexy-pouty hurt.

I grab a pot and top off table four's coffees, agree with Mr. Paiz that I am, indeed, so grown-up, and then I check in with Juno in the office. After punching Leigh's number into my phone and stashing my purse once again, I head back to the stockroom to finish taking inventory. I ignore Jake when he slides through the door, until he plucks at the apron strings tied behind my back, working at the knot. I spin around, swatting his arm away. "I *said*, not now."

"Why?" he asks, his full bottom lip thrust forward, and it's not attractive. Not even obnoxiously attractive. "You have your girlfriend, so you don't need me anymore?"

"What does that mean?"

He folds his muscled arms. "Come on. That chick! She's . . . you know. You know?" He lowers his voice to a hiss I have to lean in to hear. "You know?"

I can feel the blush coming from my scalp down. "So what?"

"So nothing." He leans back like he's proven something. "Just, you go on a date with her, but every time I ask you out, like really out, you blow me off—"

"It wasn't a date," I interrupt. "I had a thing. In Albuquerque. And we just talked, like you and I are simultaneously talking and not-dating."

He holds his hands up and laughs. "¡Cálmate! I didn't know you were one of those angry lesbians."

Fuming, I ball up a fist and drive it at Jake. I don't know where I meant it to land—probably on his stupid square jaw—but I've never punched anything, and so I pound into his stupid huge bicep instead. He twitches slightly backward, while I feel a great dull pain shoot up through my wrist.

"Jeez, loca." He blinks down at me. "I was just being funny."

"Next time be funnier, pendejo." I clutch the inventory ledger and turn my back until he leaves, shaking out the hand where Leigh wrote her phone number. Underneath the pain, it still tingles from the impression of her pen, and her fingers steady around mine.

SEVEN

"*¿Cómo te fue* hoy, mija?"

"Pretty good."

"Anything interesting happen at the restaurant?"

"Not really."

"Easy days can be the best days."

"Yeah, Mom."

Such is the typical script to our family dinners. Mom asks benign questions, I feed her scraps, she cheerfully makes a feast of them. Even as she saws through the too-tough pot roast on Dad's plate so he can spear the bits with a fork held slightly sideways, her smile never wavers. If anything, Mom is *more* cheerful in the years since Dad's diagnosis, *more* endlessly grateful for all of the challenges life presents, and the opportunity to face them as a family and whatever. As Dad's grown quieter, her undying positivity has only intensified.

And to be honest, a little has always gone a long way.

It's like the ghost peppers Dad once got as a birthday present, picked from Mrs. Mosqueda's sister-in-law's garden. I sat at the kitchen table and watched him diminish them to almost nothing. To use ghost peppers, you put on gloves, you chop them into tiny pieces, cook them a little at a time for a long time, strain out the actual peppers, put the fiery orange oil into a jar and store it in the dark for a few months. *Then* you add one drop to your big pot of pozole rojo, and you've got a really good spice going.

But you put a piece of ghost pepper right in your mouth, and you melt through your tongue, through your body, through the tile floor beneath you, through the earth to its very core, burning a hole through which prehistoric beasts emerge and retake the world.

What I'm saying is, my mother was always chatty, always the first to ask about your day or if you want one more enchilada on your plate. But Mom 2.0 talks and talks, even when it feels like she's putting on a show for some TV audience that isn't really watching.

To give her a rest, I turn to Dad, who's stabbing shakily at Mom's shoe-leather roast.

"Mrs. Reyes told me to tell you hi."

Technically, Mrs. Reyes told me to tell Dad she was keeping a prayer for him when she caught me filling up Mom's Malibu at the Allsup's. Then she flipped down her sunglasses and hustled into the convenience store, ankle-length sundress rippling around her sandals. I guess she means well, in spite of my swift exit from her daughter's life. Or maybe she's grateful; maybe she thinks I'm a bad influence, with my Christmas-and-Easter-only parents, and my halter tops, and a growing reputation I've managed to keep from Mom and Dad pretty easily, because that's the way gossip works in La Trampa. You know people are talking about you; you hear it like the rustle of bushes, feel it in the prickling hairs at the back of your neck. But nobody's there when you turn around.

Anyway, I think Mrs. Reyes's prayers are about as useful as a fake mermaid's fin, but Dad brightens. "Seen Diana lately?"

I nod. "Yeah, we've hung out."

"That's good," Mom speaks up while Dad digests the information. "We're glad you're making time for your friends, before you all go your own ways."

I could point out that the closest Diana and I come to "going our own ways" is walking down different aisles in the grocery store, but she'd only say something like, *Well, just for now, mija.* Besides, she's already off and running again, talking about work, about who heard what rumor from Mr. Binali on his stoop, or which pastor/priest/preacher will be hosting the tri-temple picnic/crafts fair/showing of *Finding Nemo* in his church's basement.

I pick at my food and try not to watch Dad stab inelegantly at his.

After dinner, I take care of the dishes while Mom helps Dad wash up—he can get around, but needs help maneuvering into his shower chair so he won't slip in the tub. Plus she likes to hover, even though we've installed this emergency pull cord by the toilet if he really needs us.

They'll be in there awhile, so I retreat to my room and pull my phone out to text Jake. It's been days since I ditched him in the stockroom, and yet he's still pissed. As if I owe him! But with no school, half shifts at Silvia's, and a shortage of chores since Mom's been home nearly full-time, I'm feeling particularly antsy. Thus, I'm preparing to suck it up and sweet-talk Jake Mosqueda, when I hear the water in the bathroom cut off, and a moment later, Mom raps on my door.

I freeze. "Yeah?"

She pokes her head into the room, phone in hand. "I just got off the phone with Xime. She can't make it for your dad's PT tomorrow, you know her mother's got shingles, and I've got to open up the restaurant. Can you—"

"Of course," I say, relieved that's all it is.

"Gracias, mija," Mom says, and sighs. "What would we do without you?"

She slips back out, and I let go of the breath I didn't know I was holding on to.

There are several doctors on what Mom calls "our team." There's Dr. Dinapoli, Dad's occupational therapist, who's all about giving my father "the tools to go through his life as meaningfully as possible." Dr. Dinapoli helps us make changes as his symptoms get worse and he moves out of the early stage of HD, like using little nonslip mats to carry plates and jars, and reorganizing drawers and cupboards so Dad can get to whatever he needs most as easily as possible. She gives us tips for when his memory and concentration slip, like making lists and calendars and keeping our questions short and to the point. And as his balance and spatial awareness get worse, she gives him strategies for things as simple as sitting down (touch the chair, then turn around, then sit). She looks like a tough little Italian grandmother, but smiles easily and often. We like Dr. Dinapoli.

The doctor we see every Friday is his physical therapist, Dr. Petrovich, who works on his flexibility and mobility. He plans Dad's exercise routines, like Pilates to keep up core strength. (I'm not saying it's funny to watch my dad roll slowly around the living room on a big silver ball while on the TV, a high ponytail in a leotard reminds him to breathe . . . but since Mom got a matching ball, they stop regularly during their workouts to make fun of each other.) Dr. Petrovich also smells like hard-boiled eggs and has ice-cold hands even through his latex gloves, which Dad points out regularly in his own clipped way.

We have mixed feelings about Dr. Petrovich.

As Dad and I sit side by side in the waiting room of the Rehabilitation Services Department at University of New Mexico Hospital, waiting for Dr. Petrovich, his sneaker taps a nervous beat against my chair leg. It makes it hard to concentrate, but it's not like I was enraptured by *Golf* magazine, so I set the issue down and turn in my seat. "Mom said Chris called from California last night?"

Dad thinks, then bobs his head. "Made it into Monterey okay. He says thanks for checking on things."

Before he left, Chris gave us his spare key and asked if someone could pop over to the place from time to time in case any of the kids who sometimes hung around the arroyo made the quarter-mile trek across his property. The worst they'd do was leave red plastic cups in his scrabbly yard or smoke weed in the garage with the glass pane missing from the back door, but Mom promised one of us would drive over every few days, make sure nobody started a skunky-smelling fire in his trash can by accident.

"Yeah, no problem. It's been a while since I was out there," I say lightly. "I don't think since that barbecue? You made puerco pibil, sí?" Pork braised in spices, orange juice, grapefruit juice, and lime juice and cooked inside banana leaves. "That was his favorite."

"Eso que ni qué," Dad confirms. "Since we were kids."

There's this picture hanging in our hallway with the family photos, of the two of them as ten-year-old boys. Barefoot and bare-chested beside a pool, they're small and brown, with biceps the size of acorns. I've heard countless stories about these kids around the chiminea in Chris's backyard. How Chris would regularly follow Dad home for dinner, and every time, my abuela would shake her head and say, "No te preocupes, le echamos más agua a los frijoles." How they'd wrestle in Dad's backyard until the day Dad slipped and cut the skin below his eyebrow on the old splintery fence that used to border the property, blood pouring down the side of his face, and Chris was so sure he'd gouged out his best friend's eye, he passed out in the weeds on his way to the house for help. And the way they used to climb the gutter to sit out on the roof of Mr. Zepeda's garage and smoke . . . cigarettes . . . while the sun went down, summer through winter and back again.

I look at Dad in his slouchy old T-shirt and sweatpants, folded into his waiting room chair, and try to imagine him and Chris with young bodies that could take them anywhere they wanted to go, that were never full and rarely tired. Bodies that chased down ice cream trucks for mango con chile paletas, and leapt into pools, and climbed tough, dusty hills out in the desert. Bodies so perfect they were beneath their notice; like the ticking of a clock you never pay attention to until the day it stops, and then it's not the sound you hear, but the silence.

Dad blinks at his watch and rocks his knuckles against his jawline, shaved with Mom's help this morning.

"I might go out with Marilee tonight," I blurt. I don't know why, except that it's an easy enough lie to back out of, and it always makes my dad happy.

"Muy bueno. Your mother's right. It's important . . . to have people like that."

I lean over and quickly kiss him on the cheek. "You're my people."

Dad pats my knee with a mostly steady hand and scrapes his throat clear. He turns to the window, watching a small brown bird flit around a hanging feeder.

I pick up the magazine and pretend to care about the politics of sand traps until Dr. Petrovich comes out to claim Dad. Then I head to the cafeteria to grab a wilted spinach salad or a dewy ham sandwich. The whole way, I have to stop myself from sprinting down the hospital halls, as if I were ten years old again.

EIGHT

That evening, I'm drying the dinner dishes while Mom helps Dad in the bathroom, when an email chimes across my phone. I grab it off the counter to read:

Hi, Savannah,

After rigorous auditions and careful consideration, I'm pleased to offer you a spot as one of the Lost Lagoon mermaids! Please let me know if you're still available for the position, which will consist of three eight-hour shifts per week, exact schedule to be determined. A full day's work on the Fourth of July is required—this is our debut show. As announced at auditions, training begins tomorrow, Saturday, June 24 at 9:00 a.m.

Sincerely,

Eric Barber

Director of Performing Park Personnel

The Lost Lagoon

I reread, then start to text Jake the good news (well, the okay news), pausing halfway through to delete it all. Instead, I abandon my station at the drying rack and slip down the hall into my room, scrolling through my contacts. Shutting the door behind me, I flop back on my bed and tuck the phone between my shoulder and my ear as it rings.

"Hello?"

"So I'm a mermaid," I announce. "This is Vanni, by the way."

"Yeah, I figured that out," Leigh laughs. "Congratulations, I think."

"It's okay. I mean, it's mostly a good thing. Exciting with a little dash of depressing. Feel like celebrating?"

"I wish. Lucas is dragging me to the movies with him and Scoop Girl."

Without noticing, I've been tracing my fingers over the palm where Leigh's number used to be. I clench my fist and snatch up the phone in my other hand. "Too bad."

"You can come to the movies, if you want."

"No, that's—"

"Seriously. It's this double feature all the way out in Las Vegas." She means Las Vegas, New Mexico, and not Sin City, I presume. "Lucas wants us to have *quality sibling time* before school starts, but I don't see what's quality about sitting in the backseat, trying to see the screen through their interlocking tongues. It'll be better if you're there."

"You want me to come?"

"Yes, my god, I want it, I *need* it."

I bite back a smile.

After we hang up, I quickly get ready in my bedroom, in the little mirror above Dad's old desk. I slick on lip gloss and pile my hair into a topknot to get it off my neck. Outside it's holding steady in the high eighties, though the temperature will sink with the sun, thank god. I change into a loose-fitting pink-and-white-striped halter top and denim short-shorts. Leigh might accuse me of wearing them to spite Scoop Girl, but I just can't bring myself to be jealous of Lucas's girlfriend, when Leigh described her to me on Monday as having all the depth of a coaster.

I poke my head into my parents' room, where Mom's rushing to put laundry away while Dad showers, so she can help him after. She's still in her restaurant clothes; she got home just before dinner and didn't take the time to change.

"Guess what? I got that job."

"At the water park? ¡Qué bueno, mija! And good for your résumé!" But she looks worried. "It won't be too much for you, will it?"

"It's only part-time, and just for the summer. No te preocupes."

"I don't want you to be overwhelmed."

"It won't mess up my shifts at Silvia's."

"We can adjust that if we need to. We'll have to sooner or later, anyway." Mom wipes a sweaty strand of hair off her face with the knob of her wrist. "You'll still have time to help keep an eye on Chris's place?"

"No problem. And it'll be great. I'm really excited I got the job," I lie.

Then Lucas is honking in the driveway, and I grab my old backpack with a sweater stuffed inside. I've got my hand on the doorknob when, feeling guilty, I circle back to the kitchen to dry the last plates and shove them into the cabinet. Then I dash out into the heat.

The Fort Union Drive-in is over an hour away in San Miguel County. Their ugly minivan squeals and rattles eastward, Lucas driving with Scoop Girl up front ("Bethany, but call me Beth," she says, and smiles) and me and Leigh in the back. Scoop Girl is, it turns out, a lot like I'd pictured her from Leigh's description. Blond and bubbly, with sizable scoops beneath her tiny maroon UNM T-shirt. A funnel of hot wind whips through the car, which doesn't leave a lot of room for small talk, but from what I can hear of the conversation, Scoop Girl is . . . sweet. Maybe not the sharpest cactus in the desert. She has a habit of chopping the ends off words, in that weird yet efficient language I didn't know girls still used. "This movie will probs be awesome. Gerard Butler is the hottest thing alive. I totes love romantic comedies."

"Oh, totes!" Leigh yells back, then leans in close and whispers, "Please beat me in the face with your back-pack until my hearing goes."

If Leigh's aiming for nice, she sometimes misses the mark. But so what? When we were in school, everyone was always going on about how Nicole Mendez is *nice*, and Kim Brentwood is a *bitch*, so isn't she the absolute worst? But there have to be more important things for a girl to be than *nice*. I was considered a *nice* girl until spring semester of junior year, when I fooled around with Nicole Mendez's very freshly ex-boyfriend under the bleachers, and then according to the third stall in the girls' room at El Trampero High, I was *nice* no longer.

Well, who needs *nice*?

Leigh might be a bitch, but she's funny, and she's sharp, and she rocks her gym-class style. And she's strong. When we park at the drive-in, she spreads one of the trunk blankets across the hot car roof, vaults onto it and hauls me up one-handed, the muscles in her thin arm hard and round like fruit. We lie on our stomachs while Lucas and Scoop Girl take the front seat, turning the radio up all the way so we can hear the movie through the open windows. As the air finally cools and the sun sets behind the big white screen, she rocks me with her elbow. "You're crowding the popcorn."

"You're crowding the Coke." We only bought one between us—she doesn't have a job, and those sweet, sweet mermaid dollars aren't rolling in yet.

Leigh holds the huge sweating cup so I can fit my lips around the straw, and then I hold out a fistful of popcorn for her to pluck from while we lie there waiting, arms crowded together and back legs lightly touching. I feel good. Like even while I'm on top of the car, looking out on the roofs of the dusty El Caminos and pickups, I'm really up above my body, high in the air and looking down and watching. That's probably why my heart's beating hard by the time the movie starts. Or maybe it's just that Gerard Butler is totes the hottest thing alive.

* * *

While the hot dogs dance onscreen in the intermission before the ten o'clock movie, Lucas and Scoop Girl unfold from the minivan. "We're going to get soft pretzels," Lucas says. "Bring you back a few?" Unlike his sister, he's been extra sweet this trip. Must be thrilled that Operation Make Leigh a Friend has borne fruit.

"Sure," we say, and Lucas and Scoop Girl stroll away, leaning into each other like they'd fall down without the other. Leigh sits up on the car roof, twisting her back until it cracks, and sighs. "What's next?"

"I think it's the one with the boy and girl who would be perfect together if they'd just get out of their own heads, and then they get out of their own heads."

"Another romantic comedy?"

"Obvs." I shiver in the desert air and pull the picnic blanket up around my right side, while my left is still crushed against Leigh.

"This is dumb," she says, noticing. "Let's just take their seats. They're not coming back any time soon."

"They just—"

"Wandered off in the opposite direction of the concession stand? Unless Scoop Girl keeps soft pretzels down her pants, we're going hungry."

We hop down off the roof and slide into the front seat of the minivan, where the temperature *is* warmer, but with the cup holders and the stick shift between us, the body heat is lacking.

The second movie opens on the lead actress falling asleep in her luxurious bed, bought on her TV producer salary, surrounded by ice cream cartons, cheese singles wrappers, wine bottles, and the remote (on a Friday night, the sad old crone!). Leigh turns the key in the ignition. "Fuck this. Let's go to Boston."

I check the gas gauge. "We have a quarter of a tank."

"Well, let's go *someplace*."

"We can't ditch your brother."

"Sure we can. For a little while."

"And skip quality sibling time?"

She inspects my face, scrunching her tanned nose I know to be lightly freckled in the daylight. "Okay. If in the next scene, Channing Tatum's out in the club being the Man, and he takes home a hottie to have meaningless sex with in his perfect apartment, where he lives a superficially happy but meaningless existence, and we're supposed to feel sorry for him even though he's happy having meaningless sex with hotties in his perfect apartment, we go. Okay?" She holds out a hand to shake, and, scanning her face to see if she's serious, I take it.

Technically, Channing Tatum meets the hot blonde at a pool party for grown-ups, but the judge (Leigh) rules that it qualifies.

"What if your brother comes back?" I ask as we jerk

forward from our spot.

Leaving the car running, Leigh hops out and spreads the picnic blanket in the empty patch of dust we've left behind. She's thoughtful that way.

I figure Leigh's plan is to drive as far as we can in one direction before time, a dwindling gas reserve, or a flurry of outraged texts from Lucas force us back. The minivan bucks down the backstreets of Las Vegas, and to keep my queasiness at bay, I focus on the darkened shapes of the mesquite-spotted hills in front of us. I'm so busy staring ahead, I don't even recognize the scenery around us until we squeal onto Route 1, and then pull off into a familiar parking lot.

"Lucas told me this was here," Leigh explains. "Have you been?"

"Yeah," I say, and nod. I haven't seen the old sand-colored visitors' center of the Las Vegas National Wildlife Refuge for a long time, but I remember it. My parents and I came here once or twice, and then sometimes I came just with Dad, which I always liked.

Not that I don't like spending time with Mom, and I spent plenty of it growing up. She was always the one to help me with math and science homework. She took me clothes shopping, made all of our hair appointments together, brought me to Blues Fests at the Mine Shaft and the Balloon Fiesta in Albuquerque and the Indian Market in Santa Fe, and chattered straight through all of it. The perfect foil to Dad, she was excitable when he was calm and outgoing when he was quiet. I love my mother, so I say this with a double-size-serving of guilt: because her words came so easily and cost her nothing, they were never quite as precious as Dad's.

Through the unlocked gate, we start down the auto loop, a paved horseshoe around the refuge. With the windows down, we cruise slowly past ponds, marshes, and cottonwood stands just visible in the moonlight. Behind it all the mountains rear up to the west, ink-black shadows against the starlit sky. When we roll up and park at the overlook at Crane Lake, I see this vivid flash of my dad. Having packed us a picnic lunch and hiked out with it, he's peeling the lid off a recycled Country Crock tub stuffed with his beef empanadas (I liked them even better cold) and uncapping a lemon soda for me as he tells me the story of meeting my mother.

Mom grew up in Round Rock, Texas, this suburb outside of Austin. Right after she and her friend Kat graduated high school, they road-tripped to Santa Fe to celebrate their freedom. One day, they drove down the trail and stopped in La Trampa for lunch, wandering into Silvia's. Just passing through on the way to someplace better, like every tourist. Mom wore a black babydoll dress sprinkled with daisies and her silver Doc Martens, and Dad was nervous while he took her order for barbacoa de pollo, because she was so pretty. But once he'd calmed down, they spent the lunch hour flirting. When he brought the bill, they exchanged phone numbers, the pencil slipping from his sweat-slick fingers. Two years of late-night calls later, Dad had taken over all of the cooking in the restaurant—his father died suddenly of pancreatic cancer in the winter—and Mom came back to La Trampa for good. She married him, helped him run the business when his mother returned to Tijuana to take care of her older sister. We visited her and the cousins right after I was born, and then maybe once a year, but she died before I could really know her. Her name was Silvia, of course.

Dad told me this story as we ate empanadas and watched a flock of mallards skim the surface of the lake. He said one of his greatest sorrows was that I couldn't remember my abuela's cooking. "Her soul was in her cooking. 'Estómago lleno, corazón contento,' she'd say."

I follow Leigh down the wooden ramp to the observation dock, where the same mounted telescope Dad and I peered through is aimed toward the glittering black lake beyond the grass. Along the railing, the same framed signs identify plants and birds. Little bluestem and yucca plants, raptors and red-tailed hawks. Leigh presses her face to the telescope, but of course, if there's anything to see you can't see it in the dark.

"I almost forgot," Leigh says. She jogs to the minivan, roots around in the trunk, and when she comes back, thunks a big bottle of Largo Bay Silver down on the railing in front of us. "I hid it in the spare tire." She screws open the cap, drinks, full-body-shivers, and passes it off to me. It is possibly the worst cheapo rum I've ever tasted, a mix of lime and mouthwash, with the burn of hydrogen peroxide on a scraped knee.

"Smooth," I say with a cough.

"Subtle hints of nail polish remover," she says, clearing her throat. "What do you want? I had nine bucks. It was this or Popov."

We sit cross-legged on the deck in silence for a while, arm to arm and hip to hip, grimacing our way through sips of goddamn Largo Bay. Slices of Crane Lake sparkle through the gaps in the railing. Between us and the water, a sea of grass whispers.

"I guess this isn't so bad," Leigh admits spontaneously.

"New Mexico is wearing you down," I giggle. The awful rum is good for something, at least; my throat feels permanently warmed and everything seems funnier already.

"I mean, in this exact spot, it's not the worst place

to be, ever." Strangling and then loosening the frayed strings of her Adidas hoodie, she sighs a little more emphatically than a sober person would. "Everything else is the worst."

"This is where you come from," I remind her.

"So? That doesn't mean I belong here."

Hoping I'm not about to poke the bear, I ask, "What was it like, where you lived?"

Leigh smiles, staring at the water. "Awesome. Our apartment was close-ish to Fenway. Like not right up in the bars and the crowds, but close enough to hear the concerts, so a couple times a year, you could lean out our window and listen to Billy Joel or the Police or someone. And we were half a block down from this awesome Thai restaurant that mostly smelled amazing, like garlic or chili or lemongrass. Except sometimes in the spring, before the AC was on and all the doors and windows were propped open, on days when they cooked a certain special, you could smell, like, fermented fish through the whole neighborhood. Lucas hated it, but I kind of didn't mind, because then it smelled like summer was coming."

At the same exact moment, we take a deep breath, and then we laugh. Here, almost-summer smells like dust, and faint smoke from some distant wildfire, but I knew that it would.

"Just wait a few weeks and it'll be monsoon season,

so it'll be like . . . what's that word for that smell when the rain hits dry soil? I think it's 'petrichor,' Mr. Garza said. Remember that smell?"

"No." She tightens her hoodie cords.

I'm not sure I believe her. "Well, it's great. Then it's chile-roasting season, and that's obviously fucking amazing, and ooh, then it'll smell like piñon in the fall, when everyone starts to burn wood. You'll love it," I promise. "You just have to wait a little while."

She pulls the cords, relaxes, pulls. "Could you keep a secret?"

"I could," I understate.

Leigh leans in, the burn of alcohol on her breath. "I'm not gonna wait. I'm going back."

"Like, you'll go back east for college?" I feel like a little girl saying it; of course that's Leigh's plan.

But she shakes her head in an exaggerated sort of way. "I'm talking September third. That's my birthday." She tugs the strings until they're tight around her neck. "There was some custody stuff going on before we left, but it was nothing, this total red-tape situation, and when I'm eighteen, I can do whatever I want. And I want to go back to Boston."

"You want to live with your mom again?"

She nods. "I'm saving up for a plane ticket—you know there's a Coinstar kiosk in Albuquerque that trades cash for, like, eighty percent of what's on your gift card? I found it when I drove you down. My nonna in Boston's always sending me these loaded-up gift cards to Sephora and Macy's and Victoria's Secret and crap. Like I'll wake up one day and hear the siren song of pencil skirts and lipstick."

I study Leigh's profile in the moonlight, her short brown hair ruffling softly in the breeze, her paintbrush eyelashes, the clean shape of her nose, and slightly chapped lips. The way she swims inside her hoodie, her strong legs and rough knees. Leigh knows exactly who she is, so why would her nonna want her to change?

I don't even really know Leigh, but already the thought of her leaving makes me sad in advance. The same feeling I get when I'm eating the last slice of the tres leches cake Mom orders from the bakery for my birthdays, and though it isn't gone yet, I know it will be soon, and there won't be anything like it for a long time after.

"Your dad won't be crushed?" I ask, taking the bottle.

"He was fine before we came. And he has *Naveen*," she says, as if the name tastes sour in her mouth.

"Your stepmom?"

"No, she's just his girlfriend. You know when they met, she was running a matchmaking service for dogs?

Our neighbor in Española wanted to stud her Weimaraner. That was before Mom and Dad got divorced. She stopped after she and Dad got together. Now she makes candles, sells them at farmers' markets and wherever." Leigh grabs the bottle from me. "Yeah, they'll be fine."

"What about your brother?" I take the bottle back.

"What about him?" she says a little too loudly. "He's moving into the dorms when the semester starts, anyway. He won't care. He probably won't even notice." Then she knocks my elbow with hers while I'm sipping from the neck, splattering my chin. "Maybe you should come, right? Go east of Texas? Maybe September is your someday."

It's a dumb idea she can't possibly mean, but the fire in my throat spreads, sinks into my chest, my heart, pumps to the farthermost parts of me. I picture Leigh pulling the van up my driveway on a sunny day. She leans out the window and laughs, *Dare you*. We stuff the trunk with our suitcases, though the only luggage I own is Mom's big duffel bag, older than me and Frankenstein-stitched back together in so many places, it'd probably have saved her time to knit a new one. We point ourselves toward the East Coast, because for some reason we're driving instead of flying, and I crank down the window as we hit the highway. Dust and wind roar through the cab. I stick one arm into the outside air, white sunlight rippling between my fingers like we're in some cheesy fucking road-trip flick.

"Would I even like Boston?"

"You'd love it," she says, and though she couldn't possibly know, I want to believe her. Because Leigh hasn't known me all eighteen years of my life (unlike the whole of La Trampa), it's like I can be anybody when I'm with her. I could even be that girl in the van, heading off to start the rest of her life, feeling the good kind of fear.

Then I blink, and the open road is replaced by the slats in front of me, initials and hearts and profanity slashed into the wood. *C likes J's dick*; *Mike* ♥ *Abbey Forever.* It all blurs together in the dark . . . or maybe it's my new best friend, Largo Bay. I pull from our bottle, trying not to cringe. "We should go back. Movie's probably almost over."

She looks at me, pupils wide in the dark, lips parted, then stands and dusts off the back of her shorts. "Yeah, it probably is."

She ditches the rum in a trash can at the end of the observation deck. Between us we've killed a third of the bottle. And yeah, Leigh more than pulled her weight, but I've been drinking here and there since I was fifteen—there's just not a lot to do in La Trampa—so I know neither of us should drive. Mom would strangle me. But I'm strangely detached from the thought. It drifts into focus, I acknowledge it, then watch it float away. Instead, I scramble to buckle my seat belt as Leigh backs the car around to the road, and I feel a little thrill as she toes the gas pedal. Every time I glance sideways at her, she's blinking determinedly, her knuckles white on the steering wheel. Once, she catches me and stares back with wide hazel eyes.

Until we hear the *beep beep-beeeeep* of a horn, and turn to see the headlights swimming toward us in the dark. With a gasp that knifes through the car, Leigh jerks the wheel so that we're safely right of the yellow line.

"That'll wake you up," she jokes unsteadily.

I clamp my shaking fingers between my knees and laugh, though I don't even know what I'm laughing at.

As Leigh glides the van up alongside Lucas and Scoop Girl in the emptying field of the drive-in, my stomach clenches. He's turned from Leigh's big brother into Mrs. Short, the high school principal, when she caught me with Oriel Trejo. With a precise cocktail of grief-stricken silence and earnest, help-me-help-myself apologies, I persuaded her not to tell my parents. My family had enough to deal with at home, she admitted.

I'm not sure Leigh will be so lucky. She hops out

to hand Lucas the keys, and through the windshield, I watch him trap her chin with his fingers to smell her breath.

"For fuck's sake!" he swears.

Wrapped in the picnic blanket, Scoop Girl pokes one hand out and lays it on his shoulder. "Don't, babe. She's a kid."

Leigh rears back and gapes at Scoop Girl. "Oh my god, you better marry rich. What's even the deal with this girl, Mucus?"

"Get. In. The. Car," he grits out between clenched teeth.

We slink into the backseat, and Lucas drives for a silent hour to drop Scoop Girl off at her friend's house in Santa Fe. Then we head south for home. Leigh and I have been very still, me with my hands tucked into my lap, Leigh slumped down with her knees shoved against the driver's seat and her palms braced on either side of her. Finally, as we enter La Trampa, she speaks up, her voice more a challenge than a plea. "Are you gonna tell Dad?"

Lucas cuts his eyes toward us in the rearview mirror. "I should."

I guess that means something to Leigh, because a slow half smile curls her lips. "You're my favorite brother," she says, this time softly.

"Shut up," he snaps, but I see his frown waver in the rearview mirror before he refastens it. "And get your shit together already. This was selfish and dumb, and it can't keep happening. 'Cause I can't help you when I'm not gonna be around all the time. You get me?"

She salutes him, then lets her hand fall and, without looking over at me, slips it into mine for such a brief moment, I've barely felt her touch before it's gone.

NINE

If Santa Cruz Lake was cold, Mermaid Cove at the Lost Lagoon is icy as a Viking's balls. Nine girls and I stand shoulder-deep in the glassy green water, pale lipped and shivering in our practical swimsuits.

"Sorry about the temp," Eric-in-charge-of-auditions-for-performing-park-personnel apologizes from his safe, dry perch on the deck, sculpted and painted to look like mossy rocks. "We're working on it. The heater's been acting up, but we'll have it running by showtime."

There's an HVAC guy I could recommend, if my teeth weren't chattering out of my skull.

Once we're moving and our sludgy blood is pumping, it's a little better. We swim some warm-up laps (literally) around the Cove, a rough oval about a third the size of Bicentennial. The bottom is black tiled to appear natural and pond-like, the water darker still because it's sheltered by giant plastic boulders—beyond those, the front gate set in a cinder-block wall painted to look like river stones. That gate will stay locked until the Fourth, when a staffer will lead park guests inside, up a narrow path, and out through a break between the boulders. They'll cross the weather-beaten-looking footbridge that arches over the center of the pool, and from there, watch our maiden performance. I haven't let myself dread it just yet.

For now, we train. We dolphin-kick while practicing soft fingers and pretty smiles. We're told how to bask gracefully on a clump of fake boulders in the deeper end, which are heated by the sun, at least. We learn to act like mermaids, coyly beckoning to visitors, then giggling behind our damp shoulders.

Soon we'll have to do this crap in public.

"What's, like, our character motivation here?" asks an ombre-haired twentysomething, one of two Camilas in the group. Camila A, I call her, because her shell bra is no Camila C's. "Are we Peter Pan mermaids or Harry Potter mermaids?"

"Can we be Starbucks mermaids?" a tall, tan girl named April mutters beside me, hugging her goose-bumped shoulders in the cold surf. "I need a hot latte or something."

"That's a very astute question," Eric calls from the deck. "The part you're playing is mysterious, yet shy. Enchanting, yet elusive. Desirable, yet unattainable. Uncatchable. You want to captivate the tourists, be mischievous, but not *too* mischievous. You do not want to drown the tourists."

We practice looking mischievous (but not murderous) until we break for lunch at noon. My fellow mermaids haul themselves out of the water, grab their towels, and cluster in the sun. They laugh about the sad state of our chlorinated hair while Eric's assistant passes out mediocre sandwiches from the Sunken Sub, free in honor of our first day of training. Throwing on a T-shirt, I take my BLT and sit on the fringe. It's not like the girls aren't *nice*. April seems funny, and Camila C offered me a granola bar while we changed in the locker room this morning. It's just that it's been a long time since I was at the center of so many girls. They haven't said much to me, and even though I remember how simple this used to be, I'm having a tough time talking to them. I consider sneaking away to Neptune's Pool to find Lucas, with whom I hitched a ride this morning.

Instead, I dig my cell out of my pocket and text Leigh.

Me: Am learning to be enchanting yet elusive

Moments later, she sends a selfie snapped at (I assume) her kitchen table, with rumpled I-woke-up-like-this hair and a mouthful of spaghetti half spilling down her chin.

Leigh: Already there

I send back a heart-eyed smiley, but it's pretty freaking insufficient.

After lunch, we gather back at the pool and watch a tough-looking woman with rough gray braids like nautical ropes haul garment bags over on a hand truck. Eric kneels and unzips one ceremoniously, then waits for us to admire the contents: lemon-yellow fabric, beads and sequins winking in the sun, narrowing and then bursting into a fin. "Naomi comes to us from costuming on a mermaid show that just shut down in Las Vegas." He means Sin City and not San Miguel County, I assume. "She'll take your measurements today, and then your tails will be fitted properly to each of you. In the meantime, you'll get the chance to try them on, take them for a test-swim. Just stay in the shallow end until they fit and you've put in the practice, okay? We'd rather nobody drown today."

I open the bag with my name pinned to the plastic and watch my future spill out: a tail the glittering aquamarine of painted oceans in Disney movies.

Seems appropriate.

We wriggle into our costumes, which are like thick, scaly, waist-high stockings for one big leg instead of two. It feels a little like squeezing myself into a giant condom. Inside, the fabric is a plastic flipper like two scuba fins glued together, with slots for each foot. Naomi clips and slides and zips us into place. My tail's a little too long for me—when she helps me up to finish dressing, I have to hoist the top above my waist to stand flat-footed on the fin. I wobble while Naomi circles me with measuring tape. Once all of my numbers are scribbled on her clipboard, she helps me sit again. I scoot to the water and slide in with some of the others. Camila A floats by on her back, while a muscled redhead with a very fancy set of eyebrows works her way around the perimeter, gripping the ledge. It seems as good a method as any, so I drag myself along a little behind her, legs and tail trailing.

I tow myself to the middle of the pool, where the bottom starts to slope toward the far end, eight feet at its deepest and off limits till we're skilled enough for flips and tricks. Here it's just deep enough to try a proper dolphin kick.

Awkwardly, I curl into position against the wall, then push off. I ripple forward, arms outstretched, chest down, hips down, thighs down, knees bent slightly. It's not my strongest move—my knees always did drift a little too far apart on the butterfly stroke—but now they're pinned together, and it's harder than I thought. I let my feet sink to the pool floor, the water around my chin. I dip down a little to shimmy clumsily back to the ledge—

—and my left leg seizes.

As my calf muscle spasms, I slip along the tiled bottom on my too-long fin. Cold water plunges up my nose before I fight back to the surface, sputtering, to see Fancy Eyebrows clinging to the ledge a little ways from me. She reaches out while I struggle forward and hauls me over to the side.

"Thanks," I say, and cough, pool water carving a painful trail down the back of my throat. I lever myself onto the deck with shaking arms.

Then Eric's hovering over me, hands on his knees, whistle dangling in my face. "Okay there, Savannah?" The whistle recedes as he straightens. "This is why you have to stick to the shallows until your tail fits properly, ladies!"

I unzip and unclip and shed my fin as fast as my Jell-O-fied fingers can. "It's fine. I'm fine."

"Take ten, all right?" He pats my shoulder.

I grab my shirt and duck out of the exhibit's back

entrance, the slap of my flip-flops uneven as I weave through tourists on a still-stiff leg. Even though the employee locker room is empty when I reach it, I slip into one of the tiny shower stalls and pull the cloudy plastic curtain closed. I squeeze the shower faucet as hard as I can for a full ten seconds without the flutter of a finger. Then I crank the water on and hold my hand below the too-hot stream, and my hand obeys even as my skin turns pink. Satisfied, I shut the faucet off and slide to the floor, both legs fully under my control.

It was just a cramp, I tell myself, breathing through raw lungs. I didn't stretch enough after lunch, and I worked my muscles too hard struggling with the tail, which didn't fit in the first place.

Cramps happen all the time.

It doesn't mean anything.

I'm strong and I'm in control. Cramps happen.

It doesn't mean . . .

When Mom finally made Dad an appointment with his doctor after a long series of spills and outbursts, he sent him to Dr. Michaels, a neurologist at the testing center based out of UNM Hospital. He explained there are two kinds of gene tests for HD: confirmatory and diagnostic testing, and predictive testing. The first one confirms you have it when you're showing the symptoms already; the other one can predict whether you'll get it even if everything's peachy for the time being.

You have to be eighteen to take the second type of test; that's the rule. Some people choose to take it when someone in their family is diagnosed. A lot of people don't.

For Dad, it was the first kind. So there were interviews. There was a vivid mapping of any and all horrible illnesses in the family. Dr. Michaels asked him about emotional problems and intellectual stumbles (already, Dad would search a little too long for the answers to simple questions, or his temper would rubber-band-snap when he'd always been unnaturally cool and calm). The doctor examined the way Dad's eyes followed the light, tested his hearing and reflexes and strength and his brain and his blood. At last in July before my junior year, Dr. Michaels sat us down and told us it was Huntington's.

That is, I know he told us, though I don't remember him saying the words.

Which is funny(ish) because I remember everything that came before. I remember the way the afternoon sun sliced through the open vertical blinds in the waiting room, and the wrinkly pink brain puzzle some kid was struggling through on the floor. I remember Mom smiling so determinedly for so long, her secretly scared lipstick cracked across her bottom lip. I remember that Dad smelled like tomatillos and spice because chilaquiles was the lunchtime special at Silvia's that day. I even remember what I was wearing: an eggplant-purple baby-doll sundress I'd just gotten for my sixteenth birthday.

And I remember after, when Dr. Michaels left his own office to give us privacy and family time, but Dad asked to be alone for a little while. So Mom and I went down to the cafeteria "for dinner." We poked gelatinous kung pao chicken around our plastic trays in silence until Mom spoke up, quietly and without looking at me. "¿Estás bien, mija? I want to make sure you heard Dr. Michaels. This doesn't mean . . . this might not mean anything for you. There's a good chance it won't, and I don't want you to live like it does. You have your school-work, your friends, your plans for college, and they're important. Your dad and I don't want . . ." She pinched her lips together, ghost pale below the worn-thin veneer of Riveting Rose. "Do you hear what I'm saying, Vanni? You need to keep planning. This doesn't change any-thing for you."

"Uh-huh." I speared a slimy, semicold mouthful that would've made Dad weep and choked it down.

If I'd wondered for even a second that things had changed, the start of junior year confirmed it. By then, everybody in La Trampa who'd never heard of Hun-tington's disease had gotten their MDs from Wikipedia. And they were all so *nice*. Diana and Marilee stuck to me like I was flypaper, like it would hurt *them* to peel themselves from my side. They walked with me arm in arm through the halls of the high school. They checked on me when I got up to grab a wooden bathroom pass, and when I came back. Diana made me promises she couldn't keep (*It'll all work out, Vanni. There are so many people praying for your family!*) and Marilee asked for promises I couldn't make (*You're okay, right? I mean, you feel fine, don't you? So you probably don't even have it, do you?*).

Every time I lied to my friends or let them lie to me, it felt like I was carving pieces out of myself to give to them.

For a while I went along, until the day I came home from school to find Mom sniffling over a ruined batch of camarones al coco. It was one of Dad's favorites, and I don't even think it was that hard to make. Just prawns caked in flour, egg, and milk, dipped in coconut flakes and cornflakes, then fried (I'd watched Dad and had a decent memory for his recipes, even if I couldn't hope to replicate them; there's a big difference between reading sheet music and playing Bach on the piano). Mom wasn't much better than me, and all the coating had fallen off, blackened crumbs of it burned to the pan, and the prawns were sad, soggy pink curls on the paper towel. She looked up at me, eyes swollen. Tried to smile and failed. Then she scooped the whole batch of them into the trash can, slammed it back under the sink, and went into their bedroom and closed the door. I stood in the kitchen, listening to the muffled squawk of a laugh track on their TV drift down the hallway.

Then I couldn't do it anymore.

The next day at lunch, I planted myself at a near-full table with stoners and La Trampa lifers and the three whole art freaks at El Trampero High. Maybe the boy with ear gauges the size of quarters was set on fleeing for San Francisco when he graduated, but none of the rest had plans to leave. None of them wanted to babysit me and ask me about my feelings while I peed. None of the boys wanted status updates on my father's slow degeneration.

And there was Jake.

That whole thing began like a strange game of Clue: the horndog waiter, by Silvia's Dumpster, with the Lucky Strikes. We were working a dinner shift together, and Marilee had just uninvited me to her New Year's Eve party via passive-aggressive text:

I really wanted you to come, but you never ever get back to me, so ur not in the headcount. Sorry ☹

Which, fair enough. But I was feeling pretty shitty down there in the mess of my own making, so when Jake took his break out back during a lull, I followed him. I asked for a smoke and, in true Jake fashion, he said, "What will you give me?"

He'd asked me this 1.5 bajillion times before, and I'd only made offers in the vein of "gratitude that cannot be redeemed for cash."

You should've seen the look on his face when I answered, "You could kiss me."

"Sure, princesita," he laughed nervously, then sucked down smoke like he was trying to wither his lungs in one world-record pull. "Don't kid about that stuff."

By then I was sixteen and a half, and I sort of knew what I was doing. I'd gotten almost as far as I could with Max, my technically ex-boyfriend, before he left for Doña Ana Community College in Las Cruces (as in we'd climbed the Rocky Mountains a few times, camped out for a while in the lower regions, but we'd never reached Pikes Peak). So I took a cigarette from the pack in Jake's fist, slipped it into my mouth, and lit it by pressing the tip to his and breathing in, the way Max had taught me, coughing a little. "Don't call me princesita."

This is what I was thinking, that first time: I was imagining water, deep and dark and cold, as if it were barely thawed or nearly frozen. I took everything I wanted but now knew I couldn't have; everything I was sad about; everything I was afraid of. Being scared all the time is *exhausting*. Like a slowly leaking faucet you can only ignore for so long, until you lie awake in the silence between drips, just waiting, waiting. When I burned my fingers freeing a too-hot strand of hair from my curling iron; when I sponged sticky white rings of horchata off the tile-top booths at Silvia's; when I slipped between my sheets at night, staring up at *GABRIEL ESPINOZA WAS HERE*. Through it all was the same dull drip-drip-drip of fear. So I imagined that fear into something solid. A bucket, a blanket, a book. I imagined dunking it in the pond, icy water swelling up around my wrists. If I let go, the thing would rise up and bob on the surface, and that was no good. But I held it under until it filled, soaked, bloated, sank. I drowned it and watched the surface glass over, and then I forgot it. For a little while, anyway.

I did it again, and then again. The boys may have changed, and some were good and some were clumsy and some were nothing, but every time was basically the same. A pond where all of my fears sank to the bottom, into a dark, frozen junkyard, and for a while the only thing left above the surface was me, and my lips, and his hands, and our skin.

Eventually, I get my shit together and get off the shower floor, already vined with mildew from the last month. Texting as I walk, I traipse back to Mermaid Cove to grit through to the end of the day. Eric hands out our training schedules—we're due to practice in half-day shifts almost every day until our big premiere performance next Tuesday, the Fourth of July. Because Eric and Naomi want us fully prepared, juggling the Lost Lagoon and Silvia's will be tougher than I realized.

Gathering my stuff and waving good-bye to my fellow mermaids, I don't bother taking off my suit. Instead, I throw on my shirt and flip-flops and scuff half-naked out to the parking lot, shielding my eyes from the sun as I scan for my ride. I'm only standing there a minute before the big dented Ford with more rust than paint clinging to the bumpers pulls alongside the curb, and I climb in.

"You're welcome," Jake says immediately, like I wouldn't have thanked him for answering my text when I haven't returned his texts in days. For driving forty minutes through Albuquerque to pick me up. For the way his cheek dimples when I ask to stop at his one-room apartment above the Turquoise Depot so I can "change into something dry." For the way I feel with the hot highway breeze in my face, my elbow resting against the burning sill of the passenger door, my legs stuck to the vinyl seat: young and strong and in control.

For all of the things I plan to forget.

TEN

My life for the next week and a half: a blur of grocery runs and laundry duty, topped-off coffees and nightly specials, waterproof body glitter and castor oil to keep my poor chlorinated hair from turning to hay.

Things are crazy enough at the restaurant. Estrella and Juno come down with the same summer cold (miraculously, Jake remains unscathed by the slime-a-thon—either he's out of Estrella's bed and can't yet bring himself to jump into Juno's or, like the poisonous gas station chili dog he is, Jake himself could survive the nuclear apocalypse). Mom has to be at Silvia's to keep things running without her assistant manager, so I pick up the slack where I'm needed. There's extra errands and chores, as well as driving Dad to appointments, or just to and from the restaurant when he gets tired or frustrated, which I don't mind.

But I'm also doing daily shifts at the Lost Lagoon to prepare for our debut on the Fourth of July. "I heard girls at that park in Florida get to train six months before their first show," grumbles Kristian, a tiny, ironically leggy mermaid with hair that dries in natural kinks I would slaughter for.

"True," Eric says patiently, "but they eat bananas underwater."

After the pool heater's fixed, it's not so bad. Sure, most days I have to pour, cram, and squeeze myself into my spangled fin and matching shell bra, feeling each of the freezer-burned waffles Mom scraped out of the toaster and into a to-go bag for me that morning. But at least I get to be in the water. We start to learn our choreography for the Fourth, practicing first in just bathing suits, then in scuba fins, and then with our tails on. Because we don't perform underwater, it's more like synchronized swimming, and a pretty simple routine at that. We learn our musical cues. We learn to float in circles and form stars with our bodies, with Eric directing from the footbridge. Each of us has short solos to memorize, and little duets. Eric and his assistant get in the water with us to teach us moves like "the tub," where we keep our legs bent with our feet and knees parallel to the surface, our faces above water and our butts below. And "the surface arch," done by arching our backs below water, with our whole tails above.

Fancy Eyebrows, a.k.a. Iris, did competitive synchronized swimming in high school, and she confirms it's pretty basic stuff. "Not that I'm complaining," she tells us while we sit poolside during a break, wringing water from our hair and spattering the stones, though we'll be wet again in fifteen minutes. "I can't believe I'm making money like this. My sister was on the team too, and she's got a summer job at a gas station. In high school, I was a waitress at Outback Steakhouse."

"You were a waitress, right, Vanni?" Camila C asks, working her fingers through my tangles, twisting the hair into an elaborate side braid. She's a single mom who works part-time as a stylist out of her trailer in Bernalillo.

"Yeah, at my family's restaurant. I still am."

"That's nice you work with family, though," she says. "When I was your age, I worked at Sonic, as one of those carhops who rollerskates your burger out to you? Then some kid I was bringing a shake to put his car in drive and not reverse. Drove it right into the side of the building. I skated out of the way, but they had to close the place for repairs, so that was the end of that job. He got my number later, said he wanted to take me out and make it up to me."

"Did he make it up to you?" I ask.

"Más o menos," she laughs. "Then he made me a mother."

"¡Que cabrón!" Kristian swears.

Camila C ties off my braid, kisses my cheek, and cries, "¡Mira que linda!" and the rest of the mermaids hum in agreement.

I admit it's almost comfortable, to be a bee in an all-girls hive again.

And when I collapse into bed at night, for the first time in a while I feel exhausted and strong, asleep even before Mom clicks off the canned sitcom laughter in the living room.

An hour before the park opens on the Fourth, the female employee locker room is stuffed. Lifeguards stroll in and out, loud and tanned and neon-ed. Paler restaurant and gift shop staff stop by to stash their crap. Anastasia, one of the rotating actors who play Neptune, the park mascot, sits on a bench and texts in half costume. She's already in her royal-blue robes with her trident propped against the lockers, but her big cloth hands and big cloth head rest beside her. I still don't get how a god with a foam crown and eight fingers fits in among the moldering ruins of the Lost Lagoon. I guess that's Eric's business, and none of mine.

We mermaids crowd the mirrors. We slick on waterproof eyeliner, press plastic jewels onto our temples, clip flowers and starfish in our hair while Kendrick Lamar pounds out of a phone someone's perched on the sink. Camila A combs out her ombre hair, then turns and cranes her neck to inspect her butt in the mirror. "Ugh, I hope Naomi can let our fins out. My fiancé took me out last night and I ate half my body weight."

Half of A's bodyweight is one of my legs and my ponytail. But I'm remembering how to have casual friends, and so with a silent apology to my curves, I deliver my line. "No, you're so skinny and I hate you."

She grins and paints swirls of body glitter on my cheeks, a bikinied fairy godmother in false lashes.

Fifteen minutes to go, and half an hour till our first show at nine fifteen. We make our way to the Cove, squeeze ungracefully into our fins, and scoot into the dark pool. I shiver and dip under, then swim to the end with the big basking rock. Eric and Naomi give us the rundown once more. We'll start the show on the rock while a park staffer leads a batch of tourists through the exhibit gates, up the stone path, and onto the footbridge that cuts across the middle of the pool. We'll flirt unattainably for a minute or two, the music will come on, and then: showtime.

Biceps straining and with my legs useless, I hoist myself onto the sun-warmed plaster boulder. We arrange ourselves in our assigned spots. Then there's nothing to do but sit in the already-hot breeze and fidget. Once I stop moving the nerves set in, the pressure building somewhere behind my shells.

On the pebbled deck, Eric checks the clock on his phone, announcing through the bullhorn, "T-minus five minutes to curtain!" and I wonder about the drama kid he was in a past life. He gives an order into the walkie-talkie clutched in his other hand. The loudspeakers mounted around the pool crackle, then play calypso-ish music that echoes throughout the Cove. Kristian sits to the right of me; she flashes a quick, queasy smile. My own smile wobbles as I wrestle for control of my lungs, command them to breathe.

¡No! ¡Vete al carajo! they respond.

Soon comes the squelch and slap of flip-flops, the laughter of park visitors being led through the gates of the Cove and up the path still hidden from view.

Lounging to my left, Camila C reaches out and squeezes my wrist.

A staffer leads the way across the footbridge, and

we see our adoring public. Well, our bemused public, anyway. Moms fan themselves with park maps and dads lift their kids onto their shoulders to see. The children squeal while their parents sweat. A boy, barely thirteen, leans so far over the railing he's practically bent in half. One of a pack of teenagers, he wolf whistles, braces winking in the bright sunshine. The girls in his group coo at us, "Oh my *god*, look at their *tails*! I totally *want* one!"

My palms are slippery on the plaster. Forget flirting. I suck in my stomach and try not to dry-heave onto the basking rock.

A serene voice like you'd hear in commercials for antidepressants blasts out of the speakers, twice as loud as the fake *Little Mermaid* sound track. *"WELCOME, LADIES AND GENTLEMEN, TO THE WATERS WHERE THE UNKNOWABLE DWELLS."*

That's our first cue. All ten of us scoot and slide into the pool, swimming for the shade directly below the bridge. Fuck pretty hands and pointed toes—I dolphin-kick my ass off for the only spot in the water where the park visitors can't see us, and so I'm the first to reach the nylon ropes that dangle from the underside of the bridge. While the rest of the girls make their way over, I cling to the middle rope, catching my breath.

"THIS IS A WORLD OF MAGIC AND WONDER,"

the blissed-out narrator declares.

Whatever she's on, I wish she'd share with me. Before today I was hardly nervous; maybe I didn't have the time to freak, or maybe I just didn't care that much. That's over now. What if I forget my twenty-second solo? What if I forget the whole routine? Fall out of place and mow down the Camilas? Panic and wallow and drown in front of two dozen children in cartoon-themed swim-suits while Mr. Orthodontia prays for my shell bra to snap off and float away?

"THESE BEWITCHING CREATURES LIVE IN A WORLD UNLIKE ANY WE'VE SEEN, HALF-HUMAN, HALF-FISH."

From under the bridge, we can hear footsteps shuffle back and forth as tourists try to catch sight of us. I twist the rope so tightly, my hands cramp.

"THEIRS IS A WORLD FORGOTTEN BY MAN."

Bobbing beside me, Iris shoves sopping red hair out of her face and twists into position.

"IT IS A WORLD WHERE MERMAIDS SWIM FREE."

That's our next cue.

All at once (or almost at once) we surge forward and resurface on the opposite side of the bridge. While the tourists rush to the railing to watch us, we maneuver into a circle, flip onto our backs and link hands. We float in place, our hair drifting to the center of us, tails flicking. The water carries my weight, just like it always does. I make my body relax, bone by bone and muscle by muscle, and it listens, and then I'm not so scared anymore.

For a debut show, it goes mostly as planned. We let go of one another, somersault, and twirl. When I look to the left and right, Kristian and Iris are on the same moves as me with our arms in roughly the same places. Then each of us runs through the short, simple solos we've learned. Mine is three back tucks in a row, which I first learned messing around with the Aquatics Club in Santa Fe. Laid out on my back on the surface, I pedal my arms to grab a scoop of water, push my hands overhead, and tuck my knees to my chest to roll under. I finish with this easy move Naomi calls "the oyster," where I lie with my hands stretched above me, then bring my legs and arms up straight to touch my fin above my hips, pointing skyward. I sink underwater, butt first, then swim back to the group without plowing into anybody. Mission accomplished.

After that, we split into pairs. Some do identical spins, some handstand in the shallowest part of the pool. Camila A and April swim back toward the bridge, where they toss up gift shop seashells the parents catch for their kids. Iris and I race each other in a half lap that skirts the edges of the pool, a duet bestowed on us by Eric. At the end of the routine, we make our way back to the basking rock, spend a minute or two blowing kisses and waving. The staffer ushers out the guests, we get a break, and the whole thing resets for the next group.

There are no disasters, no near-drownings. Nobody's iPhone falls in the water, and, miraculously, no teenage pendejos shout at us to take our tops off. And the way the little kids look at us—not like we're bartenders and stylists and dropouts and a part-time waitress with a high school diploma and no plan. Like we're magic. Like they wish they could grow up to be us, though what I wish for them is to be little and stupid and safe forever.

When we break at noon, I'm almost sad to scrape myself out of my tail.

The sadness passes the second I walk out of the Cove and into the park proper to find Leigh Clemente waiting at the gates. She wears her uniform boy's tank top and boxy khaki shorts that hang on her body—god forbid she should wear a bathing suit to a water park. But while women like Mrs. Reyes (and there are lots of women like Mrs. Reyes around here) would crow about how pretty Leigh could be if she grew her hair out and dressed like a "girl," Leigh is better than pretty. With her strong, narrow shoulders, and her sharpened collarbone, and her face, her straight nose and pink-but-slightly-chapped lips and big hazel eyes . . .

She's perfect.

"When's the next show?" she asks with a grin. "I heard the mermaids are hotties."

I tuck my chin into my shoulder and shrug, enchantingly yet elusively.

Leigh stuffs a handful of my fries in her face, and I don't blame her. The fries are the best thing on my plate—better than the overly salted fish sandwich that makes up the rest of my Flying Fish and Chips. But I *do* get a 60 percent park employee discount, so we bought our sandwich platters for cheap and brought them to the outdoor table for two we managed to snag despite the crazy holiday crowd. I lean close across the table so I can listen to her complain above the noise of the mob.

"My brother's abandoning me to go to Albuquerque and 'buy soft pretzels' with Scoop Girl," Leigh says through a full mouth. "So I'm stuck at home with Dad and Naveen on Independence Day, irony of ironies."

"That sucks," I half shout.

"It does, but if you're not doing anything tonight, you could hang out at my place. Dad will even give you a hippy beer if you promise to sleep over."

I process this. "Sleep over, like at your house?"

"We'll eat meatless burgers with eggless soy milk mayonnaise, wave sparklers, watch America-themed movies."

I snake a fry from my dwindling pile while I still can. "You really want me to go?" Because of my busy new schedule, we've only seen each other briefly since the drive-in. Once, Leigh popped into Silvia's and ordered a horchata just so we had an excuse to sit for five minutes and talk about nothing, and a few times, I slipped away from the Cove on my break and ran to the pool, where she was hanging by Lucas's lifeguard chair. Leigh's grand plan to go east hasn't come up again; we haven't had the chance, since we haven't been alone. So a sleepover feels like a big step, a scary step. Whether it's good scary or bad scary, I can't decide.

"Why do you always ask that?" Leigh shakes her head. "You think I'm being nice? Of course I want you."

If I'm blushing, maybe I can blame it on sunstroke. There's a shade umbrella over our little patio table, but like the rest of them it's tattered and holey, as if it's weathered a terrible storm or, more on-theme, washed up on shore after a wreck. Coverage is spotty at best. "I'm off at four."

"Perfect, so come around six. But don't get too hot. Remember, Lucas won't be there."

"Leigh, I do *not* want on your brother."

"No?" She pauses, and my heartbeat kind of does too. "I guess I'll see you for meatless burgers."

"And America-themed movies."

She steals the last handful of my fries and heads off, while I sit and try to sort out just what it is that I want. I'm out of practice. I've been drowning everything in my imaginary pond for a few years now, holding the big wishes under instead of inspecting them. But that's the thing about Leigh; she's the kind of person who stirs everything up, if you let her.

ELEVEN

I empty my dresser drawers and small closet, miniskirts upon camisoles upon cutoffs piled on my bed. Too dull, too tight, too eleventh grade, too the romper I wore before skinny-dipping in Jaime Aguilar's backyard pool after he accidentally finger painted my boobs orange with Cheetos dust.

None of that is right for tonight.

With the clock ticking away toward six and my mother waiting in the kitchen to drive me to the Clementes', I reach into the back of my closet for the garment bag containing a dress I've only worn inside the Macy's changing room at the Coronado Mall. Back in May, Mom wanted to buy me something for my graduation ceremony. I knew we didn't have the money, but she insisted it was a red-letter day and that I deserved it. That I was beautiful. That I was her only daughter. She kept cheerleading until I realized turning her down would pain her more than a bill in the mail the next month.

So I let her choose a dress from the rack, white with a print of faded blue carnations, a full skirt, and a teardrop-shape cutout in back. Longer than I would've liked, and tooth-achingly sweet. I hadn't been a floral kind of girl since middle school. Pre–curling iron, pre-boobs, pre–Max Binali. Pre-HD. Plus the thick straps made my shoulders look like eighties-style shoulder pads of skin and muscle. I clenched my fists until my fingertips ground the little bones below my palms, held on until my fingers throbbed and then a few heartbeats longer, then pushed through the curtain.

Mom was sitting on one of the little velveteen couches in the dressing room, and she beamed when she saw me. "It's perfect, sweetheart. It's exactly you."

I shifted in the shoes she'd picked out, espadrille wedges with wispy blue straps, and felt as if I were wobbling along a tightrope while my mother clapped below. But she was still smiling resolutely, so I nodded back.

"Right. It's me."

She bought the shoes, and the dress, and when we got home, I tucked the white plastic garment bag into the back of my closet. But I could still sense it. It plagued me like the imaginary beating in that story, "The Tell-Tale Heart." Graduation day came, and when I took it out of the bag, I couldn't bring myself to put the thing on. I told Mom it was too tight in the waist. I promised I'd bring it to Mrs. Aguilar, Jaime's mother, who worked in the Laundromat and did tailoring on the side, so she could let it out and I could wear it on another red-letter day.

It wasn't a total lie. Maybe in the next-door dimension where one tiny butterfly of a thing is different the dress would fit me, but in this life it didn't.

When I unzip the bag, though, it isn't as sugary as I remember. The carnations are still a faded blue, like flowers somehow bleached of their color by sun and wind, and the white looks nice beside my summer tan. The skirt is full over my rounded hips, the waist tight. Even the cutout between the shoulder blades seems more grown-up when I picture Leigh standing behind me, her breath on my back. . . .

But why am I picturing my kind-of-friend breathing on me? Why am I not even bothered by it? And why am I not even bothered by *that*?

I shower and blast myself with my clunky old blow-dryer until I have to stick my face in front of my window AC so I don't sweat my makeup off. I brush on a new bronze liquid liner that's supposed to make brown eyes pop, then step into the dress, slithering the silk down over my hips. I slip on the shoes Mom bought me and pace experimentally across the old red rug. Then I clomp down the hall into the kitchen.

My parents are going through Silvia's menu for next week—Dad gets full approval over the menu, even if it sometimes takes him longer to decrypt it. They raise their heads at my thunderous entrance, and he smiles. "Look at you, mi corazón!"

"Leigh says her parents get fancy for this stuff, and whatever."

Mom is watching me with one hand over her mouth, her eyes crinkled, but for once she doesn't say anything.

"Ready?" I ask.

We drive the ten miles to Los Cerrillos in the same uncharacteristic silence (for Mom, anyway). The town outside my window is like a lot of places in New Mexico. Old, dusty, and brown, but even smaller than La Trampa. Like, it's literally a ghost town. Just a few hundred people live there since the turquoise mines closed, and there isn't a lot left but ruins and trees. There's the Casa Grande Trading Post, which sells rocks and bottles and things, and there's a petting zoo next to the mining museum with llamas and goats and even a few emus. And there's a historic park where, every spring from elementary school to twelfth grade, we went hiking for a cheap field trip (Marilee first swapped spit with Donald Palmer beside the petroglyphs).

We pull down Berry Creek, more of a wide dirt path than a road. It's on the far north side of Los Cerrillos, a mile from the far south side. The houses are smallish and brown, like the town, and the yards are dirt and clay. Four Berry Creek has a bright green glider on the little adobe porch. Beaded wind chimes hang from the eaves.

"Is this the place?" Mom slows the Malibu.

"I think so."

"Beautiful. So are you, mija."

"I look like I always do."

Mom reaches over and tugs the end of a carefully shaped and sprayed curl. "I think you look grown-up."

I blush and grab the backpack I've brought with my overnight stuff. "Tell Dad happy Fourth?" I ask, half out of the car already. "I forgot."

"Of course. Enjoy your sleepover with your friend."

I shut the door behind me and watch from the lawn as she backs up to turn around. When I squint, she fades into a blur of brown hair and pale skin (paler than mine and Dad's) and I get this pang in my chest, sad but sweet. I wave at her until she drives off, then when I'm alone under the evening sun, I trudge up the slight hill of the lawn. My hair sticks to my neck in the fading heat of the day, and I pat down the curl Mom displaced.

Leigh meets me at the front door. "Ooh la la." She fans herself with her hand and slumps against the frame like a fainting lady.

"Oh, enough," I say, pleased, popping my hip casually.

She's dressed up too, so I didn't totally lie to my parents—she wears a long, loose, gray cotton vest buttoned over her tank top, and dark jean cutoffs.

I stand in the doorway under the porch lights, which are on even though the sky's the same pale blue as my faded flowers. "You combed your hair."

She ruffles her fingers through it. "I had to for company. You came just in time. Dad is busting out the veggie burgers."

She takes me by the wrist and pulls me inside, through a little tiled entryway with shoes arranged in neat rows. It's hot inside, but not horribly, and the house is as clean and bright as it is dusty on the outside. There are candles everywhere, in jars and on pillars, in all colors, so the place smells like a fruit stand turned up to eleven. In the corner over the adobe fireplace, a dozen school portraits of Leigh and Lucas hang above the candle-lined mantel. My jaw drops at one picture in particular, the earliest in the series of Leigh's. She's maybe eleven or twelve against a marbled background. Her hair is long and sandy brown around her shoulders, her T-shirt lacy, her lips so glossed I can practically see my reflection in them.

"Oh my god!" I can't stop myself. "You were so—"

"Sickening," she says with utter disgust. "Never speak of it. Naveen won't take it down."

In the kitchen, a tall, thin woman with hair dyed a cool raspberry-red bends over the counter, poking metal skewers through vegetable slices and laying them carefully on a tray. Two tiny, blond, flat-faced dogs prance around her ankles, nails clicking against the tile as they circle for scraps like small fluffy land sharks. Naveen looks up as Leigh tries to hustle me by. "Is this the famous Vanni?" she asks, wiping her hands on her shirt—a kind of purple, tasseled poncho. Her fingers shine with a collection of rings made from bottle caps, and her nails are painted tangerine.

Leigh keeps her eyes straight ahead. "No, it's one of my many other friends I have."

The woman's mouth tightens. "Well, whoever you are, welcome!"

"Thanks, Mrs. . . ." I stop short. I have no clue what to call her.

"Naveen, of course, dear."

"We're going to my room until dinner," Leigh says, already tugging me out of the kitchen and down the hall. My last glimpse of Naveen as we round the corner is the little forgiving smile she throws me before blowing kisses to her dogs.

Once we're in Leigh's bedroom and she's shut the door behind us, she seems to relax. Her jaw unclenches, her muscles uncoil. She plops loosely on the bed while I look around. I expected her room to be her sanctuary or something, a Batcave crammed with laundry and doodles and embarrassing stuffed animals. Half of my things came from my dad, but there's still my pictures and my posters of the Baskervilles album art and, okay, the hot-as-fuck lead singer with his slight but permanent smoky eye.

But in Leigh's room, there's nothing like that.

It isn't totally barren. In fact, it's strangely bright. There's a yellow accent wall behind the bed (your standard IKEA). It matches the yellow comforter, yellow wire trash can, and yellow papasan chair. Only I've never seen Leigh wear yellow. As far as I know, she has no passionate feelings for yellow at all.

If I had to guess, I'd say her dad and Naveen prepared this room for her before she moved in, and Leigh's done nothing in the weeks since to make it home. There are no incriminating band posters or sports posters or school banners on the walls, no souvenir paperweights or framed family pictures on the desk. No soccer trophies on the squat, empty bookshelf in the corner. The only books in the room are the summer reading books I saw in her car, now on her desk beside a stack of foreign language dictionaries.

I pick up *The Poem and You*, run my thumb along the edge, and let it fall open to a page:

"Little Cosmic Dust Poem" by John Haines

Out of the debris of dying stars,
this rain of particles
that waters the waste with brightness . . .

The sea-wave of atoms hurrying home,
collapse of the giant,
unstable guest who cannot stay . . .

The sun's heart reddens and expands,
his mighty aspiration is lasting,

as the shell of his substanace
one day will be white with frost

Leigh props her head on my shoulder to read—I hadn't even heard her approaching—just as I shut the book with a pang.

"Wait, I want to see how the world ends," she protests.

"I don't," I say, dropping *The Poem and You* back onto her desk. Instead, I grab an English to Dutch dictionary. "You speak Dutch?"

"Sure," she laughs. "Ik laat een scheet in jouw richting."

"Wow."

"It means 'I fart in your direction.' Or I think it does. I'm new."

"You have the basics covered."

"I want to know how to ask for a phone, a toilet, and the number two at McDonald's in every language. And I want to be able to tell people to go fuck themselves. I've got Japanese, Dutch, and French down. And Latin, but where will that get me?"

"Not Spanish?" I ask.

She shakes her head. "We had it in elementary school, but when I moved away I forgot most of it. I can say 'My German is better than your German' in German. But it's the only German I know, so it's not that useful."

"You should do Spanish again. Nobody swears as beautifully."

"Your parents speak it?"

I nod. "Mom only really learned it when she moved here to be with my dad."

She crashes back down on the bed. "Can I have a lesson?"

"Hmm. Okay. Mama huevos loco, que te pasa?"

Leigh twists her mouth around the words. "Crazy eggs?"

"It's slang for, like, 'What are you looking at, dick-sucker?'"

"I'll practice that." She grins.

"Is this, like, a self-improvement thing?"

"Definitely not." She rolls over and props herself up with one elbow, waiting patiently while I inspect her stuff. "It's totally practical. Me and Lucas are gonna travel before I go to college. We haven't decided where, but I want to be ready."

I let the dictionary close and drift over to the window. Her backyard is as wild as the front, closed in by a low stucco wall. In the middle there's a grill, and hunched over it with his tongs and veggie burgers, Mr. Clemente.

"Your dad is so . . . tall."

"Yeah, I hope I grow up to look like him."

I laugh. Mr. Clemente's tall indeed, stick straight and super skinny, while Leigh's thin, and no shrimp, but I don't think she'll grow up to play pro basketball.

Height aside, Mr. Clemente turns out to be a lot like his kids. When he talks to me at the dinner table, he gets this look on his face and leans forward like I'm the only one he could possibly be interested in listening to. Lucas has it. Leigh too.

And I'll just say it, I like Naveen. She's a little bit of a space cadet, but it's obvious she loves Leigh and her dad. She asks me questions, mostly leaves Leigh alone, and spends half the meal happily pinching scraps of vegetables off her skewer and slipping them to the dogs under the table.

When we're stuffed with non-burgers and kabobs and coconut-milk ice cream, Naveen and Mr. Clemente settle on the couch with glasses of organic wine to watch *1776* ("the second-best musical ever written about the founding fathers!" Mr. Clemente assures me). Leigh and I go outside with a box of sparklers and watch the sun crawl slowly behind the low hills to the west. We sit on the porch glider in comfortable silence, legs swinging. Her hips brush up against mine on every downswing. It's cooler now and I think about asking Leigh for a sweater or something, but I can't make myself go inside. Eventually the sky is inked over, and Leigh picks up our sparklers.

"Come on." She tugs the skirt of my dress. "I had to swear I'd light these, like, thirty paces away so we don't burn down the house." Kicking off her flip-flops, she ditches them under the glider and walks out into the yard.

I slide off my wedges and follow. There are spiny shreds of plant life hidden in the dark. After the first painful step I go slowly, without picking up my feet. Leigh scuffs bravely through the still-warm dust. Halfway down the sloped yard she digs a lighter out of her shorts pocket. She lights the tip of her sparkler and at the first sizzle of fire presses it to mine. When they've both caught, we hold them away from our bodies. Leigh watches hers blaze and I watch Leigh; tongue between her teeth, the orange blossoms of the sparklers in her eyes. She watches until they flare and fizz out.

"Meh," she says, and shrugs.

"Pretty, though."

"We can do better. Hold up a minute." She tromps back toward the house but veers off and ducks into the garage instead, leaving me behind. I'm scared to step on a beehive cactus or something, so I stand still and wait until Leigh bursts back out, carrying a box the size of a toaster oven. Under the light of our phones, I can see the fireworks on the box, their strange names in bold font, exclamation-pointed: *FORTRESS OF FIRE!!! SCREAMING MEEMIES!!! WHIRLIGIGS!!!*

"Where'd you get it?"

"Traded for them," she says mysteriously. "Want to light them with me?" Leigh doesn't wait for my answer, already ripping apart the cardboard. "Which do you want? We probably only get one shot."

I pull out a bright pink paper tube attached to a long stake that shouts: *THE GLITTERATOR!!!*

She dips her arm in and surfaces with four different tubes, hands me something called *THE SKY ROCKET!!!* "You light those. I'll do these."

Though the directions on the box definitely warn against shooting off multiple fireworks at once, I take a second lighter Leigh hands me. We stab the stakes a few feet apart into the hard earth. Then we stand, me on the right and Leigh on the left, and hold our lighters at the ready. This is dumb, maybe perilously dumb, but at least that dull and paralyzing drip-drip-drip is replaced by something sharp, something *now*, something bright.

"One . . ." she counts.

"Two . . ." I count.

We dart forward, and I hold my lighter under the short wick of *THE GLITTERATOR!!!* until it catches, then, ignoring the prickly weeds, I throw myself to the right toward the *SKY ROCKET!!!* I flick the lighter desperately until it sizzles, while Leigh darts between the other three.

Then we run.

One moment Leigh's a gray smudge in the dark, and the next our fireworks bloom in the sky above us. It's a short-lived, spectacular mess. There are pom-pom-looking fireworks, fireworks that crackle, fireworks that scream. Leigh sticks out her arm and puts her hand on my breastbone, above the scoop of the dress's neckline, and brings her lips to my ear so I can hear her over the noise. "Did you feel that one?" she asks after a bright red starburst and the loud pop that follows. "Did you feel *that* one?"

Her skin catches all the colors.

I do feel them, and I feel the warmth of her hand, and I feel her fingers press into my skin. I feel the dirt under my feet and the dry breeze through my hair, and above all that I can feel my heart. The fireworks only really last a moment, and after they're gone, I still feel my heart in my ribs and ears and fingertips, like this rocket in my body.

"I guess that's all, folks." She smiles a little sadly and drops her arm.

I jump as the front door slams open, and Mr. Clemente is a dark shape suspended in the rectangle of TV light. Naveen stands beside him, cradling a saucer-eyed dog in each arm. "What's going on out there?" she asks, not pissed so much as spooked. "That wasn't you girls, was it? Is everyone all right?"

Mr. Clemente is less concerned. "Inside," he says through his teeth in the ringing quiet, very much like Lucas at the drive-in. "Now, Leigh."

She ducks between him and Naveen, and I follow her to her bedroom, mumbling "Sorry, sorry" as I pass.

Leigh drops heavily on her bed, face lit with that hard snow-cone smile. On the floor beside her, there's a sleeping bag laid out with a pillow—Naveen or Mr. Clemente must've set it up for me. I start to sit cross-legged on the bag, but she looks over the edge of the mattress and sniffs. "Don't be stupid."

I lie down beside Leigh on top of the sheets.

Her hands shake as she toys with the buttons on her vest. "Where would you go right exactly this second, if you could go anywhere?"

I glance at the books on her nightstand, but I don't need to. "The ocean," I say easily.

"Like, the Pacific, or the Arctic, or . . . ?"

"Just *an* ocean, I guess."

"The Atlantic," she decides for me, nodding her head. "Last year, we went to Harborfest—it's, like, this four-day party from downtown Boston up to Cambridge and along the waterfront for the Fourth of July. And some of it's stupid, like eighteenth-century chocolate-making classes, and super-dramatic readings of the Declaration of Independence. But one night we went to see the fireworks over Long Wharf, and that was kind of awesome. We got there ridiculously early so we could get a spot on the dock, but we forgot a blanket, so Lucas gave me his hoodie to sit on. He had approximately one million bug bites the next day."

"That sounds nice." I stare at the ceiling. "Would I really like Boston?"

She shrugs her shoulder against mine. "Why don't you find out? You're eighteen, you're out of school. You're not stuck, like me."

I could tell her everything I told Mrs. Short when she called me into her office, advised me to concern myself less with the upholstery of Oriel Trejo's backseat and more with my future. But I *did* think about my future, I told her. I would spend meaningful time with my dad while I could, help my mother at home and with the restaurant, work and save so that when I went to school I wouldn't cost my parents anything. The same speech I gave Mom and Dad. It's pretty easy to turn a lack-of-plans into a plan itself, to turn not-exactly-lies into the truth, if you say it with *conviction*.

Except in this moment, having my only real friend not know me feels lonelier than when I didn't have any friends at all.

The air around us smells of Irish Spring, and I take a deep breath, as much as I can hold and not enough. Then I say good-bye to the Vanni who Leigh thought I was, and tell her the actual truth.

"I was supposed to go to college this fall. But my dad got sick a couple years ago. I mean, he was sick for a while before that, but we only found out when it started getting bad. And now he can't do a lot of the things he used to do without hurting himself. Like cook, or go for hikes with his friend Chris, or . . . just get himself far away from the house. And there's no cure, so someday he's not gonna be able to walk or talk or swallow, because that's Huntington's, you know? That's just what happens, and for some people it takes ten years to die of it and for some people it's thirty. But they don't think it will take long for Dad, because he got it young and it's happening pretty quick already, and he has a lot more repeats in his gene, which is this whole other thing. . . . But in the end you get pneumonia or just fall too hard or you can't swallow anymore. And that sucks completely.

"And what *else* sucks is I've got, like, a one-in-two shot of getting it. I mean not *like*, it *is* one in two. I'd already have it, it'd be in my genes. Sometimes it starts even earlier for kids of HD patients, in your early twenties or late teens, even, especially if you get it from your dad. Which is so random, right? My grandpa might've had it but he died kind of young anyway, so we don't know. Nobody knows when it can start. Or if it *will* start.

"And I could take this test to find out? To see if I have it? You're not supposed to before you're eighteen, unless you have symptoms, and then you can decide. So now I'm eighteen, and I can apply—I have the application on my laptop, actually—and then I'd have to take this psych test to prove I could live with the results and after that, I'd know. But I don't know if I want to know. I can't fucking decide, and when I try to it's like I can't breathe."

I swallow hard and drive a knuckle into my eyes.

There's a deafening silence like the quiet after the fireworks, and then beside me Leigh murmurs, "Shit."

Without meaning to, I snicker. "Right?"

"That's . . . a lot. So . . . there's a test?"

"Yeah."

"And you don't know if you're gonna take it."

"Yeah."

"Is it because you're scared?" she asks in a low voice.

"Pretty much always. I mean, lots of people don't take the test, and some people do, but I don't get it. I don't get how they're anything but scared all the time, either way. How do they all just live their lives?"

"How does anybody?" she asks, as if it's a question she genuinely wants answered.

She looks at me and I look at her, and we're both still staring stupidly at each other when there's a knock on Leigh's bedroom door.

"Are you girls all right? Can I come in?"

Naveen.

Leigh lunges for the light switch and turns it off. "We're sleeping," she calls. After a pause, Naveen's shadow vanishes from beneath the door and footsteps carry her away.

Quietly, we change into our pajamas with the lights out, turned away from each other, and I hunt blindly through my backpack for a makeup wipe. Now that we're "asleep," I can't exactly run to the bathroom. By the time I'm done, Leigh's back in bed below the sheets. I can see her outline, the peaks of her short hair and one small-strong shoulder and the shallow slope of her hip. She can't be actually asleep yet, but she doesn't say anything. Instead the room is full of our breathing, and our settling bodies, inches apart in the dark.

When I wake up the next morning I know it's early. The sky out the unfamiliar window is the blue-gray of a fresh bruise. Confused, I roll over in bed and remember where I am, when I nearly smack faces with Leigh.

"Morning," she says.

"Morning," I say back.

My hair is completely deflated and my a.m. breath tastes like last night's non-burgers. It is not sexy. Nothing about this moment screams passion.

But Leigh is smiling almost sweetly at me, and it's real, and her eyes are huge in the new light, her short hair pillow-rumpled. There's this funny feeling in my head like I'm boiling over.

I lean in and I kiss her. Her lips are dry and warm and crushable. She untangles her hand from the sheets and her fingers drift along my jaw.

I don't know what it means, exactly. This is all I know: I'm Savannah Espinoza, I'm eighteen years old, and Leigh Clemente is my best kiss yet.

TWELVE

Because Scoop Girl has to work early, sprinkling sprinkles and waffling cones for the breakfast crowd, Lucas gets home from Albuquerque while Leigh and I are foraging for our breakfast. He winks at me, steals a granola bar out of Leigh's hand, then pulls her into a gentle headlock that she elbows her way out of. I guess all really is forgiven, at least by Lucas; their dad and Naveen are drinking coffee on the back porch and murmuring at each other way too quietly to hear through the glass of the sliding doors, but I doubt they're discussing a raise in Leigh's allowance.

"Great show yesterday, Savannah," he says around a mouthful of granola. "Very synchronized. Knew you'd make a killer mermaid."

"If you're gonna write an ode to her, do it over there," Leigh snaps, shoving her brother. "You're blocking the cereal cabinet."

Since the Best Kiss Yet, we seem to have shuffled backward. Right after, Leigh practically vaulted out of bed. "Gotta piss before I spring a leak," she claimed, but she never came back to her room. After a while I forced myself out of bed, found a baggy, red, Leigh-smelling DU Pioneers sweatshirt on the floor, pulled it on over my camisole, and padded out to find her in the kitchen.

Well, what did I want? Breakfast in bed? Poetry composed in my honor? A proposal?

I wrap my arms around my chest and dig my fingers into my elbows through my sleeves until they ache. Damn it, be cool, I tell myself. So what if you kissed her? You kiss all kinds of people. If you had a diary you wouldn't even put something like this in it, because why waste ink on "Dear Diary, today I woke up, had churros for breakfast, worked at the restaurant, kissed my bazillionth person, went home, watched some inspiring YouTube videos in my bedroom, and washed my hair."

Except Leigh isn't people.

"No work today, Vanni?" Lucas asks.

"Just at the restaurant, and not till two."

"How're you getting home?"

I glance at his sister, digging some organic, farm-fresh version of Mini-Wheats out of a box by the fistful with her back to me. "My mom'll pick me up."

He pulls a bowl out of a cabinet and shoves it at Leigh. "Use it, you heathen," he says, and then to me, "I can give you a ride, no problem."

Leigh shoves the bowl back across the counter. "I can drive her, she's *my* friend. Grab your stuff, okay?" She pries Lucas's keys out of his hand, and I wonder, is it possible to take a walk of shame even if you aren't alone, you aren't walking, and (sadly) have done nothing to be ashamed of?

As we motor along the Turquoise Trail toward La Trampa, Leigh seems fine to the casual observer—she talks, she laughs, she drums the steering wheel to Carlos Santana like her brother does. But the casual observer wouldn't spend the ride studying the shape of Leigh's lips, the right angle of her spine, the just-offbeat hammering of her fingertips.

Something is wrong. So says this professional observer of Leigh Clemente.

Only a few miles to go before she drops me home. The old, slow, trickling fear is back, and in it I can hear my future. Tonight we'll pave over the awkward not-quite-silence with jokey texts, and we'll hang out again, double with Lucas and Scoop Girl, sneak away and drink in the dark. But maybe Leigh won't wash up in Mermaid Cove after last night, won't ever ask me to sleep over, won't ever kiss me again. And if I don't say something now I'll never figure out why she won't, or exactly why I want her to.

"Um, can we stop at my parents' friend's place real quick? It's only, like, a couple of minutes out of the way. I'm supposed to be checking on it while he's out of town."

Well, it's something.

I point her to Jimeno Road, just off the trail on the way into town. Chris Zepeda's property backs up against the arroyo, which must be strewn with Solo cups and smashed glass and shed clothing after the Fourth, some of it Marilee's and Oriel's. Rarely do kids get stupid enough to crawl up the slope toward the small homes spaced out along the streambed, and I only steered us here to buy time.

I don't even buy us much, at that, because everything's clearly fine. There's the big tin-roofed garage where he fixes half the busted cars in La Trampa, cheaper and quicker than the super-professional place in Rio Rancho. It's untouched, as is Chris's much smaller house off to the side, a one-story stucco home a lot like ours, but even tinier and older. The robin's-egg blue paint on the door has been leisurely chipping away for as long as I can remember. His grandfather built it when he bought the land in the thirties, probably for six bucks and a pack of gum.

I circle the place to check for broken windows or a jimmied back door, returning in thirty seconds flat.

"Done?" Leigh asks the air just to the left of me.

I can't figure out what's crawled up her ass since last night. "I want to check out the rest of the place. A couple more minutes, okay?" I jog back to the garage and let myself in with the spare key Chris left my parents to give to me. From the pegboard above the tool bench, I slip a second key ring off its hook.

Trotting up the path, I grab Leigh by the wrist and pull her toward the shed a couple hundred yards behind the house, where my key fits the padlock. I pull open the doors and we squint inside. Sunbeams pin dust between us and the two ATVs Chris stores in here. Junky Suzukis older than me, speckled and pitted with more rust than paint. The smaller one he taught me to ride is up on blocks since it stalled on us four years ago—Chris always claimed he was fixing it slowly, slowly. Dad said it'll run again on the same day the Earth runs backward. Meanwhile, metallic guts dangle from the underside. It's sad to see it this way.

Luckily, I can drive them both. And Leigh and I can fit on the bigger four-wheeler together.

"Umm," she says, standing back as I grab a pair of nerdy safety goggles and a helmet from a hook on the wall and pull them over my hair, then straddle the bigger ATV and yank the pull cord, just like Chris showed me.

"There's, like, two miles of land—this is the quickest way around." I technically don't lie. "I d—"

"Do *not* dare me. You think you're *so* cute."

I pose cutely, then pull the cord again and the machine coughs to life. Standing on the rear break, I push the lever to put it in drive, then roll out of the shed and scoot forward and wait for Leigh to climb on behind me, the metal warming under my skin. She slides on, her knees pressed against my thighs.

I twist the right-hand grip to press the throttle, and off we ride.

"You don't think anyone will notice?" she yells in my ear.

We're far enough from the Marcons', the next house over, that the guttural roar of the ATV shouldn't draw attention. Still, I shout over my shoulder, "Do you want to turn around?"

She shakes her head—I can feel her chin graze my back—and I twist the throttle so we surge forward. Her grip tightens and she squeals in a very non-Leigh way; it feels like a victory.

As we ride across Chris's land, we bounce over small hills like wrinkles in a sand-colored blanket. I haven't driven an ATV since the smaller one broke down—I'm so extremely not allowed to do this on my own—and in the rush I almost forget about Leigh until she leans in and shouts, "Go that way! Go left!" She squeezes my legs with her knees like a jockey trying to steer a horse. I turn us east and we churn up over a steep embankment that breaks out onto the flat land split by the arroyo. Leigh laughs in my ear, and I smile through the grit the wind kicks up.

By the time we've rolled the ATV back into the shed, my hair looks like something whipped out of a cotton-candy machine. Dusting ourselves off and smoothing ourselves down, we walk back up to the house. Leigh pauses to press her nose to the cloudy glass pane of the front door, palms cupped around her eyes to see through. "Can we go in?"

There's no reason to—Chris isn't a potted plants kind of homeowner, and there sure aren't any pets to feed. But the heat settles on us like wool, stifling and scratchy, and I could use a glass of whatever's in the fridge to rinse the dust out of my teeth. Besides, I still can't shake the feeling that something's off with her. I let us inside and show Leigh through the claustrophobic hallway, past the tiny, tiled living room, and into the tinier kitchen. I've been here a lot, roasted marshmallows around the chiminea on the concrete porch, but I've never seen the bedrooms in the back. It feels wrong—which it is, because I don't have permission.

Behind one door, we find a perfectly normal bedroom where Chris's denim-and-engine-grease smell lingers. Leigh opens the farthest door back into a hot sunlit room and—santa mierda.

I knew Sophia Zepeda practically ran away just out of high school, and seldom returned from California to visit. I knew Chris was a creature of habit in a town of unvarying habits. But I couldn't have guessed about this room.

Except for a stack of boxes in the corner, labels like *Spare Tools* and *Hoses* markered across the cardboard, I don't think much has changed in Chris's sister's bedroom since she moved away. My first clue: posters of bands I do and don't recognize, still stuck to the walls with duct tape. Depeche Mode, Bon Jovi, Tears for Fears. A round braided rug, pink and white, covers half the tiled floor, and on the bed, a ruffled white bedspread printed all over with pastel milk shakes, hearts, sunglasses, and music notes. On a little white desk beside the window sits a row of dusty pink jewelry boxes and tubes of makeup and perfume bottles. Dumbstruck, Leigh uncaps a bottle of something called Red Door, sniffs it, and drops it in the pile, glancing around the room. "It's like a can of super-hold hairspray fucked an ice cream truck in here."

I poke my elbow into her ribs, and regret it when she backs off. "Wait . . ." Without really meaning to, I reach for her, wrap my hand around hers, warm and rough.

"Vanni." She tugs away gently without looking at me. "You don't have to. It's fine."

"It's fine?" I ask, bruised.

"You don't have to *convince* yourself you're into this." She says this lightly, acting like none of this makes a difference to her.

Well, maybe it doesn't.

I try not to look crushed. "Sorry. . . ."

"Jesus, don't be sorry. You didn't do anything wrong," she says, lifting the lid off a jewelry box, then letting it fall. "Look, it's no big deal. You're not the first straight girl to get, like, caught up in the moment. You don't have to—"

"What?" I flinch.

She picks up an ancient bottle of blue nail polish, hopelessly dried. "You don't have to talk yourself into wanting this because of me. Or because you feel guilty. Or bored. Or scared."

That's a lot to deal with, and I'm not sure where to start. For some reason I land on, "Why would you think I'm *bored*?"

"That guy who works at your parents' restaurant."

My breath catches. My lungs are full of Elmer's glue instead of air. "When did you talk to Jake?"

At last she looks up at me, her eyes narrowed, like: suspicion confirmed. "I don't know. A couple weeks ago? I came in to pick you up after your shift, and you were still waiting on one of your tables. That guy—*Jake*—he said he was kind of your boyfriend. He said, 'Savannah's crazy, right? My girl's cool, but don't let her run you around. She does dumb stuff when she gets bored.'" Leigh drops her voice for this last part, drags out her vowels, fakes the northern New Mexico accent and adds a slight whine to her voice. No doubt, she sounds like Jake Mosqueda, but the words . . . why would he say that? I don't want to be his girlfriend; I don't believe he even really wants it.

"He isn't my boyfriend. Jake was *never* my boyfriend."

"That's not really the point," she says quietly.

I squint out the window into the dull blue sky, unbroken by clouds. If I were a crier, I'd feel like crying.

This is all going wrong. I don't want to be explaining myself. I don't want to tell her the things I've done, the reasons I've done them, what it feels like and what it doesn't feel like. I've never felt bad about the things I did with boys. Slipping out from beneath a sweating Jake Mosqueda has always been a bittersweet business, but I mean, I never felt bad about *myself*. My mother, unlike Marilee's, never told me that my body was a precious banana, and if I allowed myself to be unpeeled, my sweet white fruit might be forever spotted. Unlike Diana's parents, she never said my virginity was my contract with a holy ghost. Mom told me sex could be fun and feel good, but it's more fun and it feels better when a girl knows what she wants and knows how to take care of her body and herself, et cetera, cue the piano music they play during Very Important Moments in coming-of-age TV shows. Okay, well, I know what I want out of sex. It's my body, and I'm in control of it for the time being.

"So I'm not a virgin," I manage, my voice wobblier than intended.

"Dude, I'm not slut-shaming you." She rumples the short hairs along the back of her neck, drags her hand forward until everything stands on end, like a cat grooming itself backward. "You think you're the only one who's played their V-card?"

I smile tight-throated, and Leigh softens.

"Come here." She sits down on the ruffled bedspread in a slight puff of dust motes, a shifting halo around her.

I do, so close our shoulders bump together. In the direct path of a sunbeam slanted through the window, Leigh's eyes aren't one color, the muddied yellowed-brown I thought they were; they're rich brown on the outside, but with a bright, wispy ring that's more like amber around the pupil. I don't think I've looked at her this closely in the light before.

"I like you, Vanni," she says, and chews on the corner of her lip with her small white teeth.

"I don't want you to *like* me," I try to explain.

"Okay, so what do you want?"

Maybe my life would be simpler if the kiss this morning was just another kiss. But this isn't Jake. Or Will/Max/Oriel, or just any girl I've grown up around.

This is . . . I mean, it's *Leigh*.

I can feel my heart beating all the way up to my collarbone and all the way down. "You could kiss me," I answer. "If *you* want to."

"Hmm." She laughs, knocks her forehead lightly against mine, then looks out the window. "You know what I wish? I wish I could've met you back home. I wish it was September and I was eighteen and in Boston already. Like, we'd see each other for the first time by the Frog Pond before the pool closed for fall, and you'd buy me a hot dog, and then I'd make out with you in the fountain until the lifeguard screamed at us to go the fuck away. That would've been so much easier, I think."

Her smile is slipping, so I lean in and kiss Leigh first, right at the smooth angle of her jaw. She closes her eyes and tilts her head down and I kiss her below the jaw, my lips tracing a path toward the back of her neck. I breathe in, and a little of her hair gets up my nose.

She laughs again as I snort it out—"Okay, okay"—and turns into the kiss. Her lips are full, dry-but-not-too-dry. It's even better than the first time. I shift my feet up beneath me and lean into her until she lets herself fall backward onto the hideous bedspread. At the last moment, her fingers clamp around my shoulders, strong and slim and warm, and she pulls me down with her.

When Leigh sits up and wriggles out of her Pac-Man T-shirt, she doesn't do it the way I've seen boys do; fisting it over their heads like Will Fischer, or shrugging roughly out of it. She does it like me, pinching from the hem and pulling upward. She sees me watching, ducks her head, and kicks off her shorts quickly. Then she throws back the bedspread to slip beneath, even though it's hotter than balls in here.

"Wait," I say, catching her arm.

I remember her body from the lake, of course. Thin

but muscled shoulders, high, small breasts, a hard stomach and narrow hips, a runner's thighs, and a knee that's been skinned since I met her. All perfect. But I can see things in the hot, dusty light I never saw before, like a faint slash in the skin above her right hip bone, lighter and pinker than her tanned skin. She tucks her knees up to her chest when she sees me looking. "Appendix. Had it out when I was ten."

I slip off the bed, step out of my skirt and prop my foot on the mattress to show her the white C-shaped scar just above my left knee. "When I was nine, I stole one of those pink razors from my mom's bathroom and tried to shave my legs for the first time. I had no clue what I was doing. I bled through, like, three of her good hand towels."

Leigh reaches out and glides a fingertip across it. "Badass," she says, and nods.

I shiver in the heat.

I get the definite impression that Leigh doesn't like her body, which is ridiculous, but she loosens up as we trade scars and run our hands over each of them. The nick on her calf where she went hiking with Lucas in Massachusetts, tripped on a log, and was "slightly, temporarily impaled" on a sliver of root sticking out of the ground; the small, shiny patch of skin on my right pointer finger from a too-hot pan; the thin white line along the small of her back where she slipped and scraped herself on the concrete rim of a pool. All her scars make her look even stronger.

But then there are softer things too.

The way her whole body shudders as I trace my fingers down the ridge of her spine. The way she cups my hips with her palms. And when she pulls me beneath the covers at last, and I reach down and touch her, then stall, the way she smiles with actual sweetness, and something more, and whispers, "Wait, here, give me your hand and I'll show you."

It's not that sex is so different with Leigh. Okay, *obviously* it's different. To have the same bits and parts and still fit together so well? Leigh knows what she's doing, and I'm a quick study despite what my horrific senior year grades would suggest. But that's not what makes it revolutionary. Will was pretty good. Jake isn't as selfish as you'd think, and he's had a lot of practice, bizzaro hometown hero that he is.

It's not because I've never done it in a bed, either, though that's certainly a switch from backseats and stockrooms and boys' parents' couches.

Mostly, it's the afterward part that's so strange and new. Usually once my bones unmelt, I feel trapped. I squirm away and reassure the boys that it was great and

then I'm gone, even though I've got no place in particular to go. But Leigh and I, we lie in the heat like a
softly unraveled braid; our legs still twisted, her fingers
threaded in my damp hair, my arm across her back and
hers across my chest, her face tucked into the pocket
between my chin and collarbone, sweaty and breathing
warm breaths. Anyone else's limbs would feel like lead
weights right about now.

But—and I know it sounds extraordinarily fucking
corny—that's not how it is with her.

Leigh is like water.

THIRTEEN

I'm sitting on the living room couch with Dad a week
later while he flips slowly through this week's menu and
the order list for Silvia's, fingers scrabbling at the pages.
It's a good day—his fancy rollator walker still stands
against the wall beside his bed, unused, so it's just these
cushioned neoprene knee supports he wears. Meanwhile
I'm sloppily folding a load of laundry, but most of me is
still floating. I'm thinking about Leigh, feeling the ghost
of her hands and the memory of her taste, cinnamon lip
balm and Jarritos Limón soda. Both of our favorites,
and one of the few things in New Mexico she's admitted

to missing when she left. A better taste by far than Jake's winterfresh cigarette breath, though it never bothered me before.

I'm so zoned out, I jump when Dad fumbles and drops the ledger. "¡Puta madre!" Dad spits.

I cringe away, a reflex. It's not his fault when he gets angry, and I know it's worse for a lot of people with HD. That's the disease; when the part of your brain that's supposed to organize information starts to go, you can't control how upset you get. But the reasons are real and purely his. He's angry that he can't cook, can't drive, can't take Mom dancing even though he never really liked dancing anyway. He's angry when he can't find the word he needs, even though he was never some great wordsmith. He's angry because he doesn't feel strong anymore.

And when I was a kid, he was *strong*. This one time—I don't remember how old I was, maybe in third or fourth grade—he pretty much carried me all through Frijoles Canyon. We were doing this unit on local history in school, and for weekend homework we were supposed to visit a historical site so we could talk about it in front of the class on Monday. Except there was some crisis with the fridge at Silvia's breaking down, and both he and Mom had to be in the restaurant. I sat in the office most of the day, choked up with disappointment, stupid kid tears blurring the cartoons my parents put on the little TV for me. It wasn't even a big deal; they could've written a note to excuse me from my wildly unimportant class project. But instead, when Dad finally came to get me in the very late afternoon, he put me in his old brown Chevy we had to sell off when he stopped driving and said, "Feel like a trip?"

We motored up to Bandelier, this big national park about an hour and a half northwest of La Trampa, just south of Las Alamos. Later, it became a regular in the rotation of school field trips, but this was my first visit. Dad parked the truck outside the visitors' center, already shuttered. Signs said the park was open dawn to dusk, but we were the only car in the lot, and "dusk" was bleeding into full blue night.

"Are we supposed to be here this late?" I asked.

Dad scratched his beard, which was thick and full back then. "Sure. It's a national monument." Like that solved everything. He zipped up his jacket and nodded toward the trail, which I could see ran off into not-so-dusk. "Up for a walk?"

I peered dubiously over the dashboard.

"No tengas miedo, corazón," he said. "I was here with my dad, you know? Just once. Hadn't met your mom. Hadn't even thought you up yet."

We climbed out. It was cold—I think November,

or even later—so Dad took an old rawhide coat out of the trunk, where he kept his emergency kit in case the truck ever gave up and stranded him somewhere. He tucked it in around me and lifted me up onto his shoulders, marched us steadily down the path, which was sometimes paved and sometimes not. The trail wound through the trees alongside the thin, shimmering black path of a river. "Rito de los Frijoles," Dad said, tapping my knee so I would look. "Bean Creek."

We passed the first ruins, mostly a wide circle of stones, and then in a grassy clearing, the remains of what Dad said was a pueblo, though it looked like a flattened gray honeycomb. Soon we were out of the trees and red cliffs rose up around us, the canyon widening. On either side of the ravine, the rock was punctured by holes as tall as Dad—low to the ground, some with wooden ladders propped up to them. I thought the holes were like the pores in coral our science teacher had brought into class to show us.

Dad whistled.

"What is it?" I asked in a low voice.

"Homes. Or they were."

We later learned about those in school too. Cliff dwellings. Once they were full of people who carved out lives in the calcified rivers of old volcanic eruptions.

Then they were gone, abandoning the pueblo, and nobody was 100 percent sure why. Probably dead crops and drought and plain old enemies. Scientists or whoever have spent their lives digging for the exact reason, but what does that get them? It's not like they can bring the people back.

The trail continued, but I think I fell asleep right on Dad's shoulders, because then we were back at the truck, him shifting me into the warm cab. It felt like seconds before we were in La Trampa; the drive up had seemed to take forever, but the trip home, no time at all.

Overhearing Dad's outburst, Mom pokes her head out of the kitchen. "¿Todo bien ahi?"

"We're fine," I answer for Dad, who either didn't hear her or isn't listening as he stares at the ledger on the floor. I get up and scoop it off the floor to hand to him, then head for the bathroom while he reads over the numbers for the fifth time. I don't have to go, but I want him to think I was getting up anyway, and not to spare myself the sight of Dad climbing to his feet.

Safely inside, I sit on the closed toilet lid and tug my phone from my back pocket to text.

Me: What are you doing tonight?

Less than a minute later, an answer.

Leigh: I hate everything but you. What do you think I'm
doing?

I guess that works out, then.

For all its ruffles and ghosts of Aqua Net cans past, this
time the hideous bedroom no longer seems *that* hideous.
Maybe because it's becoming ours. We sit cross-legged
on the bed, and Leigh hands me the joint she's been
nursing so she can root around in her backpack. I take
a weak pull. Of course Leigh found a dealer right away
after Lucas caught her sampling from Naveen, though
she hasn't yet bothered to find friends.

"Did you hear about the truck?" she asks while she
digs.

My mind flashes stupidly to Jake's catastrophe of a
Ford. "Probably not."

She tumbles a bag of ripple chips and a little
Spanish-English dictionary out onto the mattress in
her search, which I try not to be flattered by. "This
eighteen-wheeler overturned and went into the Rio a
couple days ago."

"That sucks," I say inadequately, and take a proper
lungful, coughing as I hand back her joint. I'm not a
very impressive marihuano.

"The driver was fine. He said he saw a horse in his
headlights and swerved, but the guy who owned the

horse ranch nearby said it was probably a tumbleweed. Whatever, that's not the story. So the truck flipped and went through the guardrails and half into the river, and guess what it was carrying?"

"I'd prefer not to."

"Okay, well you wouldn't guess anyway. It was headed to the UFO Museum in Roswell. So the truck doors opened in the slide, and all these alien shot glasses and T-shirts and books got caught up in the rocks and the shopping carts and stuff. But there were also these glow-in-the-dark squeaky aliens and tub toys, and their boxes were smashed, and they all floated away down the river. Thousands of them." She tosses a spray can of Febreze from the backpack and finally tugs out a bottle of our old friend, Largo Bay, sparkling dangerously. "Then this morning, some doctor was rafting in the Rio, like, sixty miles south of the crash, and this little tub alien floated by. The news says they might go all the way to the Gulf and out to sea."

I take the bottle and purse my lips around the neck, grimacing through a familiar sip of lighter fluid and lime. "That's one way to leave. Maybe you can float out of New Mexico."

"Maybe I can." She shuts her eyes and leans back against the wall, crinkling an ancient Menudo poster. I study her lips as she inhales, and when she blinks, she catches me staring. She lifts the corner of her mouth just slightly. "What?"

"What?"

"What're you thinking?"

I pull my ponytail over my shoulder and start braiding down to the tip, suddenly desperate for someplace to look besides at Leigh. "I was just thinking . . . what do you think it means?"

"It?" Her dark eyebrows scrunch. "Be more specific."

With our knees overlapping, we're close enough that I imagine I can feel the heat coming off her, even in the still-hot bedroom. "You know. Me, you. What we did. What I kind of want to do now. What do you think that all means?"

"Shit, I'm not a gay pride informational pamphlet, Vanni."

I wince and take a sip. "I'm so sorry to bother you with my confusing new sexuality."

"It's not that complicated," she says, but nicer. "It doesn't have to be. Are you into guys? Not like 'You're visually pleasing and I'd look at you in a museum,' but like, 'I want to shove my tongue down your throat until I taste your uvula'?"

I think of Max Binali's football biceps and his arm wrapped around my shoulder in the arroyo freshman year; of Will Fischer sweetly playing "Going Off to College" on a used ukulele at Fender Bender when I was a junior and he was a senior; of Jake's dimpled smile and strong hands hooked around my apron straps. "Yeah? I think so, yeah."

"Are you into girls?" Her eyes catch mine, hazel and bronzed around the center. She wears long shorts and her standard boys' tank top, bright white against the tan, smooth skin of her collarbone, her slim shoulders, and the hollow beneath her throat. She takes the bottle back and her fingers dance over mine.

"Yeah." My voice comes out husky.

"Okay then," she says casually, but her whole body loosens into the headboard. "Maybe you're bi."

"Maybe I'm bi," I repeat, tasting the words. "You think I am?"

"Who cares what I think? You just have to figure it out yourself."

"When did you?" I ask, setting the stub of the joint on the nightstand and reaching for her instead of the bottle.

She slides her fingers through mine and squeezes. "Figure it out? Probably when I was six or seven and obsessed with *Power Rangers Wild Force*. Every episode, I just wanted to jump through the screen and hug the yellow ranger. She was bossy and blond and hot.

Then in third grade, there was this girl, Nina Brewster. She lived down the street from me in Santa Fe. Also blond and she smelled like grape Bubblicious. I convinced her to play Power Rangers. She was the Yellow Ranger and I was the Lunar Wolf, and I would always rescue her by, like, giving her piggyback rides out of danger. Thoroughly misogynistic." Leigh smirks. "But yeah, I was pretty sure."

I toss my ponytail over my shoulder and try not to bristle at the fact that Leigh liked blondes first. She was eight, after all, and what eight-year-old has solid judgment?

"And you just, like, came out? And it was fine?"

"Oh yeah, they built me a float out of sunflowers and made me grand marshal of the parade, and I never had any problems again," she says, and snorts.

"Sorry."

"No, I'm being salty." Leigh takes a deep sip—she's on her way to a better buzz than me, but I'm not trying very hard—and winces as she swallows. "It was mostly fine. It was okay. Just some kids . . . there was this one goblin-faced fucksicle, *Jeremy*." She says the name as if spitting out a mouthful of sour milk. "For, like, a month in eighth grade, he'd follow me around school, sneak up behind me, and shove me into random girls in the hallways and shout 'Kiss her!'"

"Ugh. Did you tell Lucas?"

"Um, no. I didn't feel like testifying at the murder trial. He acts like he's the *most* mature, like his shit never stank, but when Lucas was twelve, he tried to fight a high school senior who drove over my bike on purpose. I left it in the apartment complex driveway, but whatever—that kid was such a testicle. It was pretty sweet. Lucas was the approximate height of a mailbox and didn't weigh much more, but he was mad enough that if he hadn't gotten that concussion in the middle of the fight, he totally could've had the dude. But that's another story.

"Anyway, I didn't tell my brother. Then one day Jeremy tried his shtick outside the nurse's office, right next to the lost-and-found bucket full of textbooks and shoes and stuff, and . . . I hit him in the face."

"With a shoe?"

"With the bucket. And it was fucking heavy. Maybe I had one of those mom-lifts-car type bursts of strength."

"Badass," I declare.

Leigh smiles down at the neck of the bottle. "So. You really never got a boner for a girl before?" She elegantly changes the subject.

"Uh. I don't know," I say, searching. I've always looked at pretty girls twice, but who doesn't do that?

There *was* this summer coach for the Santa Fe Aquatic

Club when I was eleven. She had all this strawberry-red hair piled under her swim cap, the reddest I'd seen outside a TV show, and this long, cut body that sliced through the pool, peeled the water back like it was air. I think she was in college, and so I knew we'd never be friends, hold hands, have sleepovers, and breathe in each other's shampoo in the dark, but I wanted it so bad; this shockingly hot feeling in my lukewarm little-kid heart.

And there was that party in the arroyo before sophomore year, where this girl visiting from a few towns over, from Jaconita or something, asked me for a cigarette. Rather than shout to be heard over the racket of boys, she leaned in so close, the tips of her careless brown bob brushed my cheek and I could see the slight veins in her purple lipstick. I stammered back that I didn't have one on me, never mind that I didn't smoke. She smiled and sort of hip-checked me, the rivet of her hip bone bouncing against mine, before walking away. I felt like I would've traded a kidney for a cigarette to offer her, till Max pulled me by the arm to watch him play the slap game with his friends.

I figured all girls had moments like that. Maybe they do, but don't talk about it.

Leigh takes another sip, then caps the bottle and drops it on the bed, reaches forward and hooks a finger beneath the strap of my halter top, grinning as she tugs.

"Teach me how to say 'Come here, hottie' in Spanish."

Whenever a boy's commanded me: *Say something sexy in Spanish*, it's annoying as hell. But this is Leigh, and that makes a difference.

I lean back. Propping myself on my elbows, I cross my legs in front of me at the ankles and tilt my chin up to look at her, a mermaid lounging on a rock. "Ven acá, guapa. Quitate la ropa."

Even though she can't understand, she crawls forward into my lap and kisses me, tasting like lighter fluid and lime. We fall flat on the bed, her narrow hips against mine, fingers skimming the hem of my shirt, and I kiss her back and forgive her for Nina Brewster.

On the drive back to Leigh's a couple hours later, we speed with the windows rolled down and hot wind sandpapering our faces. It whisks away the fresh-linen smell of Febreze we sprayed copiously in the hideous room and on ourselves. I swallow and taste the desert in my teeth.

"Now what are you thinking?" Leigh shouts over the squall raging inside the van.

I'm thinking the same thing I've been thinking for days. I'm thinking that I want Leigh to stay. About a month and a half from now, on her eighteenth birthday, she'll go back home and my tiny world will be exactly like it was, unless I convince her to stick around. Of all the things I want, this is something I can have, something I can choose, and I'm not prepared for it to drift away.

I'm thinking that I just want one thing to be good and right, because one good, right thing can be enough.

FOURTEEN

Being with Leigh is like . . . I don't know, like halftime at the homecoming game freshman year. When Coach Garza announced the court over the loudspeakers with perhaps the slightest tug of beer in his voice. He called the king and queen of the freshman class first, and Marilee nearly shoved me over the side of the bleachers in her fervor. I tromped down the metal steps to the football field, under the glow of the outdated flood-lights they were always holding fund-raisers to replace. It was a particularly freezing November, and I shivered while someone on the student council handed me a little white bouquet of yucca flowers and draped a sash over my peacoat, knocking my beanie askew. Playing triumphantly behind us was the El Trampero High six-man band—there weren't enough kids for a football team *and* a full ensemble—and suddenly that scrabbly field was exactly where I belonged. No, it was where the better version of me belonged. A girl with a higher algebra grade and a faster time in the fifty-meter backstroke, with blond highlights and straighter teeth and better-fitting clothes, from some glamorous seaside town, with a sure and bright future. And lucky me, I got to stand in her spot for one night.

That's how it feels to be with Leigh.

Like there's a better, smarter, more interesting Savannah Espinoza in the world, one with a zero percent chance of doom in her future, and as long as nobody ever realizes she isn't me, I get to take her place.

Maybe that's why, even as the weeks go by, I don't say anything about us to anybody. It's sure not because my sterling and virginal reputation couldn't take the hit.

And it's not because my parents wouldn't get it. They're not marching in the parades or anything, but I think Dad would bob his head, as if to be like, "Do you, mi corazón." And Mom would probably throw a party to prove how happy my happiness made her in these difficult times, order a rainbow sheet cake from

Albertsons iced with *We* ♥ *Leigh Clemente.* At least, I think she would.

But I want to keep Leigh as mine. And I want to keep being the Vanni that belongs to Leigh.

Leave it to Jake Mosqueda to stick his nose where it doesn't belong.

When Leigh gives me a lift to my Monday afternoon shift at Silvia's on the last day of July, I find Jake just inside, face practically pressed to the fogged-up glass.

"¿Que pedo?" I ask, hand on my hip. The sweat of summer beads at my hairline, but I'm too busy looking tough to wipe it away, even though I feel about as tough as a melting Popsicle.

"Nada." He retreats behind his little host podium, pretending to stack and restack his pile of menus.

"No, say it."

Jake looks up, hair tumbling across his eyes. "Just," he whisper-hisses, "you guys are . . . what, like . . . is she your *girlfriend* now? Are you guys, like, *dating*?"

I lift my chin. "None of your business."

He pouts thoughtfully, teething his full bottom lip. "So you didn't like it, what we did? Together, all those times?"

There's no meanness in the question. He's a little kid, waiting for his teacher to grade a test he's sure he failed. "That's not, you know . . . it doesn't work like that, Jake."

"What doesn't?"

"I don't know, the, you know, the spectrum of . . . human . . . whatever." I wave my hands helplessly. "I can't talk to you about it. Just Google some shit, okay? I gotta go check in."

Flushed worse than I was in the blistering parking lot, I make a break for the back office, where Mom makes Mom-faces and suggests I get a cold drink before I start my shift. I grab a glass of water from the kitchen and bring it into the stockroom. Sitting cross-legged with my back pressed against the door, I let the condensation drip into my lap.

That went marvelously.

To calm myself after a delightful confab with my ex-hookup over my newly embraced sexuality, I pull out my phone and text Leigh.

Me: Still go for the garage tonight?

Leigh: You were serious?!

She answers immediately, as usual. Leigh's on summer break, has no job, and no interest in making local friends, so she's pretty available.

Me: Yes?

Leigh: Wow, you're really jumping into the deep end.

Me: I totally Googled "bi things to do in Albuquerque."

This last is not a joke; that's precisely what I did yesterday, while Leigh and I were making plans. It turns out this club in Albuquerque, the Garage, hosts queer karaoke on Monday nights at ten. It's eighteen and over, but Leigh (or should I call her twenty-two-year-old Shandi Qutubuddin from Sugarbrook, Massachusetts?) has a convincing-in-dim-lighting fake ID, which she swears worked 100 percent of the time at this place back home called Midway Café in Jamaica Plain, wherever that is.

According to my research, the Garage is neither classy enough nor dive-y enough to attract non-Burquenos, and though I might be out of touch with my classmates, I don't think queer karaoke is their scene anyway. I don't even think it's my scene.

What it is is a mission.

Leigh and I haven't used the G-word yet. We don't call each other "baby" or "honey" or "muñeca" or "querida." We're just *us*. We're together whenever I don't need to be somewhere else. Mostly we meet at Chris's, and it's great, it's hot, it's standing-on-a-football-field-while-Coach-Garza-slurred-out-the-homecoming-court magnificent.

But if I'm not ready to bring Leigh home to that rainbow cake just yet, I am starting to wish for a label, just between us. Because that's, like, the main difference between a relationship and a Jake, right? When you can't be contained inside a single night or a truck bed or bathroom stall, so you spill over into real life. And what if Leigh won't stick around town for a nebulous, unlabeled *whatever*? With the start of August tomorrow, the deadline is looming.

Bottom line: If Leigh's my good thing, then we need to be . . . something.

I need to be enough.

My phone chimes, and I check the screen.

Leigh: dude, can we just hang out at the house?

By "the house," she means Chris's place, and by "dude" she means no chance—I speak Leigh fluently enough to understand this. Frustrated, I send back some affirmative combo of emojis and drop the phone into my lap.

Lucky me, I get another chance the next morning during my shift at the Lagoon, when a rainstorm washes out the park for a half hour. The mermaids and I are in the locker room, wringing ourselves out and refastening plastic starfish and flowers and turtles into our hair. Then Kristian stands on a bench to announce her twenty-first birthday on Friday, and the whole squad's invited to her birthday party with plus-ones.

Which seems like the perfect place to finally affix a label to Leigh and me.

* * *

Kristian lives with her boyfriend in Santa Fe, in this freaking adorable one-story house they're renting on Agua Fria. Turquoise doors, strings of sea glass in the windows, rough stucco walls, ceramic kitchen tiles printed with birds and flowers. It's an Airbnb wet dream.

The birthday girl, tiny and gorgeous in this flowing purple maxi dress and flower crown, rockets into my arms when she sees us in the front room. "Vanni, YAY, you came!"

"Your place is great!" I shout over the *untz-untz-untz* of the speakers turned way up.

Leigh stands a little awkwardly at my side, shrinking from the crush of party guests. She's wearing a baggy long-sleeve button-up with the sleeves rolled to her biceps, and she just got a haircut this morning, with the soft sides cut close, and the hair on top a little longer and fluffed up. She looks so tight, I want to drag her back out to the van and peel off her shorts (which are khaki and almost knee-length, so I don't understand why it's sexy, but whatever, there it is). But I'm here on the mission. Instead, I take her hand in mine and pull her in close so she can hear me.

"This is my girlfriend, Leigh!" I yell into Kristian's face. Except it's the first time I'm saying the word aloud, unrehearsed, and technically without permission, so it comes out in a hiccup, like "g-urrrlfrin."

Leigh's fingers twitch in mine, and I clamp down.

Kristian blinks, eyes rounded with surprise and an excellent shade of blue eyeliner. "Oh! Cool, that's really cool!"

Though I'm afraid to look sideways once Kristian moves off to mingle, Leigh doesn't seem upset. At least she keeps her hand in mine on our meandering journey toward the drinks set up in the backyard. As always, it feels different from a boy's—small knuckled, she takes up much less space between my fingers, and her skin is cooler somehow—but it doesn't feel wrong. Of course, I've held hands with girls before, because Marilee was always touchy-feely, hooking arms, kissing cheeks, mounting us for piggyback rides when she was high. We even kissed on the mouth once, pursed fish lips to fish lips, in a game of Truth or Dare that was obviously for the boys around us, and not for us girls. But it wasn't a storm inside my body, the air suddenly dense and hot, my blood crackling electrically.

People are piled into the dusty backyard surrounded by an artfully jagged wooden fence. There's an outdoor bar at the picnic table, assorted snacks and bottles glittering on top, with the keg beside it. I grab a fistful of tortilla chips out of a bag—I've been freaking *starving* lately, maybe because I'm skipping a meal here and there to make time for Leigh—and lean in close to ask her,

"What do you want?"

She shrugs one shoulder, eyeing the crowd. "Depends. How long are we staying?"

Just then, Camila A spots me from across the yard, flaps an arm and shrieks, "Vanni! ¿Conoces a mi novio?"

Leigh raises an eyebrow.

"She wants us to meet her boyfriend," I explain.

"Us?" she murmurs, reaching for a cup.

I tug on her sleeve. "Hey, is it okay that we're here? And what I said—"

"Yeah, it's fine, it's a good party. I just want to get to the after-party." She kisses my jaw where my hair's pinned back, just below my ear, and the air inside my lungs sizzles.

A few of the mermaids stand together by the fence, the Camilas A and C and Iris and the Kardashian-esque Nicole, along with a scattering of boyfriends and Nicole's cousin, equally dark haired and plump lipped. The circle expands to fit us in. We talk about the Lagoon, our common denominator, retelling stories we all know about getting hit on by pubescent park guests, worshiped by little girls, shouted at by Eric, scowled at by Naomi. It's a warm night and I've got a warm buzz going from the beer that Leigh periodically disappears to fetch. She and I are holding hands while we say these perfectly normal things and talk about the epic party we'll throw when the Lost Lagoon closes for the season in September, and debate whether we'll come back next year. Though we bitch about the havoc chlorine wreaks on our hair, and joke about burning our fins so we'll never again have to squeeze inside like processed meat into sausage casings, we all say yeah. We'll do it again for sure. As little as I like thinking about the future, the promise of having a home next summer at Mermaid Cove makes me feel warmer still.

Leigh untangles her fingers from mine to make a trip to the keg, but I turn, wrap my hand around the soft, short hair at the back of her neck and pull her in for a kiss.

"*Yeah*, girls, that's hot!" some pendejo on a flyby toward the bar shouts in our ears.

I feel every part of Leigh tighten. The small tendons in her neck, her skin, her shoulders, her fingers hooked inside the front pocket of my shorts, her teeth. She snaps around to look at this guy's pink, round face bobbing above the collar of his navy-and-teal-striped polo shirt, and snarls, "Did we fucking *ask*?"

Our circle of mermaids and mer-quaintances hushes, but I bite the inside of my cheek to hide a smile. Because even I, who's never before publicly kissed a girl I actually like, know that this dude's attitude is some tiresome shit.

What *should* happen:

This guy apologizes for being a sexist jerk and assuming that every girl wakes up, gets dressed, puts on lipstick, strolls down the sidewalk, and moves through the world all so he can get a boner. Just like every asshole around here who'll honk at anything with tits as he blasts by in his truck pumping reggaetón, no matter if you're wearing sweats or have a nasty cold or your dad just got diagnosed that morning, and you need to get some air and some peace. Or like every tourist who comes into Silvia's, eyeballs Estrella and Mom and me and declares, "They sure grow them pretty in these parts!" as if we were planted and watered and picked just to delight him on his vacation. Realizing all this, the guy immediately says he's sorry, backs away from us, and shuts himself in Kristian's bathroom to reevaluate his life.

What *does* happen:

The slabs of his cheeks darken and splotch like raw marbled beef. Rooted to his patch of dust by shock or shame or both, he stares back at us. "Chill the fuck out," he murmurs, then takes a deep drink from the plastic cup crinkling in his fist. His razor-burned Adam's apple bobs violently as he watches Leigh over the rim . . . right until the moment she reaches up and palms it out of his grip.

The cup spins away toward the ground.

Unidentified alcohol drips down his chin, soaks his polo shirt, splashes the dirt around us.

Untz-untz-untz, the bass pumps from inside the house.

He stands there, bug-eyed, before stumbling toward us.

I doubt he means to throw a punch or anything, probably wants to get in her face, like any big guy used to getting his way just by existing in as much space as he does, but Leigh's already slipping away from me, out of my grasp. I'm clutching at the air where her shirt was as she slams forward, driving her shoulder into his chest, her fist into his sizable stomach with a thick *whoomph*. Bellowing "What the fuck?" he raises a forearm and knocks her across the cheek.

There is murder in Leigh's eyes as she winds back for another punch, but then Camila A's boyfriend swoops in and wraps his arms around Leigh's waist, holding her off, and I've got my hands on this guy's sweaty T-shirt, shoving him back, and people are shouting, and his friends are tugging on him, except he's not fighting to get at Leigh or anything, just bellowing, "What the fuck, I didn't do anything! What the fuck? I didn't even want to touch the bitch, what the fuck?"

And Iris is standing right behind me, saying, "Oh my god, Vanni, oh my god."

And I'm telling her, "I don't know," just "I don't know, I don't know, I don't know."

FIFTEEN

"*Not going out,* mi corazón?" Dad asks as I flop down beside him on the sofa. It's early on Sunday afternoon, the restaurant's closed and Mom's home too, outside weeding the rock mulch with her phone un-coolly clipped to her belt in case Dad needs her. Why she bothers, I don't know—will overgrown chicory stunt the growth of our luxurious pebble crop?—except that Mom's like me. She feels better when she's moving.

Tonight, though, I'm not going anywhere. "I'm vegging with you guys. See?" I gesture toward my pink Tinkerbell sleep shorts that Marilee brought me back from Disneyland three years ago. The seams now strain against my hips, but they're still perfectly veg-appropriate.

So is Dad's outfit: a loose-necked T-shirt and loosely cinched drawstring pants bulging slightly over his knee supports, so he won't have to fumble with a button and zipper, and shoes without laces. Anything to save him a little time. Sometime in the winter, I overheard Mom talking to Chris Zepeda, who'd come to visit. I passed through the kitchen where they stood, Chris with a beer, and a wineglass dangling lightly from Mom's fingertips. She smiled at me, but when I paused in the hallway I heard her say that the extra moments it took Dad to brush his teeth, to find the TV remote, to answer the phone, to slide into a car, were losses more painful to Dad because they were so small. Time that should've been his being whittled from his life. She sounded so un-Mom-like. And Dad had never said anything like that to me. My parents don't talk about Dad's HD that way. "It's not the end of the world," Mom always says, "it's just a different one."

Sure it is.

Dad and I spend the afternoon watching reruns of a sitcom, the couch shaking slightly beneath us as his body rocks against the back cushions. I pay close attention to this show about people in luxury apartments in the city, who seem to spend all of their time frantically pairing off and none of their time working. In one episode, the second-best-looking boy takes the best-looking girl to the aquarium, then falls into the shark tank to the compulsory laughter of the audience. To the girl, this is adorable, and not a troubling brush with Darwinism.

Mom finishes her yard work, showers, and joins us just in time for the end of the episode about the second-best-looking girl losing her crappy day job, experiencing a short montage of interviews for even worse jobs, and then immediately landing her dream job with the help of her friends and also a capybara that's escaped from the city zoo.

"What kind of show is this?" she asks, toweling her long hair.

Seconds later, Dad answers, "Fantasy."

I forget he's sometimes funny, even if his jokes are on a bit of a time delay. Like when Dad used to do the grocery shopping by himself, he once tripped into this beautifully constructed, eight-foot-high tree of stacked paper towel rolls—it was right around Christmastime—and I'm not saying it was hilarious. I'm sure Dad was pissed and embarrassed and scared in the moment, and I took over the shopping soon after. But later, when Mom fake-casually asked how the trip had gone, Dad half smiled when he told us that at that very moment, in the song being piped over the store speakers, Miley Cyrus sang, *"I came in like a wreeeecking baaaaall . . ."*

An episode or two later, I pry myself away from this laugh-tracked masterpiece to help Mom with dinner. It's leftover tacos de pescado from Silvia's. Mom peels back the lid on the plastic tub, spoons the cream-and-halibut filling into a pan to reheat according to Martin's scribbled instructions. I tear open a salad bag, pausing to wipe the crumbs from prepackaged croutons off my hands when I get a text.

Leigh: You around?

Me: Gotta stay in tonight. People are coming over.

Sorry!!!

For the record, I am not avoiding Leigh.

She's said she's sorry, and true, that pendejo probably deserved it, for general crimes against womanity if not specifically for being rude at a birthday party. So she didn't take his shit; I love the non-shit-takingness of Leigh. I love that she knows exactly who she is and exactly what she wants.

Except that Camila A's boyfriend almost had to fireman-carry her out of Kristian's backyard, at which point it was obvious that all she wanted was to punch, and anybody with a breakable nose would do. And that, I didn't like quite so much.

The kitchen timer beeps. Mom takes out the pan and

spoons the filling onto tortillas warmed in the microwave, because she gets too frazzled using the stove for two purposes at once. Dad would flip tortillas in the pan with his bare hands like it was nothing. For him, she puts the filling directly on his plate, then rips his tortilla into quarters so he won't have to worry about his taco splattering into his lap. "Food's ready," she says. "Go help your father up if he needs it, mija."

He doesn't, and makes his way stiffly to the table. It's a dinner like any other. Mom talks, Dad nods and bobs, I ignore my phone as it vibrates in the pocket of my Tinkerbell shorts.

"Chris sent a picture of his little niece." Mom launches into a new topic, her cooling taco hovering between her plate and mouth. "¡Que bella pequeña! She reminds me of you, Vanni, when you were little. All that baby fat, like dumplings! He says his father's on the mend, too, so he'll still be back by the end of the month, he thinks. I told him everything was fine at home, of course, with you doing such a good job looking out for the place."

Guiltily, I stuff the rest of a steaming taco down my throat. I cough, and Dad prods the pitcher across the table with both hands. I gulp water, stuff down my last taco, and stand to bring my plate to the sink. "I'll clean, okay?"

"Thank you, mija." Mom smiles quickly and warmly, and then she's off again, repeating some story Mr. Paiz told her yesterday afternoon about the increasingly aggressive pigeons in the town square.

I scrape food into the trash and wash the dishes while Mom helps Dad shave in the bathroom, then makes sure he's settled in his shower chair. There's the sputter and spritz of the water, and Mom joins me in the kitchen, still toweling her hands.

"So, no plans at all on your free evening?" she asks. "Not even with your friend?"

I glance up from the sink to see Mom studying the towel intently. In this exact moment, I realize she's figured out that my "friend" count is down to one. Here, I've been scattering white lies like super-obvious bread crumbs for the past year and a half, such as: "Sorry I stayed out so late. I went to Diana's to watch a movie and we fell asleep." Because my mother doesn't care much for Mrs. Reyes, and they run in as opposite circles as possible in a three-traffic-light town, Diana is occasionally my go-to excuse. But I haven't had her or Marilee around in all that time, and as it turns out, Mom's neither too tired nor too optimistic to have noticed. I'm not happy that she knows, that she's probably been worrying . . . but.

The fact is that my mother's not too busy or tired or

blindly optimistic to understand this truth about me, at least.

"Nope," I say for a third time, though I have to squeeze it out around this strangling little lump in my throat.

She frowns and presses damp knuckles against my forehead. "You're not feeling sick?"

"I'm okay."

"You and Leigh didn't have a fight, did you?"

"We're not in a fight." I almost laugh. "Mom, do you, like, ever want to go somewhere else? Or, like, wish you were someplace different right now? Or . . ." This is not a normal conversation for us. We don't talk much about my mom, how she's feeling, what she wishes. Maybe we used to, but not in the past few years. Still, her undivided attention's unsettled something, questions stirring way at the bottom of a deep, still lake. "Where would you go right exactly this second, if you could go anywhere?"

"I'm happy here." She folds the towel neatly against her body. "Your dad's having a good night. He's calm and enjoying himself with his family. He has everything he needs."

"I'm not asking about that, I'm just asking what *you* want."

She sets the towel on the kitchen counter and frowns

at me, a rare sight. "Love isn't always about that. Asking ourselves what we want all of the time? That's the way children love."

This makes zero sense. "So what, you don't get to have anything, ever?"

Mom opens her mouth to answer, when from the other room comes the thud of something falling.

The look on her face—pale panic mixed with resignation. The same old disaster. I follow her down the hall to the bathroom. Mom raps one knuckle against the door and raises her voice to be heard over the hiss of the shower. "Gabe? ¿Estás bien, querido?" She doesn't wait for an answer, cracking the door and ducking inside. Steam billows in my face before the door shuts again. While I wait I taste something sour and familiar, my heart trapped behind my teeth.

A moment later, Mom pokes her head out and flashes a tight smile. "Vanni, get the first-aid kit out of the kitchen, can you?"

"What happened?"

She paws a dark strand of hair out of her face, curled from the sudden heat, with one damp wrist. Her voice is calm, but her fingertips are white where they clench the door frame. "It's nothing to worry about."

"Then why do you need the kit?"

Mom's fingers flex, nails digging into the wood.

"Your father just hurt his arm. He might need to get stitches, but I have to wrap it first. It's not bad. Just get the kit, please, Savannah. Now."

I hurry to grab the kit Mom keeps fully stocked from beneath the kitchen sink and bring it to her. Then I go and sit cross-legged on my bed with the door just slightly ajar, listening to the sounds of my parents: The creak of the warped bathroom door as it swings open. The low murmur of my mother's voice. The uneven shuffle of Dad's footsteps up the hallway and toward the front door. The jingle of the Malibu's keys lifted from the heart-shaped basket on the coffee table. The quick, deliberate patter of Mom's approaching footsteps as she heads back my way. She knocks delicately. "We won't be gone long, mija. You'll be all right here by yourself?"

"Uh-huh," I say, my eyes on the ceiling.

"You're sure?" she asks, but she's gone from my doorway already.

Instead of reading or watching TV or playing the Baskervilles at top volume, I do something incredibly dumb. I sit perfectly still, staring at those words on the ceiling, and start to *think*.

It's not like I've never considered death before Dad's diagnosis. I've even thought about my death. One summer during middle school, before I was busy growing boobs and learning to wield a curling iron, Marilee and Diana and I went on this kick and read every Lurlene McDaniel book they had in the little one-room, no-bathroom, volunteer-run town library. Maybe we were too old for them, but not yet too old to feel too old. So instead, we loved them. There were beautiful teenagers in hospital gowns on the covers, bathed in pastels, glowing. Titles like *Don't Die, My Love. Sixteen and Dying. Too Young to Die. She Died Too Young.* I mean, they weren't subtle. We would all lie out on Diana's trampoline with our books, reading for five minutes, discussing for ten.

Diana: "Would you marry a boy if he was dying?"

Marilee: "No. Well maybe, if he loved me and he looked like Liam Hemsworth."

Me: "Would you tell a boy you loved that you were dying?"

Diana: "If I didn't I'd feel really bad all the time."

Marilee: "How do you think you'll die?"

The how, I hadn't much considered. I could almost make myself believe that, like the gorgeous red-haired brain tumor patient, or the young Amish boy hit by a vegetable truck, I would one day cease all activity. Close my eyes beautifully and then . . . nothing. Or something. Who knows?

But I never thought it'd be ugly. And HD is *ugly*. It's mean and it takes everything, and nights like this, when these things happen, when I think of what could happen to me, what might be happening already, and I wouldn't even know it . . .

I fumble my phone out of my pocket, dialing Leigh. Pick up, pick up, pick up, my heartbeat thumps. Pick up, pick up, pick up.

On the fourth ring, she does. "Okay, I'm really s—"

"Can you, um, can you come here?" I cut in. "Or I can go there? Can we do something?"

"I thought you were stuck at home."

"No, I'm . . ." The phone shudders in my hand, and I grip it so hard that the plastic case bites into my fingertips, jam it against my ear until I hear the low roar of the ocean through the screen. "My dad, something happened, so I'm free."

"Is he okay?" And then, "Are *you* okay?"

That hateful fucking question.

"Yeah, can you just . . . ?"

"Sure, okay," she says. "I'm coming right now."

I take a deep and jittering breath. It's okay. Leigh is coming. Things are being seen to. It's okay. I'm okay.

"What do you want to do?" she asks.

"I don't know." I grope for the right word. "Something kind of scary?"

When she answers, I hear the dare in her voice. "Want to go for a swim?"

SIXTEEN

The Lost Lagoon is long since closed by the time Leigh's van screams into the big empty parking lot. She slams us into a spot in the very back beside the stucco wall surrounding the lot, crushing the brakes underfoot, and the whole car shudders. My body rocks forward, the seat belt burns against my skin, I clip my tongue with my teeth and taste the blood. "Chingado," I hiss, but my exasperation melts away as I look over at her. Weak moonlight and the dim glow of the park through the windshield ignites just a sliver of Leigh's skin here and there—a slice of jawline, a bare shoulder, an eye, river-bottom dark—but I love the puzzle the pieces make.

"Shall we?" She wags her eyebrows and pops out of the car, pausing to grab her backpack from the trunk.

"What about cameras?" I ask. "Our contract said we'd be filmed for security."

She shakes her head. "Only at the front entrance and in the buildings, the stores and stuff."

"Which you know because . . . ?"

"Lucas. In June these kids hopped the fence after close and got caught messing around on the slides. They wanted to go down without the water running. The security guard checks those regularly—"

"So they *do* have security."

She waves one hand. "They have Mike. I casually interrogated Lucas. So stealth, right? It's almost insulting that he wasn't suspicious. He said the staff does a sweep when the park closes at eight, and the janitorial crew cleans up for a few hours, but unless there's a work crew fixing the piping or a ride or something, it's just Mike after that. When he actually caught the kids, he just yelled at them for trying to break their necks before he kicked them out. No actual cops called. Anyway, we're not going on the slides, and we're not going in through the front." Leigh starts to hike toward the park, then stops to slip her fingers through mine and squeeze, so hard it almost hurts. "Hey, you want to turn around?"

As if I'd say yes.

When we're halfway across the lot, we juke to the side, angling for a part of the brand-new chain-link fence away from the main entrance and illuminated turnstiles. It's twice as tall as I am, but not exactly impenetrable. No barbed wire curling meanly along the top, no sun-bleached skulls of past trespassers on pikes. Maybe security's so lax because the Lost Lagoon is out in the desert. It's fifteen miles off the highway, sur- rounded by scrubby, barren plains and sandy ridges and hills freckled with mesquite shrubs. Kids have to be the ambitious kind of assholes to graffiti penises onto these waterslides. But tonight of all nights, I wouldn't care if there were cameras or sharp spirals of wires or severed heads. I don't want to worry about the consequences. I don't want to worry about anything more distant than the pavement directly underfoot, still freshly laid and velvety black.

Besides, it's the frailty of our plan that makes it perfect.

We follow the fence, aiming for a spot between the public entrance and the utility entrance, which I know to be just behind the park security office. That's where misplaced children wait for their parents, or staffers scold double-parked cars over the speaker system. If Mike is chilling anywhere between rounds, it's probably in the office. When we can't see the parking lot anymore, Leigh picks a place. Hitching up her backpack, she wedges one toe of her ratty brown Vans into the chain links, curls her fingers around the new metal. I hesitate for a moment, but then I jam my tennis shoe in and I'm pulling myself up, racing to the top. She's hard and lean and I've got twenty extra pounds to haul, but my arms are strong, stronger than hers. It's a quick, thrilling climb. Leigh's barely swung over the top and started down the other side when she drops to the ground, staggering. "Ven acá, guapa," she says, stretching her arms out as if she'll catch me. I let go and hit the dirt half on top of her, the shock of impact singing up through my ankles.

And then we're both inside.

Naturally, the park looks different at night, so it takes a second for me to place us. We're in a corridor of dust behind one of the waterslides. It looms over us against a blue-black sky. The way it ripples downward, I can tell it's the one called the Tide; it shoots out park guests into a deep, circular green pool with plastic starfish and clay barnacles plastered to the walls. Leigh stares up at it; her neck craned backward, the arc of her throat silhouetted. I dart in to kiss it. She wraps her fingers around my chin and pulls my lips to her. My lip gloss squelches against her warm, dry skin.

Laughing, I shake my head loose.

I steer Leigh around the Tide, and though it's not pitch-black, it's pretty dim. There are barnacle-encrusted iron lamps along the concrete path between attractions, but only every third bulb is aglow. And all the signage on the rides and on the abandoned popcorn booths and ice cream carts scattered throughout the Lagoon is dark. I wouldn't call it creepy—though the crumbled statues look more convincing in the dark—but it *does* look unnatural. There's no evidence of people, no trampled snow-cone wrappers or cigarette butts or busted flip-flops. The janitorial crew took care of all that. But I swear, I can still detect the sweat and sunscreen smell of them.

"What if the park never actually closed, and everyone here was just abducted by aliens?" I ask Leigh. "And we're the only ones left?"

"Don't I wish," she snorts.

In that moment, I wish it too.

Lights or no lights, people or no people, I know my way to Mermaid Cove. Keeping our eyes peeled for Mike, we stick to the dirt just off the paved path. We're careful but not *that* careful—because honestly, what's the worst that can happen to us?—as we snake past

Neptune's Pool, the little temple at its center looking particularly ruinous after hours. Toward the back of the park we creep, by the looping slide called the Shipwreck, the spiraling slide called Charybdis, passing nobody before we reach the arched, fake-ancient wooden gates set in the cinder-block wall around the Cove.

I've never been in through the gate, only the employee entrance hidden in back, inside a fake cave in the rock. There's a very real metal padlock on the latch, but the painted wall isn't much taller than us. After I massacre Leigh in Rock-Paper-Scissors, she sets her back against the wall, squats, and braces herself to boost me up. I put a foot on her thigh and a hand on her shoulder as she wraps her hands around my calf. Then I can reach the top of the wall. My palms scrape rough cement. She pushes, grunting in a way that's unflattering for both of us, and I haul myself up like I've done so many times on the basking rock. Once I'm perched on the foot-wide shelf I lean down, to help Leigh drag herself up after me. Sweating and panting and scratched, we drop down the other side. There are no lights on in the Cove, only the very faint haze of the lamps on the other side of the boulders and the moon and the stars, but all we have to do is follow the path. It spits us out on the footbridge over the water. Our footsteps are hollow thuds as we cross it to the very center, where we lean our elbows on the wooden railing, peering down.

And I thought the black-painted pool was murky in the day.

"Um." Leigh's voice echoes around the boulders, unexpectedly thunderous. "You didn't tell me you worked in the sunken city of R'lyeh."

"Huh?"

"Home of Cthulhu? Underwater monster god? Possibly your boss?"

The pool looks bottomless and icy and alive, oil sequined with moonlight. Like the house bejeweled in cow skulls by the lake, I think it's beautiful, in its way.

Leigh dumps her backpack on the wooden beams of the bridge—I hope she's got big fluffy towels in her overstuffed bag, because it's after eleven by now and the desert air has long since cooled. I'm still only in my T-shirt and Tinkerbell shorts. Shaking in the dry breeze, I scuff my legs against each other and try not to recall how cold it was in the water with the heater off that first day at work. Instead, I problem-solve a route to the pebbled pool deck that's supposed to be inaccessible to tourists. If we backtrack to the foot of the bridge, climb the railing, and push off, it's only about a three-foot drop to the deck—

Leigh's shed tank top whaps me in my face. Then the sweatpants she'd worn rolled to the knees not a moment ago. Pawing her clothes off my head, I turn just in time to see her in her black sports bra and Y-fronts and bare feet, mounting the slim railing. She straightens and wobbles with her toes over the edge, brings her arms out, biceps tight, and bends forward just as I realize what she's doing.

The dead center of the bridge where we stand is at least five feet up from the water, the top of the railing another three.

"Leigh," I say frantically, "don't, it's not deep enough to—"

She snaps her arms up and dives off the railing headfirst, taking all the breath in my lungs with her, but on the eight-foot fall, does a sloppy kind of half layout just in time to fall into the pool on her back. With a thunderous and sharp *smack*, the water parts to envelope her, leaving only violent swirls of light on the black surface.

Until she rises a few feet out, swearing. "Motherfucker!" she gasps, palming her short hair back off her forehead. "It's been, like, five years since I did that. Forgot it hurt like a *bitch*."

My breath stutters and restarts. "¿Qué chingados, loca?" But she's already laughing and then I'm laughing too. "¡Esta noche estás como una cabra!"

"It's colder than a fucking Eskimo fart," she chatters. "Get in!"

I peel off my shirt and shorts and scuff out of my sandals. Before I can think about the night air on my skin, I unzip Leigh's already-full backpack and cram our clothes inside—maybe it'll keep them warm for us, at least. I wobble onto the railing, the wood grain rough and cool below my fingers and feet, and execute an extremely elegant cannonball into what feels like the just-melted ice at the bottom of a beer cooler. The cold water swallows me, plugs my ears and sets every part of me on fire as I plunge. I sink to the slick tiles, kick off and come up a little way from Leigh. She wraps her fingers around my arm underwater to tug me closer. We're in the deeper end by the big basking rock, so in a tangle of limbs we tread water, holding on to each other, her warm breath shuddering across my neck. All I'm thinking about is Leigh and all I'm hearing is the gentle lap of the pool and the animal roaring of my heart.

After minutes or hours like that, we paddle our way toward the rock. Leigh pulls herself out, scoots backward across the stone, and hugs herself, legs tucked to her stomach and arms crossed over her knees. Her teeth click together as she stares down at me. I stare back up at her, at the water beading down her neck, her shoulders, her knees, her slim, sharp ankles. If I licked them—though I won't—she'd taste like chlorine and soap and salt.

"Don't," she says.

"Don't what?"

"You always look at me like *that*."

"So?" I ask, bruised. "Why can't I look? Maybe you don't like your body, but I do."

She shakes her head and snorts, hugs her knees closer. I grab on to the rock, resting my chin on my arms. "How can you not see how fucking gorgeous you are?"

"Can't it be more complicated than that? You're gorgeous. You love your body?"

"Yes," I say at once, though it is complicated. I love how I look, I love my hips, my legs, my muscles. I love what my body can do. I *hate* that it might betray me—or that my brain might betray my body, more like.

She watches my smile fade. "Oh *god*, let's not talk about this." She forces a laugh, and then in a shivering voice says, "I just want to see you do your thing."

Leigh's never watched me swim. Even if she'd been to a mermaid show, that wouldn't be *swimming*. It wouldn't be *me*. Without my legs pinned together, I'm free to go flat-out.

Pressing my feet against the submerged base of the basking rock to push off, I do.

There's this thing that happens every time I push off the wall. It's like nothing else. From above, I probably look like any decent swimmer stroking along. I don't have the perfect body for it, and as I said, I'm definitely no Olympic hopeful. My fastest time in the 100-meter freestyle was barely less than a minute. But below, I feel like some weightless animal, something born down here. Like my body was made to slip through the cold, thick honey of the water, and this is the only way I'm really meant to move. Before I'm tired, before I'm breathless and aching, there's just potential.

If I could just stay in this moment forever, my body would never let me down.

By the time I make it back to the basking rock, I don't know how many laps I've swam. Not as many as I could, but I haven't moved at full speed—at competition speed—for so long, and so I *am* breathless and beginning to ache.

I toss my arms up onto the rock, letting air rip through my lungs. Now it's Leigh's turn to haul me up, and I drop down beside her, dripping and gasping and shivering. She rolls over, folds herself on top of me, and grabs the sopping hair behind my ear between her fingers. "You fucking goddess," she murmurs, her dark eyebrows furrowed. "What are you even doing here?"

"I'm with you," I pant, sinking into the hard plaster beneath me. "Obvs."

"That's not what I mean." Her fingers loosen.

"What?"

"You're not here because of me. Just, take the test or don't take the test, and if you didn't have *it* or if you did, that's okay, you could still come to Boston! You could go anywhere you wanted. You're so fucking strong, you can do anything."

There are so many things I could say. Casual things, flirty things, clever things. But even though my breath is settling, I can't make myself say any of them. "Sometimes I have these dreams. Like, we take Dad to the doctor's office, and they draw his blood and look at it through a microscope, and then they say 'Ah, okay, we see the problem, eat this weird turnipy-looking thing, or burn this piece of paper, or put this dead chicken under your pillow when you go to sleep tonight, and you'll be cured.' And I'm so happy. Then I wake up, and I remember it's not, it's not just a thing I can put down and leave behind." I swallow noisily, stupidly. "And I don't feel strong, just scared all over again."

"But you are strong. Maybe that's why Lucas wanted you to be my friend . . . he knew you were so tough, even I couldn't fuck you up." She untangles her hand—my head rocks painfully back without the support—and props herself up on her palms to inspect me from above. "He was right, wasn't he?"

I can feel her sinking into one of her strange moods, but I don't want to fight, or worry, or think of anything at all. I don't want to talk about how scared I am, or how stuck. I don't want to be that girl, not tonight. I just want Leigh, and to be the girl who belongs with Leigh.

The girl who has one good thing.

So I don't wait for her to answer. Instead I reach up for her, my pruned fingers skimming her arms, and pull her down on top of me. She gives in easy, her chest on my chest, her sharp hips cushioned by mine. I run my hand across the tight skin of her back, the wet band of her bra, and down to her briefs, and with an "Unf," she slides her tongue between my lips. I nip it with my teeth, and her fingers scrabble at the waistband of my under-wear and below. I crawl backward down the basking rock, and do what Leigh taught me to do.

For a while it's just breath and touch and body heat and the breeze.

We're like that until we're not. The next thing I know, Leigh's pushing off of me, glancing back over her shoulder. I don't know what noise caught her attention, but before I ask, she points to a spot of light dancing over the boulders by the mouth of the tourist's path. A flashlight, its bearer coming this way.

So I guess Mike doesn't just check the slides.

This time I'm the first to move. I grab for Leigh and slip as smoothly as I can back into the pool, newly freez-ing now that the night air has dried us. Leigh follows me in, and then under, where it's so dark and there's nothing but the water bubbling past my ears. I keep a death grip on her hand, my fingertips pressed into her knuckles. I'm trying to tell her not to surface, to follow me. I stroke one-armed, slower and smoother than usual so we won't make a sound. It's only ten meters or so till we're below the bridge; I've swam the length of the Cove so many times, I've got it memorized. Ten meters isn't far, and once we're there we'll never be seen. We can cling to the ropes for as long as it takes until the security guard moves on. Leigh's backpack is still up above, but if he finds it, maybe he'll think it was left behind by tourists. He might just drop it in the Lost and Found. I'm not excited to sneak back to the car barefoot and dripping wet in my underwear, but at least we left our phones and wallets and keys in the unlocked van, so it's not that—

Leigh's hand tugs out from mine only a meter or so from the bridge. When I turn and slit my eyes open, I can't see her in the near-perfect dark. I feel for her, but can't find her. Maybe she slipped, or got turned around, or maybe she panicked, unused to holding her breath. My own lungs are getting tight, so I surge forward until I think I'm in the shadow of the bridge. I rise as spashlessly as possible to shouting directly overhead—Mike, on the bridge. "Hey, let's go, get out of there right now!"

That's when I see Leigh, halfway out in the deep end of the pool.

From this distance and highlighted only by the guard's wavering flashlight beam, I can't see her face. I can't tell what went wrong. I guess it doesn't matter. She strokes toward the pool deck without glancing back, leaving me safely tucked away under the bridge.

But I can't let her get caught alone while I hide. I can't be Rose, floating on the only flotsam in the ocean while Jack Popsicle-izes. Without thinking—why start now?—I swim out and follow Leigh to our fate.

Water trickles from my ponytail and down my neck, along the rungs of my spine. I'm already soaked through—I tugged my clothes on right out of the pool, feeling tight and coarse and miserable, like a snake trying to slip back into its shed skin—so what's a little more misery on top of that? But I concentrate on the slow, cold trail it leaves so I don't have to feel my cheeks burning. I inspect my wrinkled fingertips, the goose-bumped brown skin on my legs, the stupid little pixies printed on my shorts. Anything so I don't have to look up at my boss.

Eric sits at the little metal desk in the park security

office while the guard hovers by the door, hands crossed behind his back, yielding command. "Savannah, I just—" Eric starts. "Do you understand how serious this is? What would've happened if Mike hadn't called me?"

I stare at a loose hem thread curled along my thigh to avoid his eyes. And to avoid the half bottle of Largo Bay atop the desk, and the twisted sandwich baggie of buds, both pulled from the depths of Leigh's backpack.

Though she sits beside me in her own expanding puddle on the seat of her plastic orange chair, I don't look at Leigh, either.

We might've gotten away free if I hadn't crammed our clothes inside her bag. When Mike ordered us out of the water, we crossed the deck reluctantly to the spot where the guard could help pull us up over the railing. He let us pause on the bridge to get dressed, cut his eyes to the side while we hurriedly yanked out shorts and shirts and sweatpants. I really think he would've shouted at us, told us we were being stupid kids and marched us out of the park, where we would've walked and then run to the car, flushed with cold and adrenaline and gasping with laughter by the time we reached it . . . if one of us hadn't tipped over the backpack in our haste, spilling out the bottle and the baggie. Then we had to give him our names, tell him our story. When he herded us back to the office, I thought he might call the police.

Instead, he called my boss.

"I didn't mean . . ." I try again. "I didn't think . . ." Another drop slides down my shirt.

"Of course not." Eric sighs. "Because if you *had* been thinking, it might've occurred to you that you're not just a stupid kid."

That startles me into glancing up at last.

"Jesus, Savannah." He leans forward. He doesn't even seem angry, just rumpled and weary beyond an unpleasant wake-up call from park security at midnight. It's because he's underdressed, I decide. Without his whistle and bullhorn and park badge, he doesn't look like the crisp director of performing park personnel. Just like a nice, tired, middle-aged guy. "You're legally an adult, you know?" he continues. "Do you understand that? And you trespassed on private property with illegal substances. *And* with a minor. That means municipal court, not juvenile. That's an arrest and a fine—you could face jail time for this. You should've been thinking about your future, at least."

"I'm sorry," I mutter, cold through my sopping clothes, through my skin, to the bone. Suddenly I'm shivering so hard I worry I'll rattle the screws loose in my cheapo seat. Leigh's smart enough not to reach for my hand, so I wrap my fingers around the hard plastic ridge to keep from shaking.

"Well, I'm sorry too." He leans back in the squeaking desk chair, scraping a hand over his abnormally furred jaw. "I truly am. You've been a great employee. A great performer. But I can't have you back at the Cove. Not this summer, and not next."

"You can't have me back," I repeat numbly as the words sink in.

I'm fired?

I'm *fired*?

I'm fired. . . .

Then his words touch bottom, unsettling silt and debris inside of me, and I realize I'm not a mermaid anymore.

SEVENTEEN

We don't go home.

Nobody's waiting up for either of us. Leigh's dad thinks she's sleeping over my place, and I called my parents on the way to the Lagoon and told them the opposite. "Buena idea, mija. Your father and I will be here for some time." Mom sighed, resigned to the eternal time suck that accompanies a non-emergency visit to the ER (we know it well).

Instead, Leigh and I head for a place in between.

It feels like it should be light out by the time we reach Chris's house, but it isn't early enough. Or maybe it isn't late enough, still a few hours from sunrise. Leigh parks the van and I climb out on tired legs. Suddenly I'm tired all over. Leigh silent behind me, I let us inside and stagger through the narrow hallway to the hideous room, blinking when she flicks on the lights. The musty, ruffled bedspread with its milk shakes, music notes, and hearts has never looked so welcoming; maybe we can slip between the sheets and sleep until Chris Zepeda comes home from California in September. Maybe Leigh will sleep right through her eighteenth birthday.

A zombie in flip-flops, I lurch toward the bed and topple dramatically onto the covers without bothering to kick them off, or to peel off my cold, damp clothes. Letting my horrifically knotted hair tumble across my face, I close my eyes, then startle at the ripe *fumf* of Leigh's backpack hitting the floor.

"So," she rasps from across the room. Beyond asking if I'm okay, she hasn't spoken since Mike kicked us out of the park.

"So what?" I mumble around a gross mouthful of hair.

The bed sinks beside me with the creak of mattress coils, and then her voice hovers just above me. "On a scale of one to ten, how pissed are you?"

"Dunno. Two. Not like Eric fired me to be a dick."

"No, I meant pissed at me."

From a sideways angle, I stare up at Leigh. Her hair dried in spikes across her forehead; it's a little longer and blonder than when we met, bleached by the summer sun. I want to reach out and brush it back, but I'm just a sack of bones on the bed, and lifting my hand seems impossibly hard, as tough as anything. "Not your fault."

"It was my idea." She looks down at her hands, thumbing a long pink scrape I've just noticed across her tan knuckles. "Plus I brought the weed and stuff."

"You always do." I laugh hoarsely. Maybe I should be mad, but there's a reason I asked Leigh to come for me instead of . . . okay, even if I'd had a more sensible person on speed dial, I'd still have chosen her. I always want to choose Leigh.

But for that to happen, Leigh has to be here to choose.

I had some time to think the problem through on the hushed ride back from the Lagoon. What would I do, if I wanted something from Jake? From Lance or Will or Max? I don't think a thick pout and a little over-the-pants hand action will get it done. I need to be smarter if I want Leigh to jettison the thing she wants most, to get back home to Boston, and stick around Nowhere, New Mexico, to be with me. I know it's not a small ask. I have to be subtler, enchanting yet elusive.

This seems as good a time as any to try.

"You could make it up to me," I say, sliding myself upright against the wall. I let my head thump back against the plaster, pretending I'm chill, and my heart isn't suddenly a heavy bass beat in my chest. "Let's go to Boston."

Her eyes flick up to meet mine, fiercely alight. She takes a breath. "You're serious?"

I ease my legs straight out and thread them around Leigh, who sits in a tight, tense bundle with her knees to her chest. "You could show me the good places. Where would you take me first?"

She grins easily. "World's End. It's a hike on, like, a peninsula outside the city."

"It's a good trail?"

"Yeah, it's okay. It's hilly, but it's not tough. But you can see the Boston skyline over the water." She leans down to dig her phone out of the backpack and flips through her pictures, tilts the screen toward me. "Here."

It's a picture of her and Lucas on a hillside. Treetops feather the background, and above them, a strip of slate-blue water, the Atlantic. Beyond that and against the clouds, the distant outline of skyscrapers like choppy, geometric mountains. Flashing smiles for the camera, Leigh and Lucas wear matching black baseball caps with Mickey Mouse ears. I point and raise an eyebrow.

She shrugs. "Had to be there."

"Where else would we go? Where would we eat?"

"Hmm . . . maybe the Boston Burger Company? They have this burger, the Porkasaurus."

"Sold." I smile and nod, but really I'm winding up to make my move. "And what about your mom, what's she like?"

"She's just . . . pretty much a mom." Leigh folds her arms over her knees and rests her chin on them.

"You think she'd like me?"

"Why wouldn't she?"

I wade in carefully, carefully. "How would you introduce me? I mean, what would you say?"

I feel the hum of her laughter where my legs rest against her hips. "Is this the Talk?"

"What talk?"

"The Are-You-My-Girlfriend Talk."

"No. But if it *was* . . . we haven't really said anything." Not since Kristian's party, anyway, but I pause before bringing that up, because I don't want to remind her of the fight.

If she's thinking about it, she doesn't let on. "How do you want me to introduce you?"

"I don't know. 'Hi, Mom, this is Savannah Espinoza. She's a really down chick. We really like each other and we're really good at sex, and she bought you these awesome slipper socks for Christmas.'"

"Why Christmas?"

"Welllllll . . ." I breathe deep, smelling dust and the faint fresh tendrils of Febreze, and of course, Leigh. "We close the restaurant for a couple days over the holidays, and you'll have winter break, so maybe we could fly up together. My parents wouldn't mind, I don't think. We're not church people or anything. I bet your dad would let you, and then we can come back in time for New Year's with our families here."

I watch her hazel eyes as the light goes out. "That's not happening."

"You don't want to visit Boston for Christmas?"

"Stop, Vanni." She starts to shift.

I squeeze my legs in closer, trapping her between them. "Just, why do you *have* to go back right now? What *specifically* sucks so much about being here, if I'm here? You're just gonna run off and leave me and your dad and Lucas? That's crazy."

Leigh's whole body stiffens. With her feet, she pushes my legs away from her until we're still close, but no part of us is touching. "I told you, Lucas won't even be here in the fall. And I thought you didn't care about my brother."

"Shut up, you know I don't. That's not the point."

This isn't working out so well.

Abandoning subtlety, or seduction, or self-respect,

or any kind of plan at all, I beg, "Come on, I don't want to fight. I want you to stay in New Mexico. Please? Stay for me," I speak the unspeakable. "You're my good thing, you know?"

"What an honor for me," she says drily.

I wilt into the wall. "Don't be mean."

"Who's being mean?" she asks innocently, eyes round. "You're stuck, and you want me to be stuck here too. Cool. I'm just so grateful for the chance to wait in the restaurant till your shift's up. And wait in your driveway while you finish your chores. And wait at the Sunken Sub while you swim around in a—" She cuts herself off with a calculated frown. "Never mind that one, I guess."

This terrible idea blossoms in me.

"Did you do it on purpose?"

Her dark eyebrows lift.

I'm trying to remember Leigh underwater. When we were so close to the bridge, nearly home free, and I lost hold of her. What did it feel like? An accident? Did she slip away, or did she pull away? "At the pool. Did you get us caught on purpose?"

With a dangerous grace I didn't know Leigh had, she slides smoothly off the bed and backs away, only a few paces before she hits the opposite wall beside the little white desk. Leaning, she examines me the way you'd check an apple for color, for smell, for rot. "Why would I?"

Her body is loose, arms dangling, but I'm not fooled.

"So I'd get fired," I say, my voice high and wavering. "So I'd have one less reason to hang around La Trampa."

She sneers, her eyes like cold river water; I guess I don't pass inspection. "First off, you're gonna come up with as many reasons as you need, and I can do fuck-all about that. Second, you're the one who calls *me* up like I'm *your* manic pixie dream lesbian when you can't handle your shit, so don't play like you didn't know what you were doing. I didn't fireman-carry you into the park and throw you in the pool, guapa."

This last word, she spits in a way I've just come to hate, and while I'll always remember the first thing I loved about Leigh, I think I'll always remember this moment, too.

My voice is stronger when I speak again, hot blood pulsing in my cheeks and the tips of my ears and twitching through my fingers. "Driving drunk and fighting and breaking and entering—that's about my shit? That has nothing to do with the shit in *your* life?"

"You don't know about my life, Savannah." Still loose, she says my full name so easily, as if it costs her nothing. "Don't act like all of a sudden you're so fucking in love with me and you know everything about me, because you don't."

Through clenched teeth, I grind out, "Don't *you* act like you're so much more worldly than me. I get that you have problems, but you don't know about *my* life. What my dad has? It could come for me at any time, and there's nothing I can do about it. It's in my blood and it's fucking unstoppable. So why shouldn't I be scared? I might be trapped forever, not just in this town but in my own fucking body. That's a *real* problem. You're just crazy."

As soon as it's out of me, I know I went too far, hit too hard. Leigh's face crumbles briefly and violently, a stone cliff sliding into the sea.

Then it smooths over, and that's even worse.

But she doesn't say anything, just bends down and reaches for her backpack.

I draw in the stale air, as much as I can and not enough. "Leigh . . ."

My whole body flinches as she slams a foot into the leg of the desk and sends it skidding into the corner, everything stacked on top tumbling off. Cheap jewelry and watery nail polishes scatter across the floorboards. An ancient vial of body glitter flies across the room, silvery-blue dust streaking behind it in a comet's tail, imploding against the baseboard on impact. The bottle of Red Door topples and cracks; a sickly strong wave of freesia and orange blossoms and honey rises up from it and I'm having a tough time breathing, though the perfume probably isn't why.

"Leigh!" I yell stupidly, frozen on the bed.

She doesn't look back at me when she hisses, "Go suck some huevos locos, you fucking baby dyke." Then she swipes a knuckle below her eyes and strides out the door, leaving me in the ruins of our hideous room.

What can I do but get up and keep moving?

I kneel, picking through the wreckage for the biggest pieces of plastic and glass and broken costume jewelry. The rest I sweep free from the cracks in the floor with the broom from the kitchen, then pound the bristles out off the back porch.

I find rags in the garage and wet them in the sink, scrubbing glitter and perfume from the floorboards until the cloth sparkles and stinks as badly as I do.

I pile what's left of Chris's sister's childhood treasures on top of the little desk in approximately the arrangement I remember, and survey the room. If I let dust collect on the furniture and on the floor for the rest of his vacation, leave the window open to air the smell until the last minute, it'll be hard for Chris to tell we were ever here.

The stars have faded and the sun is a bright yellow yolk on the horizon by the time I leave; a sky I recognize as six o'clock–ish. Only when I see the empty driveway do I remember that Leigh was my ride. I don't think she meant to strand me two miles outside the center of La Trampa and three from home . . . but I feel like a scraped-clean seashell, like there's air whistling through the cool, hard chambers of my chest, when I stop and think of what Leigh meant or didn't mean. When I think of Leigh at all. When I stop moving at all.

So instead, I walk.

It's still too early for cars this far from the town center—nobody who beats the sun to work comes out this way, and for sure no tourists are wandering off the Trail into La Trampa at this hour. The only sounds are the warble of birds, the nasal song of insects, and the slap-suck-slap-suck of my flip-flops on the pavement. I count steps by the pounding in my ankles as I make my way up Jimeno, along Calle De Vida that runs a mile into town and spits out on Calle Tamara a little way from the restaurant. Across the street from the tiny plaza: a patch of dust caught in the webbing of the main roads, where the tarnished bronze trapper and his gun glint dully in the new sun. Sitting on the wrought-iron bench at the base of the statue, canes beside them, Mr. Paiz and Mr. Armijo wait for Batista's Café to open. Before we cut our hours they'd wait for Silvia's. Now they get their horchatas elsewhere. Still, they wait exactly as they used to, same time, same place.

Mr. Armijo raises a thick, hairy arm when he sees me, then leans in to whisper to Mr. Paiz. Who can blame him? Savannah Espinoza, wandering the streets at dawn. I know what I look like—a sea hag caught in a craft store explosion.

I know before I climb the fire escape that winds up the two-story brick wall of the Turquoise Depot on Guadalupe; before I knock at the dented blue door of the little apartment on the second floor; before Jake answers, bare chested in worn plaid boxers, stubbled and shocked to see the Creature from the Lost Lagoon in all her morning glory. Knotty brown hair matted to my neck with sweat in the rising heat. Glittering up to my elbows and down my legs where I knelt to scrub the floor. Teary and red-eyed, and the smell—I stink like I've been rolling in obsolete perfume, which I practically have.

"¿Qué chingados?" His voice is just-woke-up rusty. "¿Qué pasó, princesita?"

"Nothing happened," I croak. "Can I just—can I

come in please?"

He shifts and rubs one foot against the opposite leg. For a long second I think he'll say no, and I don't want to go home, haven't even texted Mom like the thoughtful daughter I am, and I really don't have a plan B except to keep on walking—

"Fine," he says. "But like . . . don't sit on anything till I get a towel, okay?"

I make myself as small as possible in his miniature living room while he digs around in his bedroom. I know his place pretty well. It's not dirty, it never is, no dust or suspiciously crusty socks or dishes plastered with week-old eggs. But it is in a fixed state of disintegration. It never gets better, and it never gets worse. Like a condemned building just after the blast: the bomb's gone off, but the bricks have yet to hit the ground. There's the cheap TV stand bowed under the weight of a squat little set, the curtains as thin as fast-food napkins askew on their rungs, and the sagging, scratchy blue futon with one wooden arm pulled loose, clinging on by the screw tips. This futon, I know well. When Jake returns in a shirt and with a frayed red Coca-Cola beach towel, he spreads it gingerly on the cushions and gives the okay sign.

"You should put newspaper down in case I'm not trained," I say, but my heart's not in it. I sink onto the towel, careful not to touch the back of the couch.

He sits just as stiffly beside me, hands on his knees. "What happened to you?" he asks. Out of obligation, I think.

"Nothing. I told you. I um, I don't really want to talk." I rub at grime and glitter stuck to my thumbnail. My hand shakes, but I haven't slept in a while, so I forgive it.

"So you're here for what?"

"No sé." Though come on, I do know. I think that most of the time I have no idea, but at the moment, I really do. I just don't like it, or myself, very much at all. I get stomped on by Leigh, then come crawling up Jake's steps? What the fuck is wrong with me? And even now, even wondering this, I don't stop. "I guess maybe I thought you'd, um . . ."

"Oh." He scratches at his pillow-crushed black hair. "I don't think so, princesita."

"Oh," I say, a dull echo of Jake.

"You're definitely hot, eso que ni qué." He collapses back onto the cushions and throws one arm across the metal frame of the futon, easy swagger returned. He's staring into the blank gray TV screen as if it's playing a show that's infinitely more interesting than me. "But I know you think you're better than me."

"I don't. I don't think I'm better than anyone."

"Sure you do, like I'm some dumb townie."

"That's stupid. I'm a townie, right? It's my home too." The word *home* tastes like the time Dad made his traditional ensalada agridulce de jamón ibérico, but in an unprecedented and (back then) mysterious error, forgot to put in the honey. All of the sour without the sweet.

"So how come every time I ask you, you act like being my girl is the worst thing that could ever happen to you?"

"How many girls do you need?" I snap.

Jake kicks at the plastic leg of the TV stand in easy reach, and all the muscles in my throat clench tight, but he only taps it gently with his toe. "What if I said I just wanted you?"

I look down, because I don't want Jake. I want Leigh.

But Leigh doesn't want me anymore.

And I don't want to be all alone again in my own little trap.

Besides, Jake's right, in a way. He's definitely not the very worst thing.

I've never been in Jake Mosqueda's bedroom before, never slid between his papery striped sheets or mashed my face into his Jake-smelling pillows, like cigarettes and bread and some Family Dollar knock-off of Old Spice. We don't do anything more than curl up together, my back pressed to his overwarm chest, his arm an over-warm belt around my waist, big hand planted on the other side. He mumbles something softly into my shoulder and then lets me sleep awhile without even insisting I hose down first.

It's the sweetest thing he's ever done.

It's also the first time I've ever believed what Nicole Mendez once tweeted about me (without naming me, because she is Nice): *Some girls hate girls who go after their boyfriends, but I feel sorry for them because someday they'll figure out how nasty and sad they are.*

EIGHTEEN

It turns out, I can survive being with Jake.

I can survive losing my job at the Lagoon, and the drought of texts from Iris and Kristian and the Camilas that follows the tidal wave of *OMG, Vanni, I'm so sorry! That sucks so hard! We'll still hang out all the time, right?*

I can survive riding the bus or the borrowed Malibu or Jake's rust-bucket truck back and forth from Silvia's to home, where Mom is so desperately cheerful, she wears her Riveting Rose lipstick just to watch TV, or to wash and re-bandage the stitches that cross my father's brown forearm like tiny black railroad tracks.

Sure, the morning after Leigh, I woke up in Jake's bed with just this collapsed star pulsating inside my rib cage, and it hasn't stilled since. I called her once. I texted her twice. I drove halfway to her house six times before turning around again.

But I can survive without Leigh, too. Because the best thing about surviving is that it requires no extra-special effort to just keep doing it; no big decisions or choices of any kind are required. "Just keep doing it" is, like, the definition of survival, right? I mean, when I stop and look at Dad, or at the test application and consent forms bookmarked on my phone and laptop, I know that isn't literally true . . . but if I *don't* stop and look, I can keep believing.

So I don't stop.

And I don't look.

The Friday almost three weeks after Leigh, my last paycheck arrives in the mail from the Lagoon—when Eric said I couldn't come back, I guess he meant on the property, like, at all—and after feeding it into my meager bank account, I check Craigslist for job listings. The Mine Shaft Tavern in Madrid is hiring waitstaff, though the hours conflict with Silvia's. So is a car wash in La Cienega, the ad posted only this morning.

Xime's taking Dad to PT, and Jake's job at the Trading Post doesn't start till four, so he drives me out to Nick's Cars 'n' Kitsch to drop off my résumé and the printed-out application. He parks by the main office and pushes his aviators up into his stupidly beautiful black hair for a better look. "Well, this is—" He breaks off, snickering. The dust out front of the concrete wash bays is staked with every tacky statue under the sun: pink lawn flamingos, big plaster dinosaurs, windmill sculptures made from Coke cans, a chipped life-size mannequin of Marilyn Monroe. *Of course* the theme of a car wash along the Turquoise Trail couldn't be, I don't know, washing cars. "At least it's not one of those sexy places where you sponge off windshields with your boobs."

Right. I'd totally keep my dignity intact as I hosed down trucks surrounded by garden gnomes and a giant plastic doughnut wearing a sprinkle-topped sombrero.

But when I talk to Carl, the thirtysomething assistant manager with an unambitious hairline, he tells me that the hiree will work indoors only; they've already got a carefully cultivated team of high school boys to man the bays for minimum wage and tips.

"You'd stay behind the register. You got customer service experience?" Carl asks, though he has my résumé in hand. It's a quick enough read. I used phrases like "maintained high standards of service during high-volume hours" and "collaborated well with coworkers," because that's what you're supposed to say instead of "served, like, two customers per hour and occasionally gave my appreciative coworker a handy while on break." I left the Lost Lagoon off the sheet completely. I don't think Eric could give me a glowing recommendation even if he wanted to, and I'm not convinced that a month and a half of mermaidenhood qualifies me for employ at a car wash.

Though the job is water adjacent.

"Lots of customer service," I sum up for Carl.

"That's good. We had two girls, and one of 'em left to have a baby, decided not to come back after. But it's not a tough job. Mostly gets a little stiff sitting all day, but we're working on getting a better chair." Carl rolls his beat-up old office chair out from behind the desk to demonstrate, then rolls back again. "Can you do morning shifts?"

"Pretty much every morning."

"Good, that's good. Not planning on going off to school or moving any time soon? We need someone to stick around."

"Not going anywhere." I show my teeth. "Do you think I'll get an interview?"

He narrows his eyes at me, as though I asked

whether I should wear a ball gown or tuxedo to work. "Think you need one?"

So that's how I get my next part-time job, at Nick's Cars 'n' Kitsch.

Jake insists we celebrate that evening when he gets off work at nine. There's a nighttime party happening in the arroyo. Zero high school kids, just his cabrónes and their girlfriends, he says, reaching across the stick shift to squeeze my knee on that last word.

There's no good reason to say no.

To get to the dry river ditch that runs behind Chris's property, you either have to bike up Jimeno and walk your bicycle across the rough, or park your car along Calle De Vida and hike in. Jimeno's so small and straggly that Sherriff Portola and his deputy, the only police presence in La Trampa, won't notice a chain of beaters parked in the roadside weeds. I mean, they know that kids hang out there. Our parents did it in their day; Sherriff Portola probably did it. Sometimes he or the deputy come to chase kids out, scatter them into the brush like rabbits, but rarely. Nobody bothers to pick their way across the plains to bust us unless one of the homeowners nearby calls in a noise complaint. Just after the sun sets, Jake and I leave his truck in the Burrito Bandito lot and hike along the property line between Chris's place and the Marcons', far enough from either house not to be noticed, even if Chris were there. He reaches for my hand and I let him take it, though he feels too warm, his fingers too thick, like they're forcing mine too far apart.

Jake's boys are already there when we ease down the dirt slope. "¿Dónde es la peda?" he laughs, and Marcus Barela, the clerk at the Allsup's, fishes two bottles of Dos Equis out of a blue cooler and hands one to each of us. I wipe the damp from the ice off on the skirt of my dress, a swingy black slip thing with a crocheted back. I'm wearing it because I know Jake likes it. I know, because I wore it to the restaurant on Monday, and he tugged me toward the stockroom before he'd even clocked in. He would've lost fifteen minutes of pay, if my parents counted seconds and pennies. He *did* lose out on a six-top of tourists who left Estrella a decent tip.

Gathered around the cooler in the glow of a Coleman lantern are a couple of guys who work at the Trading Post with Jake. The bag boy rocking an extreme black buzz cut and pressed polo shirt, I recognize as Adrian Trejo, Oriel's big brother by a year or two. And the girl he's got his arm around—

"Hey, Vanni." Diana Reyes waves, lips curling into a shy smile.

Shocked, I raise my bottle so quickly the rim knocks me in the mouth. "Hey." I run my tongue across my throbbing lip. "I didn't know you were . . ."

"Me and Adrian?" she asks, and I remember when we were freshmen and Adrian was the sophomore she called Band Boy; how she whispered into my ear at the spring concert that he played the clarinet like a lifeguard giving mouth-to-mouth. "We're kind of new. Or not new. I guess it's been six months?" She giggles and props her chin on his shoulder.

He tips his head and kisses her cheek. "It was after we did that volunteer trip to that dog park in Albuquerque. North Domingo Baca, right? Di liked how I pulled the weeds."

"It was very sexy," she confirms.

I can't imagine the Diana Reyes I grew up a mile apart from, whose quinceañera party favors included glittery plastic purity rings, saying "sex" in any form. Not aloud, and never to a boy. *You know*, she always called it, as in: "Marilee told me Sonja Vee and Matt Wiley went to see *Jurassic World* and in the back row, they, *you know*?" Inspecting her in the lantern's wavering white-blue light, I notice her hair's escaped the frizzy clump of her traditional low bun to fluff around her shoulders, which seem . . . Diana's always had the spinal posture of a Cheeto, but outside the halls of the high school and off her parents' property line, outside of my and Marilee's shadow, she's straighter and taller.

"You look really . . ." Happy. Possibly but possibly

not still a virgin. No, probably still; unlike his brother, Adrian's the kind of boy Diana's parents are likely to approve of, if they'll approve of a boy at all. The kind who'll buy her the best Valentine's Day bouquets in the cooler at Albertsons and never expect a "present" in return. Either way, it's nobody's business but hers. ". . . really good," I finish the sentiment.

"You too!" she says.

This might be an outright lie, but it is pretty dark by now, and I'm standing just outside the globe of the lantern's light.

"You and Jake are dating?" she asks with a polite smile.

"We're new."

"I thought maybe you were dating Will Fischer."

I chug an unnecessary amount to buy myself time. "Nope. We never really went out. I was hanging out with someone else. But now we're not."

Possibly, that's all we were ever doing. Two weeks ago I would've said no, we were more, we were perfect. Still, she never bought me flowers, and I never took her home to meet Mom and Dad. Even Jake comes inside to say hello when he picks me up—Leigh never even made it to the doorbell. When we fought, she told me that I didn't love her, didn't even know her, but I know this: If a week from now on the morning of her eighteenth birthday, Leigh called me to say "Never mind, Vanni, I'm ditching my crazy-stupid plan and sticking around for you," I would drop Jake flat. Or shit, if she called to say, "Hey, I don't forgive you or love you or want you, but can you stop by my house on the way to the car wash and bring me a pizza anyway?" I'd drop him flat. I know not-so-deep-down that I'm only here because Leigh won't call, she won't change her mind, she won't want me back. That doesn't make what I'm doing to Jake right, or make me any less of a shitty person. The fact is, I'd probably drop anybody, everybody. If that isn't love, what is?

"I guess I didn't think you and Jake would ever, *you know*." Diana bobs her head. "I knew he'd asked. But people change, right? He seems like he really likes you."

I grope for a new topic; what do you say to the best friend you never talk to? "How's Grace?" Diana's youngest sister, one of the five Reyes siblings. I haven't seen her since she was five, except from afar at graduation or across the street, running errands with her and Mrs. Reyes. She's small and skinny and weirdly pale. With those white cheeks, those floating dark eyes, and a natural frown unlike her big sister's quiet smile, Grace looks like the children in horror films. Silent kids who pop up behind the refrigerator door when somebody goes to get a drink, or at the foot of a stepladder. She kind of acts like them too, so she's a pretty fertile topic of conversation.

Sure enough, Diana grins. "You know how last month, that truck crashed with all those rubber aliens inside?"

I nod while drinking.

"They did an update last week, how some of them were found all the way in the Gulf? Dad had the news on and Grace was watching. And then today she went to her little summer camp and had this assignment where she was supposed to draw the baptism of Jesus. And she did a tiny stick Jesus in the corner, and then, like, thirty aliens around him."

"She did not!"

"Flying aliens, aliens in the grass. The camp counselor showed Mom her art folder when she went to pick Grace up, and there were aliens in every drawing she did that week. All hailing Jesus. My little sister's either a genius or dumb as a mushroom," she says warmly.

"Un bicho raro," I laugh.

"Totalmente." She rolls her eyes. "She loves you, though."

Though Diana didn't mean it to, this hurts; a small and distant ache like the memory of a broken bone or vicious cramps. "Did she?"

"Why'd you think you woke up with her breathing

in your face every time you slept over?"

True enough. I once opened my eyes in the gray pre-dawn light to the sight of Grace, crouched inside Diana's big wooden wardrobe with the door six inches ajar, peering out at me. I nearly pissed my sleeping bag. "Tell her hi for me," I say, then realize what little right I have to ask this. "Or you don't have to, but—"

"I will."

I look around, and nobody's paying much attention to us. Though Adrian and Diana hold hands, he's piv-oted away to talk to the boys clumped around the cooler. That includes Jake, who's not drinking at the moment, but telling some story with big, broad hand gestures, an easy smile, and something like a hip thrust. I wonder if it's about me. *Oh, right, because everybody's stories are about Savannah Espinoza, the queen of La Trampa, the center of the world.*

"Aren't you mad at me?" I blurt out.

Diana bites her cheek, checks to see what Adrian's up to before shuffling closer to me, and now this is an official conversation instead of an obligatory fly-by chat on the way to grab another beer.

Speaking of which, I let my empty bottle slip to the dust at my feet to tuck my arms around my waist.

"I'm not mad, Vanni," Diana says carefully. "I think it really sucks, because we were friends, and then we just suddenly weren't. I know you had stuff going on—"

"I—"

"Okay, sorry, you had *big* stuff." She leans farther from the light to say quietly, "How's your dad doing?"

She must know. Sit in on any chisme session with the church ladies, and you'll hear updates on anyone of interest in La Trampa. "He's okay." I give her the resigned, trapped-in-line-at-the-grocery-store answer. "He hurt his arm a couple of weeks ago, but not too bad. His doctor says he's walking pretty well, so he'll get around on his own and then use the rollator for as long as possible before he switches to the wheelchair, and his medicine's helping with the, you know, involuntary movement, so that's—"

"But I mean, how is he other than all that?"

Squinting, I study her face in the shadows. "Other than what?"

Diana shrugs. "Like, that's not really your dad, is it? 'Cause I mean, he's not just his body, right?"

I close my mouth with a *click*, not sure how to answer.

Then Adrian comes up behind Diana, untucks her hair from the collar of her pink plaid button-up, and she nearly glows in the dark.

Maybe I could be like that.

I'm no better than Diana—definitely worse, as I've

never de-pooped a dog park in an orange vest for fun on a Saturday—so if she can have a life here, can't I? I can be somebody's girlfriend for once. Run my fingers through Jake's hair while we watch stolen cable at his place, and bake for him—well not *bake*, obviously, but at least buy him something from that awesome bakery in downtown Santa Fe. Become the top administrative assistant that Nick's Cars 'n' Kitsch has ever had. Show up at the Reyes' next week with a box of Swedish Fish for Diana and a James McAvoy movie, and then she'd take me back (even if Marilee never would). None of us in this ditch are leaving La Trampa, and they're all okay with it. Really, how hard can it be to just . . . be?

Half an hour later, I tell Jake I'm not feeling great, that my mom cooked dinner and it's now in full-scale revolt against my small intestine. But when he bends his arm around the back of my neck on our walk to his truck, I purposefully soften my body against his. He squeezes me tighter, and I can tell he's pleased.

See? I'm off to a solid start already.

It's not that late when Jake pulls up my driveway, but the house is dark. His hand rests on my knee, so I shift a little to slide out from under it. His grip tightens. "Hey, hold up. Am I gonna see you tomorrow?"

"Don't think so. I have work at noon, and I have to bring Dad to the dentist and do some stuff around town." Then I remember that I'm trying to be my best La Trampan self, so I tack on, "Call you after I'm done?"

He bends halfway across the stick shift to kiss me, and I lean in to meet him. The faded, stale-bread taste of beer hangs on our tongues. I wanted this once, I remind myself. I can want this again. I can want him.

His fingers flex over my kneecap. "Sure I can't make you feel better?" Even in the weak glow of the street-lights strung intermittently across Jemez, his dimples are almost supernatural.

I shake my head, sliding out of the truck.

"Okay, no problem. Buenas noches, princesita."

"Don't . . . yeah, night." I smile and shut the door.

Stopping in the kitchen to sniff around anything left over from dinner, which I skipped, I find only a big Tupperware of green beans. I head to my room empty-handed. I slip out of my smoke-smelling dress and flip-flops, and then I brush my teeth with the tap on low so Mom won't wake up on the other side of the thin bathroom wall; she's a light sleeper of necessity. I scrub off my mascara, hook my phone up to the charger in my room without bothering to set the alarm, and unmake my bed.

All the little routines that make up a perfectly survivable life.

* * *

Instead of sunrise, it's the buzz of my phone on my nightstand that wakes me.

Clumsily I grope for it, tilting it toward me to read the name on the screen. *L—* is as far as I get, and that's enough. Ripping it off the charging wire, I press the phone to my ear. "Hey!" It comes out as a gasp, the last air expelled from the shriveled red balloons that are my lungs all of a sudden.

"... Hello?" a gravel-deep voice answers hesitantly.

Not Leigh, then. The stupid bright star inside my chest collapses all over again. "Sorry, who's this?" This time, I remember to whisper.

There's a pause, and then, "It's Lucas. How's it going, Vanni?"

"Um, cool, yeah, thanks." Smooth as a fucking train track.

"I was just calling to ask, is Leigh over there?"

"No. We, um, we're not really hanging out anymore."

"I know." He does? "I mean, she's been home all the time lately, so I figured you guys weren't . . . There were clues."

I reach behind my head to yank out my pillow and slap it down over my face. The sooner I suffocate myself, the sooner this horrifically awkward call will be over.

"She took off with the van when I got home from

work this afternoon," Lucas adds, "and she isn't back yet. And you know Leigh."

I shove away the pillow and lift the phone from my ear long enough to check the time: it's 10:34 p.m., and way earlier than I thought. "I haven't talked to her."

"Her phone's off." He sighs. "I was just hoping. I mean, shit. Dad and Naveen are pissed, and the only reason they haven't called the cops is because I told them she was probably with you. Shit. *Shit*. Okay. I'm really sorry, Savannah, this isn't your problem."

"But you think it's *a* problem?"

"Would you think so?" he asks, sounding absolutely exhausted.

I can't say, *Don't worry, Lucas, she would never do something balls-out crazy like running away.* Still, it's only August 25. Over a week left until the deadline; the one I was afraid might pass without ever hearing from (much less about) Leigh. She's smart enough not to take off before her eighteenth birthday, on a night when her dad would notice her absence. With her escape so near, she would wait a measly week. Wouldn't she? Could she even buy a plane ticket before her birthday?

Crap, a quick Google search tells me she can.

But even if it were my job to worry—which it isn't, because I was fired from *that* position as well—I probably shouldn't be.

Yet five minutes later, I'm out of bed, sliding into my flip-flops, easing open my bedroom door. I snatch the car keys out of the basket and leave a note on the kitchen table, saying Leigh needs a ride home from a party a few towns over, where her DD got wasted.

And then I'm gone.

NINTEEN

Leaning my chin atop the steering wheel of the Malibu, I yawn and squint down the dark, dusty corridor of Berry Creek. According to our not-at-all-desperate plan, Lucas is telling Mr. Clemente that both my and Leigh's phones are off, but he's almost positive we're at my place. A friend's giving him a ride to La Trampa to drag his sister's ass home, so Mr. Clemente and Naveen can go to bed and yell at Leigh tomorrow morning.

Mr. Clemente might be annoyed at me by association, and if Mom does wake up, she might think a little less of Leigh. But spoiling future Clemente-

Espinoza Christmas dinners isn't exactly a primary concern anymore.

Soon, Lucas's bright shape swims out of the dark and into the range of my headlights. With a small wave, he jogs toward the car in a hoodie and shorts, muscled legs pumping loosely. I straighten up as he opens the door and slides into the passenger seat. "Fucking Leigh, right?" he says immediately, smelling familiarly of sunscreen and a little bit of his sister's clean soapiness.

The star pulses painfully. Mierda, this night is going to suck. "What happened?"

He spreads his palms in front of him. "Not much. She and Naveen got into it a little this afternoon, but that's not a rare event. Naveen wasn't even doing anything. She asked what Leigh was wearing tomorrow, and if she wanted to go back-to-school shopping with her. Leigh was *Leigh*, said she was all set on tie-dyed skirts and Birkenstock/sock combos. And then Dad said Naveen was just trying to help, and if she couldn't be nice about it, she could wear a grocery bag to school. That was about it. Leigh said she'd go shopping by herself and asked for the car. But that was at three. And I don't know where else she'd go, or why she'd stay gone, unless she was with you."

I dial Leigh again, and of course it goes directly to the generic voice-mail message of a person who hasn't bothered to record their own. I drop my phone into the cup holder, defeated.

Now I have to tell.

"I don't know either, but Leigh had this plan. On her birthday." I rub at a stain on the steering wheel cover with my thumb. Pressing down, the stain becomes a snag in the vinyl. "She said she was saving up for a plane ticket so she could go back to Boston." The snag becomes a tear.

I feel stupid and guilty that I didn't rat Leigh out sooner, and just as guilty for ratting her out now. Worse yet, this tiny, selfish, whining voice (the same that whispers, *What about me?* whenever I look at Dad) hisses: *Now she'll never want you back, you traitor.*

"Of course she did," Lucas says roughly, scrubbing a hand down his face and up again, through his dirty-blond, Leigh-like hair. "She thinks we can't tell her what to do the second she turns eighteen?"

I trap my hands between my goose-bumped legs so I won't make the tear worse.

"Fucking Leigh," Lucas repeats with a sigh. "I should've told Dad. Probably should've told on her a long time ago. I was just . . . I really wanted to take care of my sister." He slumps back in his seat, looking so sad, a smaller version of the boy in the lifeguard chair I would've swum fifty laps to impress on graduation day.

That seems like a really long time ago.

"We'll look for her," I promise him. "Maybe that's not what she's doing."

"If she ran away—"

"If we don't find her really soon, then we tell."

Lucas drops his head back against the headrest.

Throwing the car into drive and pulling a decisive K-turn to point us away from four Berry Creek, I ask, "Where should we try?"

"I don't even know anymore. Someplace you guys hang out a lot?"

A vision appears, then vanishes in a puff of glitter and perfume and cracked glass. "She won't go there. She hates me."

"She doesn't." He shakes his head and shoves his hands into the pockets of his sweatshirt. "Leigh doesn't hate anybody like she hates Leigh. Let's try it."

Either we make a move, or I go home, put on some Adele song about regret and missed calls and aging, curl up on my bed, and wait for a summer monsoon to pour down so I can stare out the window into the rain, feeling sorry for myself. Continuing to feel sorry for myself, actually, because I can't really remember the last time I didn't. So without much hope, I head for Chris's house. As I drive, we peer stupidly out the window, like we might spot Leigh on the side of the dirt streets, out front of the adobe church, in the disintegrating archway of a ruined home.

"Whatever happened between you guys," he breaks the quiet inside the car, "it's not your fault."

My stomach twists. "But you don't know what happened." *I* don't even really know.

Lucas rubs his fingers across his chin, callused skin rasping over his nighttime stubble. "Okay, true. At least it's definitely not all about you. I love Leigh, you know? Pretty much the most. But she scares the shit out of me." He laughs once. "The stuff she used to get up to in Boston? Everything that happened between her and Mom, you'd think she'd be so thrilled to come back to New Mexico. But she acts like it's a freaking life sentence."

"But she loved it there," I protest.

He looks over at me.

"That's what Leigh told me. She said this was just custody stuff."

All of a sudden, he's extremely interested in the knob on the glove compartment. "It wasn't a great situation." He toys with the knob, examining it closely. "Mom and Leigh would fight about big stuff. When Leigh went to high school, she cut off her hair and stopped wearing skinny jeans, and they fought about that. Mom didn't like Leigh's girlfriend, either, and then she thought Leigh was too pissy when they broke up, so that was another thing. But they'd also fight about nothing. Like, just *nothing*. If Leigh didn't separate her laundry by cold water and hot, and accidentally shrunk her shirt. If mom didn't ask before buying Leigh a new shirt. On and on.

"And if things were quiet for a while, Leigh would pull some stunt. This spring, she went to her first-period chem class drunk—seriously, so drunk her breath could've set the lab on fire if she'd coughed on a Bunsen burner. It's like Leigh was almost relieved to have something new to fight about. Like, I don't know, she was scared to *stop* fighting for even a second, 'cause then she'd have to pause and figure out why she was fighting at all, or what came next. I was living at home while I went to UMass, so I tried to get her out of the house when things got dark, but I couldn't be there all the time."

"So—what, your mom kicked her out?"

"She didn't. I called Dad. I asked if we could come back home, and he called Mom. She wasn't exactly thrilled."

"But she said yes."

He nods, then sits in silence for a few minutes before adding, "I thought things would be better for her in a new place. Then she's driving drunk, and breaking into the park—heard about that, by the way—and fighting with you. Maybe I was wrong, if she loved Boston so much."

We bump across the town line to La Trampa, where the roads are instantly worse thanks to our lowly town budget, scarred by the heat and the cold.

"I don't know if you were wrong," I tell him. "Every time she talked about the stuff she loved back home, she talked about you."

"Yeah?"

"Yeah. Like you guys at World's End? In the Mickey Mouse hats?"

He rubs his chin again, staring out the windshield, and murmurs, "That was a good day."

Who knows what I'm bargaining with, but as I turn left onto Jimeno, I propose a deal: Let Leigh be at Chris Zepeda's. Let the boxy bulk of the van shadow the driveway when we pull up. Let her have shimmied open the window, and be waiting for me to find her in the hideous room on that musty patterned bedspread that now smells the opposite of us, and I promise whomever or whatever it takes, I'll *make* things better for her.

The driveway's empty.

Just to be sure, we hop out and survey the house—me shivering in my pajamas in the cool night air, Lucas with his hood pulled up like an amateur burglar. I let us inside and click on the hallway lights, but there's no evidence that anyone's come through since I cleaned up after us two weeks ago. No dripping faucet in the kitchen; no lingering, oily herb scent in the air; no tracked-in dust on the tiled hallway floor. I don't have to check the back bedroom to know it's unoccupied.

"She couldn't make it easy," he says, grinding the toe of his sneaker into the mud rug.

Back in the car, we idle by the curb, without another direction to head in. Lucas stares at his phone. Winding himself up to call their father, I guess.

"Why do you think she does it?" I ask. "All of it?"

"I have some ideas. But you have to ask her."

If we find her before she flies away, that's the first thing I'll do.

"My sister can be amazing. She's funny and smart and strong. She was one of the best center backs in the region when she played. Short, you know, but totally fearless on the field. That's why I left Boston and came home with her. She's not just the worst things she does," he says pleadingly.

Diana thinks we're not just our bodies, and I don't even believe what she believes. But I hope she's right, and Lucas, too.

I hope we're not only our mistakes, our diseases, our disasters.

We both jump as Lucas's phone chimes. He fumbles

to pry it out of his sweatshirt pocket and read the text. Bathed in the blue-white glow of the screen, his face changes—fear to relief, his jaw loosening, dark eyebrows unstitching. "Fucking Leigh," he says as he exhales, and it's the sound of a heart restarting.

Instead of the Turquoise Trail, we take I-25 North because it's faster, and get off onto the quiet streets of Santa Fe. Just about everything shuts down by eight, and it's almost midnight now. Lucas directs me toward 285 North toward Chimayo, which we take for a half an hour. He cradles his phone and fiddles obsessively with the volume, even though Leigh's battery was on its last gasp forty miles back, so it's super unlikely she'll text again.

We rise into the foothills of the mountains. Somewhere up there is Santa Cruz Lake, and I remember that night, Leigh's body in the cold water, how she made me feel. I want us to be there again, but we don't need to go that far before we see the van on the side of the road, listing toward the flattened front left tire. The cabin light is on, but the driver's seat's empty.

"Keep going," Lucas says, anxiously juggling his useless phone between his hands.

Within a mile, we're winding through a narrow gap in the hills and into the town that none of us can name, the small houses looming above and below us, a dog trotting aimlessly through the narrow street, summer bugs under the porch lights. Around a tight corner, the bone house looms. That's where we find Leigh: sitting on the narrowest possible strip of earth just outside the fence. Our high beams illuminate the cow skulls skewered on the fence posts. They light up Leigh's skin too, because it must be in the fifties this high up and after dark, but Leigh's in shorts and a tank top. I'm already cold as soon as I leave the car, half a step behind Lucas.

Her head drifts up as we approach, eyes flickering over me and settling on Lucas. "I didn't mean to," she says, her voice low, kind of compressed, like her mouth isn't working quite right. A little like the way Dad sometimes speaks.

I stop, but Lucas stands over her. "You were drinking?" he asks. "Or are you on something?"

She looks down at her ratty Vans, pulls on a loose thread. "Are you gonna tell Dad?"

"*Of course*, Leigh-Bee." He kneels in the street, strips off his hoodie, and wrestles it onto his little sister, who almost disappears inside its folds. "We love you, you asshole. Don't you get that?" He laughs low and thick.

This is what I want: to rush forward and elbow Lucas out of the way, wrap myself around Leigh and bury myself in her at the same time. To take her back to the hideous room and tell her how much I miss her. That I'm sorry about everything I said to her. That I forgive her. That I feel so much better and bigger and braver with her than without her. That I need her, and I want to be with her, the way things were on the Fourth. That I want to fix her, and for her to fix me, and if it's not possible then I want us to just keep hiding away together.

I want, I want, I want . . .

But because what I want isn't what's important right now, I walk back to the Malibu. By the time I slide behind the wheel, Leigh has her face smashed into her brother's shoulder and he's murmuring things it's not my business to hear. I close the car door. Flicking on the turn signal so I'm visible on the wildly unlikely chance that anybody else is driving through the hills this late at night, I click off the headlights and let Leigh be with the person she loves the most in the world and who knows her the best, for however long she needs.

TWENTY

Three things worth mentioning happen on Sunday, September 3.

Okay, not three things in *the world*. According to KOAT Action 7 News, the standard sound track to our breakfast cereal, there are notable happenings outside of La Trampa. A congressman is arrested for embezzlement and insider trading. This past August is confirmed as the warmest on record in New York City. A giant flock of turkey vultures drops dead in the Florida Keys. Reporters uncover an actress's on-set affair with her married costar—she plays a high-powered chef who spends her nights alone with tubs of frozen yogurt, wine bottles, and Netflix; he plays an underachieving club rat who has meaningless sex with nameless hotties until a chance encounter with the chef rearranges his priorities . . . and his heart—and it's established that the actress has "ruined" the actor, at least until the film comes out and breaks the box office.

But within my little ten-mile orbit, it's just the three.

Happening #1: Finally, the heat breaks. It'll linger in the eighties till late September and could spike back up before then. But when I step outside at noon, my lungs feel like lungs instead of twin magma chambers seething within a volcano, and that's not nothing.

Happening #2: Having returned home from Monterey late the night before, Chris Zepeda comes to reclaim his spare key and stays for lunch. While he and Dad watch TV—the Buccaneers and the Rams are busy trying to break each other's bones on a bright green field—Mom and I churn out ham and cheese sandwiches in the kitchen. I grab the mustard out of the fridge, and she presses a kiss into my shower-damp hair. "No sé que haría sin ti," she says. I don't know what I would do without you.

I slap mustard onto slices of bread, blushing. Because what I'm actually doing is courageously hiding out from Chris.

By now he's had a chance to inspect his house, and if he peeked into the hideous room, he might have noticed the dust gone from the floorboards where I swept and scrubbed them, the reduced pile of his sister's things on the little table, maybe a stray starburst of eye glitter I somehow missed. Besides which, I'm feeling super guilty about using the house Chris entrusted to me as a hookup pad. I guess it was more than that—a "reevaluating my sexuality and falling in love, or so I thought at the time, and maybe I still think so" pad—but I'm not sure if that's any better.

We gather around the table during halftime, and while Chris casually slides Dad's chair up and then settles into his own, I search his face. If he suspects anything, he's totally stoic behind the wild shrubbery of his beard. "This looks great, Melanie." He smiles broadly at Mom, tucking his paper napkin into the collar of his faded Allman Brothers Band T-shirt as if he weren't facing down bland sandwiches, but a plate of costillas adobadas con mole poblano; the messy pork spareribs Dad smothered in sauce made from Mexican chocolate, four kinds of chili peppers, Kahlúa, and unidentified magic. I don't know if anybody misses my father's cooking quite like Chris.

He devours half a sandwich in two bites and washes it down with instant coffee, pausing long enough to grunt, "Sophia says hello," before leaning in for the finishing bite.

Mom slides a second-round sandwich onto his plate without being asked. "¿Cómo está tu hermana?"

"Está bien. She's finally, how do you say it, when you're getting the baby to bed on a kind of schedule?"

"Sleep training," Dad says, rocking himself toward the table.

Mom blinks, but Chris doesn't skip a beat. "Yeah, right, sleep training. So now she's not so pooped during the day. She can go out, get a haircut, go to the park. They're in a great place for kids. The whole area, it's nice. You'd like it, Vanni. Nick—that's Fee's husband— he does something fancy in software." He nudges Dad. "You picture my sister marrying a tech nerd?"

After a few seconds' silence, through which Chris waits patiently, Dad tips his head. "Sure can't."

Chris reaches for a third sandwich, and Mom meets him with the platter halfway. "Nick has a good job, so they have a nice little place in this condo park called Ocean Forest. Couple of miles from the beach, actually. You even get a peek at the water from their balcony. Now that Dad's up and around and back in his senior apartment where he's happy, they've got a spare bedroom."

I resist the urge to panic.

"I'm sure Fee'd love to meet you," he continues, catching my eyes over the condiments, "if you get out that way. In the future, you know?"

"What a nice offer!" Mom says. Then they're off and talking about Chris's whole summer, the weather out west, his jet lag, and Mom's secret recipe for her wonderful ham and cheese sandwiches (spoiler alert: it's ham + cheese + a guest with low standards in a very generous mood).

After lunch I head to my room to get dressed for the evening. I spend a good fifteen minutes staring into my drawers before I pull on a pair of bone-white denim shorts and a soft button-up with blue and red checks. A Fourth-ish ensemble for a special occasion. I braid back my hair, then do my makeup in my spotted bedroom mirror, bending over and bracing my elbow on the desk so my hand won't shake while eyebrow-filling and lip-lining. This, I'm sure, is not flawed genetics but the strain of no-makeup makeup that takes half an hour to apply.

I'm pretty sure.

After the finishing touches, I track down Mom to say good-bye. She's at the screen door in the kitchen, looking out to where Dad and Chris sit on the lawn chairs permanently stationed in our backyard. There's not much to see out back but a small, grassless, rocky plot like most yards around here. It's hemmed in by a coyote fence made from spindly wooden poles, set in concrete and bundled together with galvanized wire. Dad and Chris built it themselves, with the brand of help from seven-year-old me that some would consider unhelpful. But they got it done, and for eleven years they've been sitting out back in various lawn chairs exactly like these, nursing a beer each, staring at that fence like it's an ocean view at sunset. Mom watches them as if her view's the same.

She turns at the slap of my flip-flops across the kitchen tiles. "¿Te vas, mija?"

I nod. "I'll be back after dinner."

Mom nods back, and then says carefully, "It was nice of Chris to make that offer."

"Monterey? Yeah, I guess. It's not like I'm going, though."

"If you wanted to . . ." she starts, pushing away the loose hair that flutters against her cheeks in the breeze through the screen. "I didn't mean what I said before, you know, in the kitchen. I know it'd be tough for you, but your father and I would be okay."

"I know." I scuff at the tiles. "Maybe you and Dad should go to California. On a vacation or something."

"Maybe," she says in the same sweet, high voice she uses to assure Mrs. Reyes she'll try to stop by the prayer circle organized on Dad's behalf. "Long before your father was sick, he was happiest at home."

"You think Dad's happy?" I ask, more drily than I meant to.

She turns back to the screen, staring out. "I don't know, mija. Why don't you ask him?"

Feeling as brittle as a husked peanut shell, I head into the backyard.

"¡Que linda!" Chris exclaims when he sees me.

"Yeah, yeah."

"Going out? Hold on, I'm parked behind you in the drive." He pats my dad on the shoulder and levers himself out of the lawn chair with a groan, as if he's been there so long he's grown roots. "I'll move it to the street. Got to hit the head anyway. Back in a few, Gabe."

Dad toasts him with a bottle of beer he's only half emptied in the past hour.

Inspecting the plastic seat for dust, I swat away a light cloud of gnats and plop down beside my dad in Chris's empty chair. "I start that new job tomorrow morning," I say to fill the quiet.

His own chair creaks gently as one leg bounces up and down without his doing, one elbow jerking out of time. Chorea, it's called—it means something like *dance* in Greek. "The park?"

I toe at a weed sprouting from the dust with my tennis

shoe. "No, I quit that place. Remember? Too many hours."

"I meant . . . what really happened at the park, corazón?"

I slouch down and tip my head back and squint into the blinding blue wash of the sky above us. I'm not shocked that Dad suspects. Maybe Mom doesn't, but I'm pretty sure she still believes I've stayed home the past few months for all of the reasons I claim: to save money, to help in the restaurant just a little longer, to spend just a little more time with Dad. If those were my motives for kicking around town, then I might actually go off and start my life someday soon. Mom's hoping *hard* for that. But Dad . . . I think he knows the truth.

I think we just don't talk about it.

"I got fired," I sigh. When he doesn't speak, I'm not sure if he's processing or waiting for more, so I keep going. "I did something stupid. Leigh was there, but it wasn't her fault. I wanted to do it."

Another pause. "Are you sorry?"

Now it's my turn to process. "I'm sorry about what happened after."

"Do you—" His left elbow slips off the plastic arm, threatening to tip his bottle. He swears under his breath and tucks it back in, and I stiffen in my seat, but he lets out a wobbly breath. "You want to talk about it?"

I don't, and I do.

Because if he's not exactly the dad I remember growing up with, and he's destined to become less so very
soon, he's still my dad. We're not just the worst things
we do *or* the worst things that are done to us, right?
Just because he and I can't go hiking, or ride ATVs with
Chris Zepeda . . . just because we can't be in the kitchen
together, him cooking and me happily watching, not
learning but marveling at my dad . . . just because we've
never needed to talk before much, and I'm scared that
it is and always will be too late for us to learn how. . . .

So tell him *something*, I command myself. Something true. Tell him I broke up with Jake a couple days
ago by the Dumpster behind Silvia's, and it was hid-
eously awkward and I felt truly awful about it, but now
he'll be an even worse peak-hours waiter because he'll
spend half of his shift vengefully trying to hook up with
half the customers; an admirable goal, but Jake lacks my
time management skills. Tell him about Diana, and how
we've been texting for the first time in over a year and a
half; nothing deeper than Buzzfeed lists that remind us
of each other, but you have to start somewhere, somehow. Tell him about the Fourth of July. Tell him about
Leigh. Tell him what Mom said about wanting things
only for yourself being the way that children love, and I
didn't get it then, but I might be starting to.

Just say something.

"What would you have done, if you knew you would get sick?"

We don't talk about this. We rarely talk about his sickness, let alone the possibility of me being sick. We're supposed to—we had a few family counseling sessions after Dad was diagnosed—except that Dad is Dad, and Mom's so busy being optimistic, and I'm busy being, you know, busy.

But that isn't working for me anymore.

Dad takes a long time to think, and when he speaks it's a little bit slurred, but slow and mostly clear. "Run the restaurant. Married your mother. Had you."

I scrub at a patch of grime on the plastic with my thumb. "No, but what would you have done different? If you knew, when you were my age, when you could go anywhere you wanted?"

"I would've—" His head jerks forward and back. "Run the restaurant. Married your mother. Had you."

"Okay," I say, my voice watery.

"Don't regret . . . that would be the worst thing. I don't want that for you."

"Okay."

The slap of the screen door against its frame announces Chris's return. I kiss my dad's rough cheek, swallowing raggedly, my throat too tight to say good-bye. For once, we've probably said enough.

TWENTY-ONE

Happening #3: At 3:45 p.m., Leigh Clemente turns eighteen years old.

Leigh's not a birthday-party type, but if she were, I still don't think Mr. Clemente would be renting out the Rockin' Rollers skating rink. These days, Leigh is solidly homebound except for school, which she's driven to and picked up from, and for the therapist her dad found and made her go to pretty much immediately. (Leigh had her first appointment last Friday, but all she said when I asked about it was a single texted emoji: 💣)

On the drive to Los Cerrillos, I'm bouncing with

nerves. I have this slick, hard knot in my stomach, like the pit inside a peach. At each stoplight I check and recheck my makeup, sliding a finger along my lips and below my eyelashes to smudge away any imperfections. I haven't seen Leigh since Sunday night, and I'm allowed over today solely thanks to Lucas. After he and Leigh wobbled down the mountain on a spare tire and a prayer, me following behind them all the way to be safe, he put her to bed with water and aspirin and a trash can on standby, then woke their dad to tell him the whole story. The only editing he did was on my behalf. According to him, I'd had no inkling that she might go missing, that she had ever planned to go missing once she turned eighteen. When he went to my house that night to find Leigh, I selflessly leapt out of bed and drove him back and forth across the county searching for her.

He claims he kept it simple because I'm a good influence on his sister—maybe the only time I've been called *that* in years—and he understands why I kept her secret, so why complicate things in his dad's eyes? Leigh's theory is that her brother is shipping us, and doesn't want to mess up those Clemente-Espinoza Christmas dinners I so brazenly risked.

We are not back together. I didn't dump Jake to date Leigh; that I did because it's one thing to sleep with him, which I don't feel bad about, but another to lie to him, which I've been feeling consistently crappy about. So now there's no me-and-Jake, but there's still no me-and-Leigh. She asked me to come today, and of course I said yes. But everything between us that used to feel so easy now seems so tough. We haven't talked on the phone yet, haven't texted about anything serious. Even my stupid jokey texts land weirdly. This morning I sent her a GIF of Taylor Swift in a party hat, astraddle a banana, hurtling through the galaxy, and she sent back a laugh-face emoji. Which is *not* like her. It's as if we're standing on opposite shores and shouting, but half of our words are whipped away by the wind, and what makes it across is barely recognizable as our voices.

Why does it have to be so hard all of a sudden? Why can't everything just vanish again, leaving only us, on an ugly ruffled bed in a hideous room?

I hear high-pitched yipping and the scrabbling of nails against the wood in the seconds before Naveen answers the door to four Berry Creek. She joins me out on the porch, her raspberry hair flashing in the sunlight, and the dogs circling our shoes. She smiles and leans in for a sweet if awkward hug right on the porch—all arms, the big bell sleeves on her purple top enveloping me, one of her feathered earrings sticking to my lip gloss as she presses us cheek to cheek. I sort of pet her back where

I can reach it. She lets me go and we step inside, where the air is warm and sugary with the smell of a cake baking. There's other evidence of her efforts to make this a totally normal birthday celebration—a bouquet of silvery balloons drifts along the ceiling by the fireplace, yellow streamers dangle from the archway between the living room and the kitchen.

"Savannah, honey, we're so glad you came," Naveen says. Her voice is balloon-like itself, sweet and floating.

I feel guilty for the gratitude I don't deserve. But whatever we do or don't "deserve," it doesn't stop the bad stuff from smashing down on us. So I take this good thing. "I'm really glad Leigh's okay," I tell her.

She squeezes my hands between her soft, pale ones. "She's in her room. I can grab her for you?"

"That's okay." I shake my head. "I'll find her."

I follow Naveen into the kitchen, where she returns to the stove. As I pass the sliding door to the dusty backyard I see Lucas and his dad huddled together around the grill, probably over blackening squash or bell peppers. *We'll eat meatless burgers with eggless soy milk mayonnaise, wave sparklers, watch America-themed movies*, I hear past-Leigh say, and get that same pang in my chest you get looking at photos of your old stupid, sweet, little-kid self.

In the hallway outside Leigh's bedroom, I hover. I

sweep a hand down the ridges of my French braid, raise a knuckle to knock, stop, shift my weight, tug my shirt down over my hips.

"Oh get the fuck in here," her muffled voice drifts through the door.

I crack it open and lean in to find Leigh lying on her bed in a blue Henley and black nylon gym pants. Her head hangs backward off the edge of the mattress, tanned face pinker with blood, short brownish-blondish hair dangling, legs crossed and propped up against the wall. She holds a comic book straight up above her with the pages pointed down. Just seeing her, I let out a breath. Things might still be terrible and weird, but I miss her. I miss her the way I miss the water. I can pretend I don't, that being a performing fucking mermaid was a joke and now I'm better off. But I know the second I'm back in a pool, it'll be a held breath released.

"This page," she says, "it's supposed to be the same picture when you look at it upside down."

"Oh." I lean against the door frame, pretending that makes sense. "How'd you know I wasn't Naveen?"

"It sounded like you on the floorboards. Naveen flutters. You kind of sink down."

I pop my hip to the side for old time's sake. "I *know* that's a fat joke."

Tossing the book down on her yellow bedspread, she

snakes around until she lies on her stomach, feet drumming back and forth against her ass . . . which is looking pretty tight, though it's certainly not mine to look at. "I guess I should say some stuff now," she says, examining her knuckles instead of looking up at me.

"You don't need to."

"I want to, though."

Realizing I'm still in the hallway, I step into her room, easing her door shut behind me. I perch straight-backed on the edge of the papasan across from her. "Me too. I should say some stuff." Then we sit in the loudest kind of silence. A warm breeze slithers the curtains; Naveen bangs a pan around in the kitchen; dog-day cicadas rattle drily out in the scrub. I watch dust motes drift through a sunbeam that slants by the bedpost and think, oh god, we're going to sit here not talking until the veggie kabobs are ready.

"You want to go for a walk?" she asks at last.

"Definitely."

Leigh fishes her Vans out from under her bed and leads me toward the front door. "We're going outside," she tells Naveen when we pass her in the kitchen.

Naveen pauses in the middle of sponging off the floury countertop. "Lunch will be ready pretty soon."

"We'll turn back when we reach the border," Leigh says, and I cringe. But then, in a peace offering that's basically a gold-plated olive branch, she adds, "I can take the dogs out if you want."

"That would be very helpful." Naveen smiles and goes back to sponging.

I wait while Leigh gets their vinyl leashes out of the hall closet, a pink one speckled with purple hearts and another, purple with pink hearts. The ankle-height dogs dance around her while she hooks the leashes to their collars, and then she sweeps them gently enough toward the door with her foot.

"Nice she's making you a cake," I say as we burst out onto the front porch.

"Yeah," Leigh agrees, swatting at the tinkling copper wind chime hanging from the eaves with her free hand. "My nonna sent me another gift card."

"Sephora?"

She pulls a tragic face. "Banana Republic."

So we walk. The cicadas click and the breeze rattles mesquite bushes in the front yards. The dogs' paws whisk back and forth over the dirt, pebbles skittering away from them.

"What're their names?" I think to ask for the first time.

"Coconut and French Vanilla." Leigh's lips twist, burying a smile. "Don't ask me which is which, though."

A few houses down, Leigh stops, because her road

isn't actually that long. We're at the dead end of Berry Creek. Right in front of us, the dirt that's been packed and sculpted into a road tapers off into pale desert prickled with spiny plants, studded with rocks in the distance. She loops the dogs' leashes over a rough fence post outside the last house on the street, checking them twice, then sits down along the fence, sort of the way we found her Sunday night. This time I sit beside her, though a solid foot away.

"M'sorry," she mumbles. "I was a megabitch."

"*I* was a bitch," I argue.

"I got you fired. I really didn't mean to, but it's my fault. And then I went and got so pissed at you just for pointing out the pretty obvious fact that I fuck things up."

"I didn't mean it like that, though. And I'm sorry I said you were—" The word catches in my throat. "Crazy. That was so shitty of me."

Silently, she tugs down the sleeves of her Henley, tucks her fingers inside. "You're not wrong," Leigh says at last. "I have that therapist now, you know, my dad's making me go? This guy."

I watch the dogs snap at a tuft of purple wildflowers, then at each other, then at the light breeze. "Is he, like, helpful?"

"Eh. He says when 'teens' abuse 'substances,' and 'act out,' it's often to escape 'emotional struggles,'" she says, air-quoting liberally.

I smile at this because I assume I'm supposed to, but Leigh doesn't. "What struggles are you escaping, exactly?"

"I don't know. He asked me why I wanted to go back to Boston, and what I thought I was going home to, and whether I was actually happier there. Then we talked about Lucas, about how he's moving out to go to college. He says it's technically a kind of loss, so I'm technically grieving, or whatever."

"Maybe you are."

"Maybe." Leigh leans forward to swirl one finger in the warm dust, scribbling a meaningless language of shapes and squiggles. "My brother's just always been there, and now he won't be, and I miss him before he's even gone. He didn't know everything about me, but he knew more than anyone. And he still liked me, which is weird. Like, not just loved me, but *liked* me. Sometimes I don't think anyone else does."

"I do," I tell her.

"Yeah, well, you don't really know me."

I want her to be wrong, but she isn't, not completely. Because part of what I've loved best about Leigh was that she didn't really know *me*, and so with her I could be strong, and special, and brave. I loved the girl I could've been in the next-door dimension where one tiny butterfly of a thing is different.

But this is the world we have, and this is the girl I really am. So I just say, "I want to."

Leigh seems to think about this as she draws a big circle in the dust. "You know what you said, that night after the Lagoon? When we were fighting?"

I wince. "What in particular?"

"That you didn't want to be trapped in your body."

"Yeah. I remember."

She smashes the circle clear with the palm of one hand. "I feel that way sometimes too."

"What does that mean?"

"Like . . . I've known I was into the ladies since practically forever. Then I'm eight, right, and the girls at the back of the bus are saying Shelby Leroy's mom told them that the lady on *Sex and the City* is a lesbian, because *she's* into girls. I thought, hey, that's me all the way down. I'm a girl who likes girls—I'm a lesbian—good to know. But that doesn't even feel completely right. I don't know if it felt completely right back then."

I must sound dubious as I say, "You think you like boys, too?"

"*No.*" She snorts. "I'm definitely not bi." She draws my name in the dirt, my whole name, with little polka dots around it.

"So you like girls, but . . ."

"But sometimes I don't, um, *feel* like a girl. I mean

a lot of the time, I don't." Leaning back against a post, she dusts off her fingers against her gym pants, leaving light handprints on the black fabric.

Rather than stare at them, I lean down and rake my own fingers through my name, watching all the tiny rock particles glitter in the sun overhead. "Do you feel like a girl right now?"

She gives the smallest toss of her head. "I think I always knew *something* was wrong with me. And then I got older, and it started to piss me the fuck off."

I try to picture tween-Leigh, the way she was in school pictures: her long, silky hair, shiny lips, frilled shirt. Angry all the while. I guess I'm not surprised she started fighting back, and just fighting, period.

"Have you told Lucas?"

"I sort of did, in Boston. I tried, but I didn't know what I was saying. It's like . . . I've been reading this English to Spanish dictionary," she switches tracks out of the blue.

". . . Oh?"

"Yeah, I got it after the Fourth. There's this part in the beginning about Spanish words that don't exist in English. Like, there's no translation."

On this subject, at least, I know my lines. "Yeah." I fold my arms across my knees, sitting the way Leigh sits. "Vergüenza ajena, that means when you're really embarrassed for somebody even if they're not embarrassed for themselves. Or te quiero is sort of in between 'I like you' and 'I love you.'"

"Right. It's all this vocabulary, and I never knew it, and I could've talked around these words forever without really describing them. Then I start to learn this new language, and I find exactly the word I've been looking for. I mean I've known *this* word for a long time, I just didn't . . . I never really knew I was looking for it. Does that sound amazingly stupid? I'm messing this up."

"No." And though I've already guessed, I ask, "What's the word?"

Her eyes are like river ice when it's first melting, just after the water shows through the cracks.

"Sorry, you don't have to say."

But then she bends down, dips a finger into the dirt, and spells it out. *Genderqueer.* I know that word. I came across it in my bisexual-and-generally-queer-related Googling, which I was zero percent kidding about.

Okay, so Leigh is genderqueer. I nod, and reach over to wind my dusty fingers through hers.

"You probably think I'm crazy."

"Stop. You're not crazy, that was the worst thing to say. This is, yeah, it's a lot, but it's *not* crazy. You know that, right? There's nothing wrong with you."

Her throat clicks as she swallows. "I want to be

okay. I just don't think I am."

"I don't think I'm okay either." I give her a half smile that hurts; shakily, she returns it. "What can I do? Should I be doing or saying something different? Like, should I call you anything—"

"No." Leigh grinds the heel of her free hand into her eye, sounding tired beyond tired. "I don't know. I have to figure it out. That, or keep fucking everything up all the time."

I know exactly what she means.

"But, um"—she squints over at me—"if I looked like a boy when we met, like if I was a boy then, would you still have wanted me?"

To make her laugh, I almost joke about my failed seduction of her doppelgänger brother, but stop myself. Leigh deserves much better than that, and needs me to be better. So I tell her what I've decided. "We're not just our bodies, right? You'd still be *you*."

After squeezing my fingers between her own, she peels away. "Um, can you take something?" Without waiting for an answer, she reaches into her pocket, pulling out a piece of paper folded in on itself so many times, it's a tiny white block.

"What's this?" I ask as she presses it into my palm.

"Homework. Kind of. The guy, the therapist, he wanted me to do this thing, transactional writing or . . .

whatever, it doesn't matter. I'm supposed to write letters to the people I care about, and I don't have to send them until I'm ready, or ever. But I wrote this thing for you. For us, kind of. So I'm giving it to you, but can you not read it until I tell you I'm ready?"

I nod, and I must be making heart-eyes at her, because I am a person Leigh cares about.

"Oh, *stop*." She taps my cheek and turns my face away. "For all you know, I farted in an envelope and folded it up."

"Are you *trying* to seduce me, Leigh Clemente?"

"Like it's hard."

We sit with our backs against the fence posts, and I close my eyes as the sun toasts the top of my head pleasantly. For the first time in a while, I don't feel like meat cooking on a spit.

Leigh clears her throat, and says in the loud cartoon voice of a game show host, "So! Savannah Espinoza! Thanks to your bitchy ex, you're no longer a performing mermaid. What are you going to do next?"

Again I resist the joke (have awesome sex with Leigh in a semi-public place) and picture that stupid cold pond where everything I ever tried to sink is bobbing along the surface. There are so many things I want. I want Dad to drive and talk and cook again; I want to buy a plane ticket to Boston, or California, or Tokyo, with

Leigh in the aisle seat beside me; I want, at the same time, for us to hide away together in the hideous room forever, never worrying about what we were or what we are or what we'll become.

But what's really stirring at the bottom of the water, what's been stirring for a week, or months, or years, is this:

"I think I am going to find out if I have HD," I say, the words only wobbling a little.

"Shit," she breathes.

"Right?"

"I've been reading this other thing—"

"Jesus, really?" I laugh. "A month ago you owned five books, and you'd read none of them."

"Well, now I'm grounded for eternity, so I need something to do. Anyway, it's not a book, it's online. About Huntington's." She looks up through her eyelashes, as if confessing. "Are you mad?"

I can only shake my head.

"I read a bunch of stuff online, actually. Some of it was about getting tested. You were talking about it, so I just wanted to know more. This one article, it said something like, 'Most people would rather live with the question of Huntington's than the answer.'"

"Yeah. I get that." I squint up into the turquoise sky. "A lot of people do just fine and have great lives without knowing. And me, I think I could totally survive without knowing. I can be too scared to go anywhere, and work one thousand awful jobs just to keep busy, and eat defrosted leftovers forever. Or I could go somewhere and do something and get some damn tamales. Probably most people could do all of that without taking the test, but I've tried, and I don't think I can. I think this is what I need to get un-stuck." As I say it aloud for the first time, I know it's true; terrifying, but true. "Do you think that's a good reason?" I ask.

Though I didn't notice it happening, we're all of a sudden right next to each other—either I've been inching closer, or Leigh has, or both—so it's nothing for her to reach up and take my hand in hers again. "It's your reason, right? It's what you need. Good enough for me."

Happening #4: Sitting at my laptop that night, I pull up the bookmarked guidelines for predictive testing in a new tab. Just before it loads I catch a flash of an article on my homepage, the KOB 4 local news blog, and click back over for a moment. It's a picture of a rubber alien, bright Crayola green, big-headed, binocular-eyed, and a two-sentence blip of a headline:

The Tub Aliens Have Landed. Bath Toys Spotted in Mexico, Washed Ashore at Last.

TWENTY-TWO

One thing you don't think about when you sprint head-
long into a big, change-your-world-overnight decision:
how unbelievably goddamn long it can take for the
world to catch up with you.

I didn't expect a big neon sign to descend from the
heavens the second I made my choice, flashing *POSI-
TIVE!* or *NEGATIVE!* But October's halfway through
by the time I sit down with Dr. Janowitz for our next-
to-last appointment. Familiar by now, her office is
white, lukewarm, and brightly lit. Having a pretty big
sampling myself, it is almost what you'd call Generic

Doctor's Office™, except for this picture filmed over a single fluorescent light panel in the ceiling above her desk. A bright sky view with what look like those big saguaro cacti, their arms uplifted, flowers white and open, looking up out of the corners of the frame, as if you're lying down in their shade. This being my third visit, I've had some time to study them. Which must be exactly the distraction Dr. Janowitz—the genetic counselor Dr. Michaels recommended to Mom and me—was hoping for when she stuck the picture up there.

Not that I spent the first two visits staring at the ceiling. Since we got through my whole family history and retreaded the story of HD, Dr. Janowitz has been asking questions; questions are what the counseling's all about. Do I believe I'll be negative for the disease, or positive? Have I been obsessing over possible symptoms? Did I know that it's incredibly common for potential HD carriers to symptom-hunt? Who have I told that I'm getting tested aside from Mom, who waited during the first appointment, and Diana, who sat through the second, and Leigh, who's out in the waiting room now (still grounded, but given special permission for the occasion)? What have I done to prepare for the outcome? What are my immediate plans and my life plans, either way? Who am I planning to bring to my test results? How will I tell the people I love if I'm negative? If I'm positive? Here, I remembered that middle school summer when Diana and Marilee and I lay on the trampoline in our morbid little book club, plotting the melodramatic or cool or practical ways we'd tell our imaginary boyfriends about our imminent deaths. *Diana: I am about to die, but don't cry, my darling, because I had your love! Marilee: Since I'm dying, can we please go to second base after the dance tonight? Me: Hey baby, you know how the milk at the Trading Post is always, like, a day away from expiring?*

I don't love answering all of these, but I know why Dr. Janowitz is asking. I know it's important. It's also kind of a relief. Nobody in this room is slapping on lipstick and pretending we're fine, that life is the way it's always been, that everybody's okay and there's nothing to be afraid of. If I'm scared, I tell the doctor I'm scared. Sometimes I tell Mom, too.

When we're not talking, we've been doing little tests, too. I've walked with one foot in front of the other across a hospital room, walked on my heels, held my arms out straight, pressed my head into the doctor's hand from each side to make sure I'm not showing any signs of the disease yet. All scary, all pretty simple.

Today's the big one.

On the other side of her desk, Dr. Janowitz follows my gaze up to the saguaro, glances back down at me, smiles. She has a Jake-like dimple in her plump left cheek, though none in the right. She's also professionally kind and smells like yogurt. All of which could be much worse.

"We were going over the repeats?" she reminds me.

"Right." In my chair across from her, I fiddle with the strings on Leigh's yellow Bruins hoodie—the one I love—which she gave to me on the car ride over.

"I know you've heard this before," Dr. Janowitz says sympathetically, "but I don't want you to have any questions going into the blood draw."

"I get it."

"You know we'll be testing the gene that holds important information for the brain in its coding. Part of that code is repeated in the normal gene, but even more so in Huntington's patients, where their mutated gene grows larger—we call that expansion, remember—causing brain cells to malfunction and die."

I nod, my right leg bouncing up and down against the lip of the desk. I spread my palms straight across my skinny jeans and press down to stop it, then reach into the pocket of the hoodie. Inside is the smooth, solid rectangle of Leigh's folded-up note, which I don't yet have permission to read, but take with me to every appointment. For luck, I guess, or something like it.

"When we get your test results in the next few weeks," Dr. Janowitz continues, "we'll know the number of repeats in your gene. Again, fewer than thirty-five means you're negative. There should be fewer than twenty-seven to show that your children would be at no risk, but the risk would still be very small. From thirty-six through thirty-nine repeats, we're in more uncertain territory. This means you're positive for the disease, but if symptoms do appear, it'll happen much later in life. Perhaps in your sixties or seventies. More than forty repeats—"

"I'm totally, completely, absolutely positive, right?"

"It means symptoms will definitely appear in your lifetime." Then she folds her hands atop her desk. "You know that you don't have to get these results, Savannah. We don't even need to draw blood today, or next week, or next year. And if we do, but in the time before the results are in you decide not to find out, then tell us so."

"I want to," I say. "I know a lot of people don't need to know, but it's what I need."

"Okay then." She smiles in her kind, professional, yogurty way.

When I push through the frosted-glass door to the waiting room, Leigh glances up at me from her corner chair. "Hungry?" she says, without asking how my session went, without even pausing to level the hazel moons of her eyes at me in sympathy, and for this I love her a little bit more.

"Starving," I say.

Leigh and I sit on barstools at the Mine Shaft Tavern, squeezed between big-shouldered bikers in leather and a pack of big-haired, frost-blond fiftysomethings in summer dresses. But just because we can sit at the long pine bar doesn't mean they'll serve us booze.

"Do you really care how old we are?" Leigh hassles the tattooed bartender. "I mean, do you *really*?" The guy isn't paying us much attention. He's new, but he's not dumb, and Leigh isn't even trying all that hard. The second he strolls away, she turns cheerily back to me. "Figures we'd get the tough case. But you were right about this place. Check out the ambiance!" She sweeps her arm. A buffalo head hangs above the fireplace, and railroad spikes and pickaxes and coiled lassos decorate the wooden walls. Over the bar, framed paintings show the history of Madrid. Almost all of them are coal-related. In one, fat angels fly a banner over a huddle of tired-looking miners. Leigh, who tells me she's taking Latin II this year, says the banner sort of translates as "It is better to drink than to work."

"Latin?" I screw my face up. "Where will you ever use that?"

"Meh." She ruffles one hand backward through her hair—chopped closer than I've seen it yet, so the back doesn't nearly reach the collar of her gray jean jacket— and the strands stick up in little blondish hedgehog spikes. "Italian would've worked with my schedule too, but I already took Latin in Boston, and it's not like I'm going to Italy."

"You think you're more likely to time travel than travel?"

"Yeah, good point. Maybe I'll switch next semester."

Next semester might be the furthest into the future that we've spoken about. I get that, because we're both still figuring things out, and waiting to hear what the other needs. But Leigh's told me she's been working on it, thinking more about pronouns—like how she wants to be called instead of "she," which doesn't feel right anymore, if it ever did. In the meantime, Leigh says she's okay sticking with she/her. I'm definitely not pushing, but I'm ready the second Leigh decides.

For now, I ask, "You're sticking around, then, right? For the rest of the school year?"

"Yeah. I kind of promised Lucas when we moved him into the dorms."

I simply nod, when I want to say: *Who cares about figuring our shit out, let's just go into the bathroom and smoosh our utterly flawed bodies together until we forget all about it.* But I don't, because I can't hide inside Leigh forever. And I can't tread water forever while telling myself I'm swimming.

"You?" she asks.

"Me what?"

Leigh leans forward over the bar top, looking intently into a bowl of peanuts. "Will you be around?"

"Maybe," I say without thinking.

"What does 'maybe' mean?"

"Where would I go?"

"To college, if you wanted to start in the winter. A lot of places have rolling admissions."

"I know."

"You applied anywhere?"

"Not yet. It's not like I don't want to, but if I got in anywhere, then everyone would expect me to go."

"So?"

"So, I'm scared I'll back out if I'm positive," I admit, because even if Leigh's not my girlfriend or my boyfriend (not anymore, or maybe not quite yet), she's still my person.

She shakes her head firmly. "I don't think you will."

"You know for a fact?"

"I just know you."

Then our plates come, and when I take a bite of my Shroom Burger, I'm pleasantly surprised. I haven't eaten here since I last came with Mom, and I forgot how good the food tastes. Even when we're done and stuffed, we still order dessert, and then another one, because we want to make the most of Leigh's day pass. It's like Mom said—one of the worst things about HD is the time being carved out of Dad's life, bit by bit at first as his symptoms get worse, and then years from now (but who knows how many) all at once.

Fuck that. This is today, and this time is ours.

The same can't be said of the weeks between the blood test and the results. They slip by slowly, slowly. And let's just be honest, they suck maximally. It's not hard to keep busy at the restaurant, at the car wash, at home, with Diana, at Leigh's. But constantly moving doesn't distract me like it used to, and I think about the results all the time, and feel every passing minute until my cell phone rings in the last days of October, flashing Dr. Janowitz's office number.

Mom and Dad come with me to this last appointment. We sit in the waiting room together—Mom on one side, Dad fidgeting on the other, and Leigh texting me stupid selfies every time she escapes to her locker—until the doctor pokes her head out and calls my name. We move achingly slowly toward the room so Dad can keep pace. I perch on the end of the padded table, and Dr. Janowitz asks me one final time if I'm ready to hear the outcome of the blood test.

I nod.

And then, I know.

After Leigh meets me in her driveway that night, and asks me how I'm doing, and I still don't quite know.

After we walk as far as we're allowed to, down Berry Creek, all the way to the end.

After I tell her the test results, and she cries and smiles at the same time, so when we kiss once, for the first time in months, her lips taste like salt and cinnamon.

After we say good-bye, I drive home alone but smelling of Leigh Clemente. The road is without streetlights, and I can't see very far along it but everything I *can* see is familiar and new at once, and with the bugs catching my headlights like low little stars, everything seems to be moving, flickering, alive.

TWENTY-THREE

My nose stays glued to the cold cube of the window as we rise, the roads below us like gray rivers fringed with trees, then ribbons, then higher still, a delicate web. When we break through the choppy mist of the clouds, rough air lifts us and dips us, leaving my stomach in twists, and I still can't stop staring. It turns out Mom hates planes, was scared of me tumbling out of the sky, but honestly.

What's up here to be afraid of?

The seat belt sign dings off as we level out, but even as people unclick themselves to meander toward the bathroom or drag their laptop bags out of storage, it's a good hour before I can tear myself away from the view. When the sun flares over the wing and the suited businessman in 32B cringes dramatically, I lower the shade. It's cool. Over an hour to go until Denver. Then another hustle through an airport packed with travelers returning home after Christmas and New Year's, a two-and-a-half-hour connecting flight to L.A., and an hour-plus plane ride to Monterey; the sky will still be there.

In the meantime I dig for my backpack beneath the seat and haul it into my lap, trying not to elbow the businessman, but not trying *that* hard. I take out my phone, now in airplane mode, and scrolling for the millionth time through the saved email from Chris, I go over the Plan. When I touch down in the Monterey Regional Airport at 6:43 p.m. this evening, I'm supposed to call Mom and Dad immediately, to prove my continued existence. Chris's sister, Sophia, and her husband, Mark, will be waiting to pick me up in baggage claim.

It is ridiculously, unreasonably cool of them; Sophia says she's happy to help a friend of the family and a fellow La Trampan (meanwhile, I'm super curious to meet the original occupant of the hideous room and find out who she became). I'll stay with them for the night, and then Sophia will drive me an hour up the coast to help me move into the dorms at Hillview U, home of Division II women's swim team the Sea Snakes. I certainly haven't had Sea Snakes posters tacked to my bedroom wall since I was a kid, but Hillview had scholarships for low-income students *and* a bilingual scholarship. And it's not so far from the beach, either. Walkable, if you have the time.

Not like a part of me isn't hurting. When my parents said good-bye at the airport—Dad folding an arm around me and accidentally shouldering me in the chin, Mom pressing a lipsticked-kiss onto my forehead and whimpering, "Te extrañaré. Estoy orgullosa. Te adoro, mija"—it was everything I could do not to duck out of the security line, sprint to the short-term parking garage and hide in the trunk until we pulled back into La Trampa, where everything and everybody waited.

There's so much I haven't figured out. Most of the time I think I've got absolutely nothing figured out. But I've figured out how to move forward anyway, and that's not nothing.

The suited businessman starts to snore, head tipping forward into his chest. I slide my window shade back up to see, slide it down when he jerks awake and fiddles with the TV on the seat in front of him. The screen plays that sitcom Dad and I sometimes watch; an old episode where the best-looking boy agrees to babysit the third-best-looking-but-still-gorgeous girl's baby nephew, then accidentally leaves him in a grocery store, having mistaken him for a sizable butternut squash.

I fish out the sweatshirt folded at the bottom— Leigh's Bruins sweatshirt, specifically. The thick fabric smells like Leigh, that clean Irish Spring scent that nobody's going to bottle and sell at Sephora for fifty bucks an ounce, but I don't think I'll ever get enough of it. I smash my nose into it, then pull it over my head despite the too-warm, canned air of the cabin. I tried to give it back this morning, when Leigh met me in the driveway to say an unfairly brief good-bye, but she wouldn't take it.

Which reminds me . . .

I stuff my hands into the pockets, and when paper crinkles, I pull out the folded-up notebook page. As she helped shove my suitcase into the trunk of the Malibu, she gave me permission to read it, but only once I was in the sky.

Flattening it in my lap to see familiar handwriting scratched across it, I feel the ghost of her pen tip against my palm as I read:

> *"Little Cosmic Dust Poem" by John Haines*
> *(I know, I know, but don't stop reading. I dare you.)*

Out of the debris of dying stars,
this rain of particles
that waters the waste with brightness . . .

The sea-wave of atoms hurrying home,
collapse of the giant,
unstable guest who cannot stay . . .

The sun's heart reddens and expands,
his mighty aspiration is lasting,
as the shell of his substanace
one day will be white with frost.

In the radiant field of Orion
great hordes of stars are forming,
just as we see every night,
fiery and faithful to the end.

Out of the cold and fleeing dust
that is never and always,
the silence and waste to come . . .
This arm, this hand,
my voice, your face, this love.

Okay? So now you've read, and now we know
what the end of the world will be like (it'll be sappy

as a motherfucker). So we don't have to be scared anymore.

> *All my love,*
> *Leigh*

Part of me wishes I'd cheated and read this when Leigh and I were separated by four miles of dust and three traffic lights . . . but part of me is so glad I waited. Glad that Leigh knew just what I needed. And we'll see each other soon-ish, when I come home for summer. That's the next Plan.

What will it be like when we're together again? Who will we be by then? Where will we go from there? I have so many questions, and no answers on the near horizon.

But I can live with that.

ACKNOWLEDGMENTS

Thanks to Lana Popovic, my agent and queen, for answering every insecure text and email and for making each book better.

Thanks to Jordan Brown, my genius editor at Balzer + Bray, for believing in me and in Vanni and in millennial anxiety.

Thanks to the team at HarperCollins and Balzer + Bray, including Alessandra Balzer and Donna Bray, Kate Jackson, Viana Siniscalchi, Alison Donalty, Stephanie Hoover, Bess Braswell and Tyler Breitfeller, Bethany

Reis, Caitlin Garing, and Oriana Siska—you guys make everything possible.

Thanks to Xaviera López for her gorgeous cover illustration, and to Sarah Kaufman, who designed the cover. You both captured the heart of the book, and every time I look at it I fall in love.

Thanks eternally to Rachael, Ashley, Kristian, Noemi, and Vee for making sure that *Like Water* is respectful to all its readers.

And from the bottom of my heart, thank you to LGBTQIA+ readers everywhere; you matter, and you are loved.

ML   11/2017